How NOT to Date an ANGEL

CAUTIONARY TAILS BOOK FOUR

LANA KOLE

CONTENTS

CONTENT INFORMATION

Thank you *so* much for picking up this book! I am thrilled to go on this journey with you!

While this is a lighthearted rom com, the delicate subject of domestic violence is broached beginning in chapter twenty-three. The violence is not detailed, it is not between the main characters, and the situation is resolved before the end of the book.

Please be advised that Rami *is* an angel, and some subjects around purity culture are discussed. If you happened to be worried about the implications of religion in this story, fear not. These halos are not used for holy reasons, ya'll.

Rami is gender fluid, non binary, and uses they/them pronouns.

For a full content list, please check my website.

And most of all, enjoy!

Putting the horn in horny and making halos unholy.

1
KNOCK KNOCK

Rami's steps were slow and calculated, so as not to rush the woman they were leading to the exit.

"Thank you so much for your time today," Melissa said.

Rami paused by the backdoor as she collected herself, and smiled soothingly.

"No thanks necessary. This is what you pay me for, you know," they teased, and leaned in to elbow her casually.

It got a chuckle out of her, and what a relieving thing to hear after such a hard session.

Melissa, like many of Rami's clients, would find that their bills were lost in the mail, never to be inquired about again.

It wasn't like Rami needed the money, but their clients needed the help, and, well. Rami liked to be helpful.

"Get home safe. Are you alright to drive?" they asked.

Melissa stuffed the last of her tissues in her purse. "Oh, yes. I'm fine now. Thank you, though." She cupped her hand over theirs and squeezed. "Thank you."

Rami felt warmth swell in their chest at her genuineness. "You are so very welcome, dear. I'll see you next week, same time?"

She nodded, and stepped through the doorway when

Rami opened it. "I'll see you and those pretty birds next week."

Rami chuckled politely and sent her off with an extra little blessing of safe travels home to her family and her struggling marriage, and ease with her newly discovered childhood trauma. Despite the fact that Melissa was still holding something back, she was making tremendous progress.

It was that progress, and clients like Melissa, that made Rami love Earth.

They shut the door only once they saw her get into her car, her headlights splashing their drive as she reversed into the street.

Once they were alone, Rami locked up and retrieved their mobile device from the office. It was a night-in kind of night, so they ordered food right to their door.

Humans—they'd thought of everything.

In the meantime, they tidied up their session room, turning off the incense and lights and making note of their appointments the next day. Before they pulled the French doors shut, they glanced toward the tall arched windows on the opposite wall, an old tree visible through the panes. The branches were empty, not a single bird in sight.

What was Melissa on about?

With a soft snick they locked the office and retreated to the kitchen, where they retrieved a bottle of wine from the rack and a single glass.

They poured themself a healthy drink and headed upstairs to change into something a little more comfortable. Less buttoned-up, fewer layers.

It was in moments like these, when they donned cozy pants, a rather basic tee shirt, their cardigan, and their feathered wings, that they felt most human.

They knew what it was to take a disguise off at the end of

the day and finally relax in their own skin, like many of their clients. Rami sipped their wine and sighed as it burst over their taste buds.

Humans had a lot going for them down here. Technology, community. Rami just hated that so many of them were so… *hurt*. By each other. Parents and children and family and friends and lovers. So much pain, passed from one to the other.

They'd never understand it.

But they could try. It's why they were here, after all.

Pushing the thoughts from their mind until the "work" hours tomorrow, they made their way back downstairs, checking their device for the timing on their food.

Their wings twitched, the eyes amongst the feathers blinking slowly as they sensed a shift in the air, the energy of… *everything* stuttering, caught, snagged for a moment before smoothing out again.

They froze, wondering what that was about, finger hovering over the black screen of their phone, when they heard it.

A knock.

It wasn't a normal knock. It was continuous, slow, ominous.

Thump, thump, thump.

Their feathers shifted in irritation, and Rami hid their wings once again before making their way to the door. Their heart rate picked up, breath going short as memory transported them to another time, another *century*, another knock on the opposite side of Rami's door.

They prayed this wouldn't turn out the same.

Through the peephole they failed to see anything besides their own hedges, and frowned, steeling themself as they unlocked it and twisted the knob.

The door was heavier than usual, and as it fell wide open, they finally saw why.

A demon was on their doorstep, though he did not stand. He collapsed backward, where he'd been resting against it, and sprawled out in Rami's doorway.

"Oh dear," Rami whispered, and knelt down. Their hands fluttered over the surface of his golden skin, unsure of where to touch. "I suppose you're responsible for that hiccup of energy, then?"

The demon's face was swollen and one of the wings crushed beneath him did not look right. Blood poured from a wound on his head, matting his hair and covering half his face in a haunting visage. But the worst atrocity was the broken horn on the left side of his head. It was noticeably shorter than the right, and jagged where it had snapped off.

Rami shivered in empathy. They couldn't imagine how painful it'd be if their halo cracked.

"What happened?" they asked, because they didn't know what else to say.

The demon's eyes fluttered open, though they didn't track very well.

"I d-didn't know where else to go," he breathed, clutching at his side.

"Oh *fuck*," Rami cursed, and barely spared a second to notice the furrow of the demon's brow at their use of the foul word before they gripped the demon beneath the shoulders.

"This will probably hurt—do brace yourself," they warned softly, and then pulled.

The demon did not brace himself. He groaned, the sound pouring from the very depths of his soul, as Rami dragged him through the door and safely into their entryway hall, wings scraping beneath him.

Oh dear, oh dear, oh dear, a voice chanted in Rami's head.

Carefully, they stepped around the demon and shut the

door, vanishing the blood staining their steps with a wave of their hand.

Then they turned and stared down at their unexpected guest, hands on their hips as they tried to decide what to do next, heart pounding.

Who could do such a thing?

"Okay, well. First, we need to get you all better."

The demon glanced up at them expectantly; meanwhile, Rami stared at him patiently.

A handful of long, slow moments passed. "Well?" Rami prompted, waving their hand. "Heal yourself."

For angels and demons it should be nothing but a moment of concentration to heal any injury, a bit of magic.

"Can't," the demon said, breath wet and quite concerning.

"Why the heavens not?" Rami asked.

They could have sworn they saw the demon's lips twitch before he said, "I'm not allowed."

"Well—well!" Rami sputtered, flustered at the sight of this hurt, bruised, and bloody demon. No one deserved this, even if they were from Hell. This suffering was unnecessary. "Fine, then I'll have to take care of you myself."

Only when they waved their hand to take care of it themself, nothing happened.

Their lips pulled down into a frown, and they tried again to no avail.

Which could only mean one thing. "What is going on? Were you cast out?" From *Hell?*

Rami didn't even know if that was something that happened—they certainly hadn't ever heard of it. But why else wouldn't a demon be able to draw on Hell's power, and why wouldn't an angel be able to heal him?

And what could this demon have done to earn such a punishment?

"No… I don't think so," he muttered, though his gaze was closing again.

Rami crouched down and snapped their fingers. "Stay awake. That's important." Though they couldn't remember why at the moment. "We'll have to do this the old-fashioned way, I suppose."

They *were* able to conjure a bowl of water and a clean cloth, as well as bandages and antiseptic ointments for all the open wounds. Rami had to help; they couldn't just stand here and watch the demon suffer.

"What's your name?" the angel asked.

"Julian," he muttered, eyes drifting shut again.

"Nah-ah," Rami said, and carefully poked his cheek in an unblemished area. "Awake." His skin was soft.

"What's your name?" he slurred.

Their manners took over. "I'm Rami. Pleased to meet you."

The demon still had horns, golden skin, wings, and that tail, so he wasn't human, which meant he wasn't likely to die from his injuries. In that case, Rami quite literally couldn't mess this up, and they found relief at the realization.

"Julian, then. Do you remember what happened?"

"Pretty sure I pissed off the boss."

Rami felt the blood leave their face. "L-Lucifer?" they whispered.

Julian scoffed, and then groaned, clearly regretting the action. "N-no. I'm not that high up."

"Oh, well. Glad to hear that," they said, though they weren't sure why they said it. What were they glad to hear? That the demon wasn't as evil as they'd thought?

All demons were evil, that was just… how it worked. They were part of Hell, and Hell itself was evil, and therefore they were evil. It just made sense.

Rami liked when things made sense.

It was part of why they liked to study humans, how their brains worked. Psychology, they called it.

It was also why they loved helping humans understand why they were the way they were. Why Rami was a therapist, of all the human professions they could've chosen.

There was a reason for everything humans did, and it often tied back to their childhood. It was like solving a mystery.

Rami liked mysteries, too.

And it seemed the greatest one had just dropped onto their doorstep.

"Who is your boss, then?" Rami asked, for lack of another question coming to mind.

"Oh," Julian said, a little garbled, like when humans had too much to drink. "You wouldn't know 'im."

"I don't see why that much matters," Rami muttered.

Carefully, they blotted the blood from the demon's eyes and forehead, discovering it was a shallow wound, like he'd been hit with a hand wearing a sharp ring. The gash was across his forehead, so the assaulter hadn't had very good aim.

"How did you know to come here?" Rami asked.

"What d'you mean?" Julian's brow furrowed in thought before he winced as the wound on his head crinkled. That couldn't have felt good.

"You said you didn't know where else to go. So you came here, to an angel. How?"

Julian managed to wave a hand lazily before it dropped to the floor. "Felt you," he mumbled. "All your goodness and whatnot. Knew it'd be safe."

Rami's cheeks flushed at the blind faith the demon clearly had in them.

A demon with blind faith. The irony was loud.

And despite the fact that this was, in fact, a *demon,*

someone an angel like Rami shouldn't even bother giving the time of day, they felt inclined to help.

It *was* quite a damper on their evening plans, but, well. What was Rami to do, throw the demon out? Not very likely.

His dark, wavy hair was tacky with dried blood and Rami decided they'd have to somehow get the demon upstairs in order for him to be truly clean.

"I'll have to get you upstairs somehow, in a moment," Rami told him. "So mentally prepare yourself for that. Where else do you hurt?"

Julian chuckled at that, and once again regretted it with a groan.

"Everywhere?" Julian guessed.

Not very helpful. Rami blew out a breath, and once the demon's face was clear, they realized he was quite handsome. Sharp jawline and cheekbones, ruffled brows, a delightfully angled nose.

Which, of course, was just an observation, by human standards. It meant nothing.

"Did they break your wing?" Rami asked, shuddering at the thought. Who would be so cruel?

"Something definitely isn't right," Julian mumbled, eyes falling shut.

"Don't—"

"Not falling asleep, just resting my eyes," he said, cracking one eye open.

"Fine, fine. If you start snoring, I'm throwing you right back out on the street." It was a lie. Rami was going to help this demon regardless. They were powerless not to. It just wasn't in the fabric of their being.

"No, you won't," Julian responded, lips twitching.

Rami sighed and shuffled on their knees down the demon's body, carefully lifting his hand away so Rami could get to the wound beneath.

"And why wouldn't I?" Rami asked haughtily, as they carefully lifted the demon's shirt.

"You're too selfless," Julian said.

And, well. He wasn't wrong.

"I am an angel, after all," Rami muttered, but that didn't mean they were happy about all this nonsense. "I'm no doctor, so I have no idea what could be wrong beneath the surface here. You're better off going to a hospital, where they can treat you properly."

He could have broken ribs, which could pierce his lungs or something, and always sounded quite serious on the shows Rami had discovered on the television.

"What the hell is a human doctor going to say about me, a demon?" Julian challenged.

They winced at the sight of the mottled bruising along Julian's right side, and guilt lanced through them. It looked painful, and Julian was right. Humans couldn't very well treat a demon patient.

"They weren't trying to kill me," Julian said. "So I'll heal up eventually. Just needed somewhere to crash."

Then *what* exactly was Hell trying to do to this demon, if not kill him?

"Well, I don't run an Airbnb!" Rami reminded him.

"A what?" Julian asked.

Rami felt his cheeks heat. "An Airbnb?"

Julian stared blankly at them.

"Have you never been here before? To Earth?"

"Of course I have. I'm a messenger, after all."

Ah. A messenger. Messenger demons were sent by hell to do just that: deliver messages. "You should be familiar with Earthly things, then."

He shrugged, which, in his state, was quite impressive. "I am, a bit. Just not familiar with an Airbnb."

"It's a website where you book someone else's home like a

hotel."

"Why would you want strangers staying in your home?" Julian asked with a frown.

Rami shook their head. "The homeowners aren't usually there when the visitors are. In fact, from what I understand, companies buy homes exclusively to offer them to strangers for profit."

Julian grinned up at him, teeth still bloody. "Diabolical."

Rami didn't answer, because yes, they thought so, too. But it felt wrong to agree with the demon.

"Oh, I get it," Julian continued in their silence. "You're saying I'm not welcome here," he guessed.

"I—well…" When the demon put it like that, it sounded a bit heartless. And Rami very much was *not* heartless. They sighed and pulled the demon's shirt down to cover his bruising. "You are in need, and I am not one to turn someone away. So I suppose you are welcome here while you heal."

Then he could be on his malicious way out.

"How kind of you," Julian scoffed.

"I've spent long enough here to know sarcasm when I hear it," Rami scolded.

"Good for you," Julian muttered.

Rami rolled their eyes, a very human expression of annoyance that they'd never had to borrow before.

They had a feeling that as long as this demon was in their home, they'd be using it quite often.

2
A DEMON'S JOB

Julian sighed at the brush of the cool cloth against his skin. He winced at the dab of the gentle finger along his wounds, coated in a clear antiseptic gel. He slumped forward at the pain of the angel resetting his wing, maybe even sweated a little.

Fuuuck.

"There you go," the angel said, voice utterly, despicably soft. They were so disgustingly *good* it was ridiculous, though Julian supposed it was working in his favor, so he couldn't complain.

The relief was instant, though he knew the wing would be sore for days to come.

He could see now, without blood dripping into his vision, and he let the angel help him to his feet.

"Where're your wings?" Julian asked, frowning at the absence of them at the angel's back.

He pressed a hand gently into his own side, wishing they'd gone a little easier on the ribs. It wouldn't kill him, really, but it sure as hell hurt a lot.

"I tucked them away before I answered the door. In truth, I thought you were my—"

There was a knock at the door, and they both froze,

sharing a single stare, the angel's filled with fear, and the demon's brimming with irritation.

"Stay put," they told him, and leaned Julian up against the wall by the stairs.

Julian watched as the angel walked away and peered through a hole in the door. Their shoulders relaxed, and so did Julian.

Then they opened the door and accepted a plastic bag carrying a delicious scent from a human who did not smell so delicious.

"Thank you. Have a good evening," the angel told him in a kind voice.

Julian didn't bother hearing what the human had to say. Instead, his attention was all on the angel.

They were dressed… rather human-like. It was surprising. He'd expected robes and wings and a halo to go with their pompous attitude that matched their lofty status but, well, Julian supposed that would be rather obvious, even to humans.

Instead they were in plaid pajama pants and a cardigan. They looked… cozy. Soft.

Julian sneered as the thought passed his mind.

So that was how the angel turned to find him once they'd shut the door quietly. Sneering at them.

Julian tried to mask his expression but didn't quite manage in time.

"You were the one who interrupted my night, I'll have you know," the angel said. "I was waiting on dinner when I found you on my doorstep instead."

"Sorry for the inconvenience," Julian drawled, gesturing down his beaten and bruised form.

The angel, Rami, shot him a frown as they deposited their bag of food on the table.

Julian wondered what it was they'd ordered. Whatever it was, it smelled good.

One of the things he was most excited about visiting Earth was the *food.*

"If you want help up the stairs, you've got to put your wings away," Rami reminded him. "It'll be easier to get you up the stairs."

"Right, yeah," Julian said, and propped against the wall. He grimaced at the ache as he tucked them out of sight, molding into his back once more. His tail also melted away, and his skin changed, too, from demon gold to pale human. "There."

"Now, come here," Rami said, and looped an arm around his waist. It pressed into his ribs, but Julian really didn't know if he could make it up the stairs by himself. In fact, as they took the first stair together, he knew he couldn't.

Grumbling, groaning, and cursing the whole way, he leaned into the angel. His knee was sore, too, and in the haze of memories he was pretty sure he remembered a bat being taken to it at one point.

Had the bat been totally necessary?

For just a moment, he was thankful the angel was there. They were surprisingly warm and soft against his side, their other hand held out in case Julian wanted to take it.

He didn't, gripping the handrail all the way up instead.

"Nice place for an angel," he muttered as they made it to the second floor. It all led to a loft bedroom and a huge bathroom.

"Thank you. I quite agree," Rami said, pleased with themself.

Julian resisted the urge to roll his eyes, and instead huffed out a relieved sigh as they stopped moving, finally.

"Your hair is disgusting," the angel told him, and Julian let all of his distaste show in his expression. "I think a bath will be more comfortable for you, though it will hurt to get in and out. I can assist you."

"Lucky me," Julian drawled.

The angel's face went all pinched before they turned away. Then the hush of the water filling the bath was the only sound in the room. The angel's water. Which, from what he understood of humans, was quite a precious thing. And here this angel was, sharing their own.

And even though they were technically enemies, and he should revel in the angel's discomfort and hurt little *feelings*, even though it was what Julian was counting on, something in his chest… itched, and he feared it had nothing to do with his injuries.

He sighed.

Damned selfless angels.

Julian swallowed as Rami fiddled with the bath. Julian *did* have an assignment here, and if he was going to succeed, maybe he should try being a little nicer to the angel. It was a start, after all.

"Thank you—for helping," Julian said.

Rami's shoulders stiffened, and when they turned to face Julian their expression was carefully blank, as if they cared not what happened to the demon. Their features were soft and unassuming, neither masculine nor feminine but somewhere in the middle. Their skin looked smooth and Julian found himself wanting to touch them.

That's not what you're here for, he reminded himself.

"Just doing my heavenly duty."

Julian couldn't stop his lip from curling. The angel seemed more open to Julian when he was being *himself.* Maybe he didn't need to be nice after all.

"Come on, then, get undressed," Rami said, turning their back to face the tub again. "I won't watch."

"Wouldn't care if you did," Julian responded. The angel's

shoulders stiffened again, and—how had they lasted this long on Earth if they were so easily flustered?

Julian lifted his shirt, all bravado, until he got about chest-height, and then groaned and dropped his arms, clutching at his side.

"Serves you right," the angel said, suddenly appearing by his side.

They had a pair of scissors in their hands, and they grabbed Julian's shirt by the hem and placed it between the two blades.

"Do be still—wouldn't want to hurt you." Their brow furrowed before they said, softer, "Seems like someone's done enough of that."

Then the angel was cutting his shirt off, and Julian didn't have to lift his arms at all. Rami was close, closer than they'd been so far all evening. They smelled nice. Clean cotton and vanilla and clouds. Which shouldn't have been a surprise, since they were an angel and all.

Julian shouldn't have found it pleasant, but he did.

He caught his breath, holding it as the angel moved even closer, and for a second he thought the angel was… embracing him.

But then the fabric of his sleeves was slipping over his shoulders and down his arms and Julian realized the angel was simply removing his shirt.

Julian shivered.

The angel noticed. "Sorry about the temperature. I like it quite chilly in the house."

"Why? So you can wear your cozy little sweaters?" Julian meant it as a sneer, but it didn't quite land how he'd wanted it to.

"Exactly," Rami said easily. They stepped back. "Can you get your pants, or should I help with that, too?"

Their expression was pinched. This was a challenge.

Julian wanted to laugh. The angel was challenging *him!*

He did not laugh. Instead he unbuttoned his pants and held the gaze of the angel as he did so, beginning to work them off his hips.

Rami's eyes flickered, something passing through them that Julian couldn't read. But they never wavered, not even as Julian's pants dropped to the floor, and he toed off his shoes and managed to kick them away in a pile.

"Are you quite finished?" Rami asked, arching one perfect brow.

Julian pouted. "You're not even a *little* tempted to look?" he teased.

The angel... well, their lips twitched, but they simply turned to face the tub and held out their arm. "Would you like some help or not?"

"Fine, fine," Julian growled, and grabbed onto their arm.

Rami led him to the side of the slowly filling tub, and then moved behind him. Julian stiffened at first, unsure of having someone at his back.

The angel noticed that, too. "Just giving you something to brace against," they said, tightening their grip on his biceps before sliding lower.

His knee throbbed, a constant heartbeat of discomfort, and he held on tightly to the angel as he stepped over the lip of the tub. Julian could barely put weight on his hurt knee, and Rami seemed to sense that.

"Forgive me," Rami said, and gripped Julian's hips.

His breath caught as Rami caught him, offering support as Julian managed both feet into the tub.

"Down you go," Rami said, and Julian wanted to be annoyed by the commentary, but found he wasn't. He was appreciative, instead.

"Careful," Rami murmured.

Julian felt like an infant as he gripped the sides of the tub and let himself be lowered into the hot water.

He hissed at first, but once his skin adjusted to the temperature, he found it was rather delightful.

"Oh, I missed baths," Julian remarked with a sigh. "Holy shit."

"Ugh, I rather despise that phrase," the angel said, shutting off the water and stepping away, then even further, until they were out the door.

I'll just keep using it then.

Julian assumed the angel was gone, and let his head rest against the edge of the tub, finally wincing at the throb in his head and knee and side and horn and back and—fuck, everywhere.

A throat cleared, and Julian picked his head up, squinting at the angel. In the bright light of the bathroom, Julian made a completely ambivalent observation: the angel was attractive.

Eyes as silvery as the sky upon the day of creation, and hair as gray as the shades angels refused to acknowledge they all lived in.

Okay, fine. It was blue-ish gray, down to the root as if it was a fresh dye job the internet had made popular a few years back.

If anything, the angel looked outdated with their tidy hair. Short on the sides and long and curly on the top.

Julian had let his own hair grow out after despising every moment of the buzz cut he'd experimented with. His hair now proudly brushed his shoulders, and was long enough to put in a bun when his horns weren't in the way.

"Here are some towels and clothes. I'm going to give you some privacy; try not to waste it. Yell when you're ready and I'll be back to help."

Julian hummed and watched the angel turn and go,

pulling the door until only a crack remained. With a sigh, he turned his head up and glared at the bright light of the bathroom, only for it to dim to a comfortable setting.

His gaze snapped to the door once again, Rami's hand slipping from the light switch and away.

Julian's brows furrowed, and his head smacked against the lip of the tub.

Stupid, thoughtful angels. All *kind* and *pure* and fucking… fucking *selfless.*

With a groan, he sank beneath the water, bubbles rising as he let out his frustration.

When he came back up, the water was a muddled pink, and he grimaced before dipping under again.

He scrubbed his right hand through his hair, keeping the left one pressed to his probably-bruised ribs. When he couldn't take it anymore, he came up for air and decided that would have to do until he could properly wash it.

He inhaled the steam from the hot bath and studied the bathroom, trying to learn more about this angel while he had the opportunity.

Well, that explains the vanilla scent, he thought as he read the label for their body wash. Their shampoo and conditioner—they didn't use a three-in-one, Julian noted—looked like it should be used on a horse instead of their delicate angel hair, but who was Julian to judge?

Julian didn't relish the thought of smelling like a dessert, but since it was his only option…

He lathered up his palms and scrubbed them over his skin instead of using the angel's fancy sponge-looking thing.

Actually. On second thought. He grabbed it from the hook and poured more soap on it before sudsing up.

He chuckled to himself as he washed the dirt and remaining blood from his skin. The warm air filled with the scent of vanilla, and by the time the water was cooling, he was squeaky clean. His wounds hadn't magically disappeared, but he imagined the hot water had loosened him up, made him feel a little better.

In fact, he felt so refreshed he didn't even need some stupid angel to help him, so he unplugged the drain with his toes and then braced himself on either side of the tub before—

"Ohhhh fuck," he groaned, teeth gritted as he lifted himself up.

His arms shook and his side throbbed, and his knee felt like someone had stuffed cotton between his joints.

But he did it—he made it to his own two feet, heavily leaning one hand against the wall as he stepped over the edge of the tub and onto the fluffy white mat.

Water dripped off him onto the floor anyway, and he swallowed a grunt as he lifted his other leg out of the bath, knee protesting the whole way.

Everything was going well until he tried to put weight on that leg and walk. It just… didn't work, and he careened into the wall with a thud and a curse.

"Now, I told you to call out for me when you were ready," Rami said, pushing into the bathroom like they owned the place—they did—and coming to Julian's rescue like he'd asked them to—he hadn't. "You're going to hurt yourself even more if you're not careful," the angel scolded him.

Scolded! A demon!

Julian would have laughed in their face if he weren't huffing in pain.

Rami draped the towel over him before helping Julian back to his feet. He had to lean on the angel; he had no choice in the matter as he was dragged from the bathroom to the bedroom, and carefully lowered to the bed.

Without another word, the angel walked over to the

dresser and started rummaging. When they turned again, a stack of clothes in their arms, their gaze… dipped.

Julian followed it, lightning-quick, and discovered the towel had not stayed in place like the angel had probably intended.

Rami's pale cheeks flushed a delicate pink as they averted their gaze. Julian grinned, target locked.

Maybe, just maybe, tempting this angel wouldn't be so difficult after all.

3
HOST WITH THE MOST

They should've known the demon would be too stubborn to ever call out for help.

And yet, when they'd heard the water drain after unpacking and reheating their food, they'd thought surely Julian would be calling for them any moment.

They'd even ascended the stairs, anticipating his call. Expectant, Rami had paused outside the bathroom door, waiting, up until they'd heard the thump and a hissed curse.

They'd rolled their eyes—should they start keeping count?—and pushed through the door, chastising the demon for being so unreasonable. Honestly, he was *hurt,* why wouldn't he—

Ah. Yes, that was it. He had been hurt, probably by someone higher up than him, someone he knew, was relatively close to. Well, as *close* as Rami imagined one could get in Hell. Rami's chest ached at the idea.

Why would this demon trust anyone?

This is what they were pondering when they turned, the clothes chosen for Julian suddenly heavy in their arms. The demon was sprawled across the bed that *Rami* slept in—or read in—every single night. Across *their* blankets, the demon's bared skin was displayed, from his bruised chest and side to his hips and thighs and—yes, that was certainly...

Heat rushed to their cheeks, and they averted their gaze as they stepped forward, dropping the pile of clothes beside Julian on *Rami's* bed.

"Here are some clothes for you. Do you think you can manage?"

Ignoring the demon's cheshire grin, they took a step toward the stairs.

"Sure I can," the demon drawled, and he did not sound like he intended to dress one bit.

"Well, cover the bits you want protected from hot pasta, at least," they snipped, and left the bedroom, steps thudding down the stairs as they retreated to the kitchen.

Rami poured themself another glass of wine and drank it impolitely quickly.

Then they continued what they'd been doing while Julian was bathing.

On Earth, humans had to eat to survive. Angels didn't. Likely, demons didn't either. But it most certainly wouldn't *hurt*, and Rami wasn't going to feed themself while Julian went without.

That was just *rude*.

Food was a... luxury to Rami, and they weren't ashamed to admit it.

So they gathered an item from the freezer and added it to the tray with a single bowl of reheated carbonara, the remaining breadsticks, and a healthy glass of water before making the trek back upstairs. They counted the steps again, telling themself to remain calm.

This might be a demon, but he was also someone in need.

The last time someone had been at Rami's door, knocking that frantically, they hadn't been able to help.

Rami didn't want to live that again, so they'd be damned if they wouldn't help this demon, no matter how frustrating he might be.

Maybe once the demon was well enough on his own two feet, Rami could return to their regularly scheduled program of operation.

They could taste the freedom already.

But for now, they would help this demon get back on his feet.

Much to their surprise, when Rami knocked on the wall at the top of the stairs and was granted entry into their own bedroom, the demon had dressed properly.

He was sitting on the edge of the bed, palms pressed into either side of himself as he eyed the stairway.

Rami became the focus of that stare, those deep golden eyes practically flaming. His mocha hair framed his strong cheekbones, brushing at his chin and shoulders as he tilted his head in Rami's direction.

"What's that?" he asked.

"Pasta carbonara," Rami answered reflexively. "And breadsticks, water."

They crossed the room and placed the food on the nightstand.

"Up you get," Rami directed, and motioned for Julian to sit against the headboard.

Julian narrowed his gaze, but did as he was told. "What's that?" he asked, and Rami lifted an oven mitt, letting it hover over Julian's knee as he stilled.

"An ice pack for your knee. The mitt is so you don't get cold burns," they explained as they balanced it.

"Cold burns," Julian scoffed. "Please."

Rami's lips twitched as they raised up and stepped away. "Right. You're from Hell. Probably used to all kinds of burns."

Julian pursed his lips, and it was quiet for a moment. His attention trailed to the nightstand containing the bowl. "Actually, we did away with the hellfire a few centuries ago."

"Really?" Rami asked, their voice three octaves higher in surprise. "Marvelous. I'm sure that's been quite the improvement to morale."

"Morale," Julian echoed, shaking his head up at the angel.

"Yes, quite. Here," they said, and handed Julian the bowl. "Let me know when you're finished. I can come get the dishes."

Julian's lips twitched. "You make quite the little servant."

If Rami's wings were out, they were certain they would've bristled.

"How long do you anticipate staying?" they asked sharply.

"I dunno," he said, and messily dragged a bite of pasta to his lips.

He *moaned* rather dramatically at the first bite. "Holy shit, this is good."

Rami's eye twitched.

"An estimate, maybe?" Rami pressed.

The demon shrugged and then winced, regretting it, and guilt pierced Rami. The demon was *hurt,* had been cast out, or—or something! And here Rami was trying to push him out the door already.

"However long it takes to heal?" Julian said, turning those big brown eyes up to them. "I've never *not* been able to heal myself. So I don't know."

Flustered by the effect those pretty eyes were having on Rami, they hummed, and turned their back.

"Where are you going?" Julian called out.

Rami paused by the doorway. "Downstairs. I've got some work to finish."

"Work? Celestial work?"

Rami glanced over their shoulder. "No, I need to update client files with today's notes."

Julian arched a brow. "Clients? You a hooker?"

Rami caught their eye roll before they could complete it. "If you *must* know," Rami said slowly, "I'm a therapist. I'll be downstairs if you need anyth—"

Julian's howling laughter interrupted them, and followed them out the door as Rami turned away, cheeks aflame, and retreated down the steps to the solitary peace of their office.

They shut both doors and locked them for good measure before they stalked over to their desk and sat down with a flourish.

"What am I doing?" they mumbled to themself. Housing a demon?

Absolutely ridiculous.

Rami had spent many lifetimes witnessing injustices, unable to step in because of the natural order of things.

And this demon, Julian, was hurt. And in need.

This time, Rami could help.

So no matter how annoying he might be, Rami was going to, whether the demon wanted it or not, whether *Rami* wanted to help a demon or not.

With a chuckle, they released a much-needed sigh, and let their shoulders slump before filling their lungs again.

Once they felt more settled, less rattled, they cracked open their laptop and began transcribing the notes they'd made during sessions.

Melissa had made some major realizations today, and they were so proud of her! They made themself a note to prepare a little treat for her before the next appointment.

It didn't take very long at all, and then they focused on sending automated texts and emails to cancel all appointments for the next week. Surely it would take the demon a few days to heal, and Rami couldn't have clients visiting if there was a demon in the house.

Demons and angels were still kept secret from humans. And even if they seemed alright with werewolves and vampires and dragons and all the other creatures, Rami wasn't going to be the one to accidentally reveal them.

Their chest ached as their finger hovered over the *send* button, and their gaze trailed overhead, to the ceiling, wishing the demon knew they were glaring.

Because of *him*, Rami had to press pause on their clients who were making great headway.

With a sigh, they added that they could still contact Rami for any emergencies and finally sent the notifications.

As if the demon had some sixth sense—it wouldn't surprise Rami if he did—he called out.

"Hey, Feathers! Hellooo!" he practically sang.

Rami took a breath, prayed for a bit more fortitude, and shut their laptop down. They were finished with work anyway. After grabbing a pillow from their client couch, they made their way upstairs.

Upon reaching the second floor, they found the demon had cleared his bowl and even finished all his water.

"How's the knee?" they asked, watching the demon adjust the mitt.

"The ice feels great," he said, looking pleased with himself as he lounged back against the headboard, hands clasped over his stomach. "And the carbonara was really good."

"Glad to hear it," the angel said, and put the slim pillow on the bed. "Up," they said, and slid it beneath the demon's knee. Then they gathered his bowl and glass. "More water?"

The demon was staring at them, and the angel did not enjoy being under his spotlight like a bug beneath a lens.

"Did you give me your dinner? The one the human delivered?"

"I ate my portion while you were bathing," Rami told him. "Not even I'm so angelic as to sacrifice all of my pasta. I'll bring you some more water. Keep the knee elevated."

The demon offered no more witty retorts as Rami did as they'd said. They were an angel of their word, after all. The night was wearing on them, and they looked forward to sleeping. Another necessity of the humans that Rami treated as a luxury. Maybe they'd wake up tomorrow and it would all be a dream.

They knew it wasn't likely, but they could hope.

When they made their last ascension to the second floor loft bedroom, they were relieved, and placed the glass on the night table.

"Water. Now, I'll be downstairs, but if you need anything else, let me know."

"Where are you sleeping?" he asked, and patted the bed next to him with half-lidded, suggestive eyes.

Rami pretended they didn't see.

"I'll be on the couch, downstairs. It's quite comfortable." It wasn't a lie, technically, but anywhere away from this demon had to be more comfortable.

"Aw, come on, now, I can't take your bed," Julian drawled. "Look how much room there is."

"You can't do much of anything with all your injuries," Rami retorted.

"Don't be like that," Julian said, a teasing note in his voice.

"I'm not being any certain way except helpful," Rami noted. "Now. Goodnight," they said, and turned on their heel.

The demon let them go, blessedly, and Rami soaked up the silence of the lower level of their home, staring at the couch as if it was a challenge.

It *was* comfortable, if you laid a very specific way and placed the pillows in just the right position.

So that's what they did, and they prayed for the demon's

healing and well-being, as well as more patience in the coming days.

They had a feeling they were going to need it.

Rami hadn't thought they'd actually fall asleep, not with a demon in their home. However, next thing they knew, they were blinking their eyes open to the soft light of the morning.

They stretched, groaning softly, and arched their back to stretch out the ache that had formed over the night.

"Keep making noises like that and I can't be responsible for my actions."

Rami startled, pulling their arms down by their side and simultaneously attempting to sit up and locate the demon. The pillow beneath their hand slipped and they slipped with it, spilling onto the floor beside the coffee table.

For a second, they considered staying there and pretending the demon didn't exist.

Instead, they pressed themself up by their hands and sat back on their knees, glaring at the demon who was standing by the stairs. His arms and ankles were crossed, casual as can be.

"How long have you been standing there?" Rami asked, a familiar heat rushing to their cheeks no matter how much they wished it wouldn't.

"Long enough," the demon said with a smirk. When he walked forward, it was with a limp, though the gash on his forehead seemed to be healed, his skin smooth and unblemished once again.

"You've healed overnight," Rami noticed, and got to their

feet. They picked their pillow and blanket up and made the effort to fold them and place them neatly on the edge of the couch.

"Some of me has," Julian said. "Knee still hurts. And my ribs."

"And your wing?"

Rami asked more out of politeness than anything. They didn't expect Julian to free them and stretch them out in Rami's crowded home.

His wings spanned from the kitchen to the doors of his office. Without hesitation.

"Seems fine now," Julian murmured.

"Glad to hear it. Now put them away before you break something."

"You could just fix whatever I break," he said, waving his hand about as if performing a bit of the magic they were privy to.

"No, actually. I'm not supposed to be frivolous with it. I'm here to study humans, not perform magic tricks," they informed the demon, and then passed by him to go upstairs.

"Where are you going?" Julian asked, a frown in his voice.

Rami paused on the steps. "I am going to dress for the day."

"Oh, right. You have *clients*," the demon sneered.

Resisting the urge to snap at the demon, Rami didn't bother correcting him and continued to their room, where they gathered clothes for the day and then locked themself away in the bathroom.

At least it's quiet in here.

But it would only be a short reprieve, they knew. How were they going to entertain the demon all day and keep him out of trouble? He was already up on his own two feet. Granted, he wasn't very fast.

He's like a toddler.

Rami chuckled at that. The demon, toddling around and causing chaos.

It was only their problem while Julian was here, at least. Once he was well enough on his own, the angel could go back to their regular proceedings, never to waste a moment thinking about the demon again.

With a sigh, they dressed.

4
A NOTICE

I *can do this,* he told himself, standing in front of the coffee pot.

In hell, it wasn't necessary for demons to eat, especially the lower-level ones. However, Julian's frequent trips to the human realm as a glorified postman meant he'd gotten to… cheat, every now and then.

Coffee was one of his favorite ways to cheat. He'd just never had to make it himself before.

As he stood in the angel's tidy kitchen, staring at the little coffee maker, he told himself that it was easy.

If the angel could damned well do it, so could Julian.

But when he opened the top of the machine, there was no coffee to be seen, and his brows furrowed.

With a huff, he began pulling open cabinets until he found a bag filled with beans.

What the fuck was he supposed to do with these?

I don't have time for this, he thought.

With a wave of his hand, he conjured up a paper cup with hot, steaming coffee inside.

"Much easier," he said with a smirk, and turned, ready to abandon his attempts.

"Having fun?" Rami asked him.

Julian refused to show his surprise at the angel's sudden appearance. "Now that I have coffee, almost."

"You didn't make that yourself, I take it?"

Julian stepped to the side, hiding the machine and the bag of dark beans from the angel's gaze as they approached.

"Are you going to keep me from making myself a cup, in my own kitchen?" Rami asked, pausing a few steps away.

They had dressed for the day, just like they'd announced. They were good at blending in, looking human. *Frumpy,* some might say.

Slacks and a plain shirt and a large sweater draped their frame. Only the tips of their fingers were visible in the sleeves and the demon thought to himself, *They look... soft. Sweet.*

They're an angel; that's how they're supposed to look.

Amusement framed their silvery eyes, supple, full lips curling slowly as Julian tried to hide his attempts at coffee.

Rami took another step forward and lifted their hand, the sleeve slipping back as they motioned the demon aside.

And, well, he went, and didn't really have an excuse as to why he obeyed.

"Fine," he conceded, offering just enough room for the angel to get to their coffee machine.

The angel first gathered a kettle from the stove and went to the sink, filling it with water before replacing it and turning the stove on.

Next, they opened their cabinet and pulled out a mug, as well as *another* machine.

They were close enough for their shoulders to brush. Julian refused to move. Privately, he enjoyed the warmth of the angel so close as they fiddled.

Curiosity broiled beneath his skin, and Julian gave up pretending not to watch Rami work.

They used a measuring cup to collect the beans from the bag and dumped them in the second machine. Then they placed a lid on it and plugged it in, before pressing at the front of it.

Julian startled at the loud whir, the grinding noise as the beans were turned into grounds. His own coffee sloshed up the sides of his cup.

Ah. Ground coffee. Makes sense.

The angel's lips twitched as Julian settled back down, and the demon cleared his throat to hide his surprise.

Soon, the horrible noise shut off and Rami opened the cabinet yet *again*. This time they pulled out a round cone-shaped thing, and placed it over the top of the mug, followed by a paper cone that went *inside* the first cone!

Julian frowned.

The angel paid him no mind, going about their business as if they didn't have a demon watching their every move. They unhooked part of the second machine in order to dump the ground-up beans into the paper cone.

"Seems like a lot of work just for coffee," he mused, gaze narrowed.

"It tastes better when the grounds are fresh," Rami retorted.

The kettle whistled, right on time, and the angel hummed as they retrieved it and then poured the hot water over the grounds. The water filled the cone quickly and then… they waited.

Julian watched the water slowly disappear, and deduced it must be dripping through the cone into the cup below. The seconds that passed were not quite as painful as the ache in his side, but it was a near thing.

"This is ridiculous," Julian scoffed as the angel filled the cone for the third time. "You could've magicked a dozen cups of coffee by now."

"I find this process rather soothing, especially first thing in the morning."

"But there's… so many steps! How do you even remember them all?"

"I do them every morning—it's become routine. I hardly think of it anymore."

"What the hell is this for, then?" Julian asked, and pointed to the first machine, the one with the glass pot.

"That's just a regular coffee machine. I use it for clients."

Julian rolled his eyes. "Why don't you just use it? Surely it's simpler."

"I told you, the coffee tastes better when it's fresh. And nothing is fresher than a pour over."

"Coffee grounds. Pour over. Humans really got creative with those names, didn't they?" Julian drawled.

"Well, I can't imagine why it needs to be complicated," Rami snapped.

Julian resisted the grin threatening to twist his lips. This angel was so easy to rile.

"So you give your clients second-rate coffee, then? Saving the good stuff for yourself?"

The angel bristled. "Well, no. I—"

"Sounds selfish, Feathers," the demon teased, and sauntered out of the kitchen, to the very couch the angel had slept on.

"I am not *selfish!*" they called out, indignant, cheeks flushing prettily.

The demon hummed in response, kicking his hurt knee up on the coffee table. It was… quiet, here. In the human world.

Outside, the birds sang, and behind him, the sun streamed in through the windows, casting a glare upon the television he figured the angel didn't get much use out of.

Not compared to the overflowing bookshelves framing it, many of the books' spines cracked and lined with use.

When the angel eventually followed after him, their coffee cup steaming, they frowned at the foot on their table.

"What? You said keep it elevated."

Rami's jaw ticked. Julian added a tally to the scoreboard in his mind.

"I'll have you know that my clients get the most expensive brand of coffee on the shelves," Rami said haughtily.

Julian arched a brow. "You pay for it yourself, do you?"

He knew the angel didn't. Just like they hadn't paid for this house, or even the coffee they'd spent so long making.

"Well. It makes the humans happy either way. They enjoy the coffee. Or tea, if that's their preference."

"Oh god, how long does that take?" Julian asked, poking fun.

The angel chuckled at that and the demon frowned. There was no laughing allowed. *Stop that.*

It made Rami's eyes crinkle, and the demon didn't like it.

Their sleeves were covering their hands again, cupped around the hot mug.

Ah, they used the fabric as protection from the hot mug. Now *that* made sense.

Maybe this was their coffee-drinking sweater. It wouldn't surprise Julian if they had a sweater for each part of the day.

"Why don't you just magic yourself a cup of coffee every morning?" Julian asked.

The angel paused before they continued taking a seat in the leather chair near the double doors of their office. The sun shone on them from that angle, and it occurred to the demon that maybe they'd placed the chair there on purpose, to take advantage of the morning rays of the sun.

How... simple of this angel to find pleasure in such a

small thing. To arrange their living area around the sun's rays.

Worshiping a false god? Julian smirked. Humans had the silliest notions.

"That would be considered a frivolous use of magic," Rami answered.

The silence stretched on. "Okay, and?" Julian asked.

Rami frowned at him, lips pursed to blow at the top of the mug, steam dissipating. "It's not right to use magic frivolously."

"Who in the world told you that?"

The angel didn't answer, and honestly, Julian didn't know why he'd asked a question he knew the answer to. He was just so… flabbergasted.

And, well. Maybe it was time for a proper temptation.

"It's not like using magic leaves less of it in the world, Rami."

The angel's name felt odd on his tongue. Sticky.

He took a sip of his coffee to wash it away.

"There's not someone up there," he said, whirling a circle in the air and pointing *up*, "keeping track of what magic you use when and where and for what. Using it doesn't take it away from someone else." It was hardly the least selfish thing Julian was going to tempt the angel into, but he had to start gently, ease them into it.

The angel was still as a statue, averting their gaze to their mug and blowing the steam away once more. They took a sip, and then spoke. "Even if that was my concern, it matters not. I'm supposed to blend in and help the humans. Hard to blend in if I'm using magic all over the place."

Julian narrowed his eyes. The angel was being purposefully obtuse.

So Julian waited, and let the subject drop for the moment. The angel picked up a book from their side table, and traded their mug of coffee for the contents within. It didn't take long for the steam to disappear, the angel too lost in their book to notice.

The rustle of pages turning was the only sound in the home for a long while. The sun tracked across the couch, and left the angel in shade eventually.

Only then did they reach for their coffee, and frowned, their gaze falling to the cooled mug and then to the clock in the corner.

The demon stood, stretched, and then regretted it as his side protested.

With a snap, he reheated the angel's coffee and watched as surprise filled their face. Then their features went all pinched as they met the demon's eyes. "You didn't have to do that."

"Easier than watching you have to do another *ritual* in order to heat it back up," he teased to cover his tracks.

The angel stared for a few moments longer, and then slowly lifted the mug to their lips. Their gazes were still locked as they took a noisy sip.

Julian held out his arms as much as he could without aching, and shrugged. "See? No smiting necessary for a tiny bit of magic. Enjoy your coffee, angel."

"And where are you going?"

"Is it any of your business?" Julian asked.

Rami shrugged and sat back in their chair, sleeves still covering their fingers where they held the book gently in their hands. "I suppose not."

"I'm bored. I'm going for a walk because I'm tired of watching you read," he grumbled, unsure why he was answering.

"Are you sure that's smart?" Rami asked. Their brows were ruffled, tight in the middle as they quit pretending to read and stared at the demon over their book. "What with…" They lifted a hand to motion at him. "Whoever is after you."

"I'll be fine, but I'm touched you care," Julian drawled.

He watched Rami process, lips pursed. "If you feel well enough to go out on a little day trip, don't you think you're well enough to leave?"

Julian cocked his head to the side. "And go where? I'm clearly not welcome back in Hell, and I have no connections here. Why, Rami," Julian cooed. "You want me out on the street?"

Rami's expression went all tight. Adorably bitchy. "You could just use that magic you're so partial to. Set yourself up."

Julian pretended to consider it. "You might be right. I could just magic some human into giving me their car keys. Maybe house keys, too. Oh, now, that's a good idea, Feathers. Best one yet," he declared. "I think I'd like to try out a mansion." That would be one way to enjoy his time on Earth while he could.

Panic was slowly filling Rami's expression, and Julian spun on his heel as if he intended to hunt down the first human he found and magic all their possessions into Julian's hands.

"Wait!" Rami called out, frustrated. "Don't mess with the humans. You can stay here. Just—don't expose yourself to them. They don't know angels and demons exist."

"I may have been stuck in Hell all this time, but I at least know that, Feathers."

Rami's expression went perfectly blank, smoothing out once again. "Whatever. Enjoy your day."

Whatever.

"I'll be sure to make it home for dinner, don't worry," he informed the angel as Julian snapped his fingers and changed his outfit to one that wouldn't draw attention.

"Wasn't worried," they retorted without lifting their eyes from the page.

"Sure you weren't," Julian said, sarcasm dripping, and then let himself out the very door he'd appeared on the step of the night before.

He'd planted the seed; now he just had to wait.

Outside, the world was even prettier than he remembered.

The night before, he hadn't been able to see very much, on account of it being dark and all.

Everything was different in the daylight.

Once he'd stepped out onto the sidewalk and made his way over a tiny bridge, the city opened up before him.

Cars honked, and people shouted at one another over trivial things. Humans and monsters alike were buried in their devices as they hurried from one destination to the other. They were taking it all for granted! They needed to pick their damned heads up and appreciate what they had around them.

The sun still shone, but it wasn't cast artfully over a leather armchair; it was blinding. He passed a human and magicked the sunglasses off the man's face and onto his own.

It was nice to be here, even if it was a bit too warm, and he regretted the extra layers he'd added. That's what he got for trusting an angel who loved sweaters regardless of the weather.

He magicked a tee shirt beneath his pullover and stripped his top layer off. He considered just dumping it in the next trash bin he saw, but instead, he missed by about two feet or so, and the human sitting nearby grabbed the sleeve and pulled it closer to claim it as his own.

The man needed it more than Julian did, so he kept walking. One little act of selflessness wasn't going to get him into trouble.

At least, he hoped not.

He studied the humans he passed and nosily peered in the shop windows. At clothes and food and a hardware store. He even passed a sex shop and gawked at the window for a moment before committing the location to memory and moving on.

Humans and other monsters—Julian knew there was a different word they preferred, but he couldn't think of it just then—didn't know how good they had it here, on Earth. Free to do as they please, go where they want. He passed a tree, leaves stained orange with the passing of summer. It was just as lovely as it looked on television, and Julian plucked a leaf down, spinning it between his fingers.

Humans got to enjoy their simple little pleasures as much as they wanted.

Like a cup of coffee, he thought bitterly.

As a messenger, Julian didn't get to do *this*. To take his time and experience the Earth and all it had to offer. Julian held onto the leaf as he walked.

As he passed an alleyway a few moments later, a flash of light caught his attention. It was so bright in the day that most humans probably wouldn't have noticed it. But the hue of it was one Julian had seen countless times, as he'd delivered summons and news to whoever needed it.

He glanced to the left and saw a messenger awaiting him.

With a sigh, Julian turned into the alley and met the demon at the end.

"I have a notice for you," the demon said.

"Great, what is it?" he asked.

The demon pulled out a… clipboard?—clearing his throat as he prepared to read it.

Oh god, was this what Julian had always looked like? How annoying. He snatched the clipboard from the demon, eyes scanning the ancient paper beneath the metal bar.

"What happened to the scrolls?" Julian asked. This was a new development.

"The Seventh Devil's doing, sir."

"Galen?"

The messenger nodded. "He claimed it would help us blend in."

Julian missed Galen something fierce just then. Galen was a lucky bastard, getting his promotion, using it to meet Maeve, visiting Earth whenever he wanted.

His new boss, Carl, was an asshole, but the promotion in temptations hadn't been in Galen's territory. So even if it meant leaving his friend, Julian had taken it anyway.

And it had landed him… here.

The words embedded themselves on the page as he watched.

ATTN: Julian

It has been more than twelve hours since we assigned the angel Ramiel to your temptations. Have you any updates?

Julian rolled his eyes and spoke at the scroll. "Twelve hours is hardly enough to do much more than annoy the angel, which, it turns out, is going quite well."

More words burned themselves into the paper.

Are you in position to continue the temptation?

Julian swallowed what he really wanted to say, hands tightening on the plastic board. "I'm in place, as we discussed. I can handle it from here."

You will be the first demon to ever tempt this angel.

Yeah, Julian knew that. When had demons started tempting angels, anyway?

Julian kept his thoughts to himself. "Okay, and?"

Due to the difficulty of the mission, we will accept your resignation, if you so choose.

"But it's only been twelve hours," Julian hissed. "I haven't even gotten to the good stuff yet!"

Twelve hours was hardly enough time to do anything, let alone tempt an apparently *pure* angel.

Do you wish to continue?

"What happens if I return?"

You will be added to the waitlist for temptations.

He'd been on the list for decades before now. Only demons who were successful in their temptations got to do another, so the list rarely shuffled. His gaze flicked to the current messenger, patiently waiting a few steps away, content to watch the humans pass at the end of the alley.

Julian didn't want to return to Hell yet. He didn't want to be a messenger, only catching glimpses of humanity—of Earth—and living vicariously through the internet. He wanted to *experience* it. He'd only just gotten here.

"And what if I'd like to continue the temptation?"

That is your prerogative. However, if you choose to stay and fail in your temptations, you will be demoted.

Julian's chest went tight. "To what?"

To your previous role: a messenger.

Resisting the urge to groan, Julian stared at the clipboard so hard he hoped he burned a hole in it.

No such luck.

He could return now, give up on the angel, and wait a hundred more decades to get another chance—*if* he got another chance. Or he could continue, fail, be demoted, and wait anyway.

Or. He could try, succeed, and remain on Earth.

Julian lifted his head to the sun, felt the warmth on his skin.

There was no warmth beneath the florescent lights of Hell.

"I'd like to continue the temptation," Julian said.

A pause extended as the scroll remained silent. Julian tensed, half expecting to be sucked back down to Hell anyway.

You have until the end of the week.

Julian nodded. "Yes, sir," he said.

The text on the paper all vanished in a puff of smoke, and Julian waved a hand to clear it. The messenger took the clipboard from him and nodded before disappearing in another flash of light.

Spinning, Julian glanced around, but found the humans none the wiser.

He relaxed in the face of their indifference, noses too buried in their phones to glance up and notice what was going on around them.

One week, he thought.

He could tempt the angel in that time, right?

Well, it wasn't like he had a choice. Hell did *not* like being disappointed.

5
A TINY INDISCRETION

After the demon left, it was like the sun shone a little brighter through the windows. Their shoulders finally relaxed despite the ache in their neck, and they sank deeper into their chair, reluctantly sipping their now hot coffee.

It was still delicious, to their dismay.

But the caffeine did little to boost their mood, and they glared at the couch responsible for their aches. The cushion was still indented from the demon's presence all morning, the ghost of him lingering.

Rami placed their bookmark before closing the book altogether and setting it on the side table, exchanging it for their mug. The warmth was perfect against their hands.

It had been… not so terrible to spend the morning alongside the demon, they supposed.

At least Julian was quiet.

Waiting, Rami realized, to show off his little magic trick.

Rami's sip of the hot coffee was loud in the quiet of their space. It was nifty, they admitted. Coffee didn't always taste the same once reheated, and this had been a particularly perfect, smooth pour, leaving nutty and cocoa hints behind. They would have hated to waste it, so they couldn't say they didn't appreciate the demon's gesture.

Still, they were not one for frivolity when it came to magic. They'd been sent here to masquerade as a human, to study them, and overall, that was just easier when they knew what it was to *be* a human.

And what better way to learn than by listening intently to their life experiences, their process of emotion, as they sat on the yellow couch and played with the pillow tassels?

Besides, Rami must have been doing something right, because they hadn't heard from Heaven in quite some time.

Why change what was clearly working?

Their mug clicked on the tabletop, and they stood, socked feet padding as they stepped toward their office, pulled open the French doors, and took a seat at their desk.

This office was their favorite room. The walls behind and across from them were bookshelves, filled to the tip-top with books they'd collected over the years. The wall to their left was nothing but arched windows, the stained glass tops casting a beautiful glow over the yellow couch.

They did have curtains, but rarely did their clients request to use them.

The desk was more for show, except for when they were doing admin work—of which there wasn't much. In sessions, they preferred to sit in the chair in front of their desk so the clients didn't feel so disconnected from them.

A lot of trust went into Rami when someone entered this room, and they truly respected the humans for it.

Pulling their gaze back to their laptop, they read through a few emails and replied when needed.

In the monotony, their thoughts traveled to the demon. Where had he gone in the late morning? Was he meeting someone? He was still injured, so surely he wouldn't have gone far.

Rami realized they had no way to contact the demon. He

said he'd be back, but as the hours passed, Rami began to wonder.

What if Julian had been taken by the people who hurt him? What if he was being hurt again?

What was he even doing on Earth? He'd said he was a messenger, but messenger demons usually remained in Hell until they had a message to deliver.

You could ask.

Oh, but that felt like an invasion of privacy.

Then again, the demon certainly didn't mind invading *their* privacy, slinking around and showing up bloody, making them *worry.* The audacity.

It might not be any of their business, but this demon was staying in Rami's house. If he was going to bring trouble to their doorstep, Rami deserved to know ahead of time, right?

As they contemplated, they stared toward the arched windows, the branches of the tree swaying softly in the breeze, empty of birds.

Mind made up, Rami opened their desk drawer and pulled out a piece of very special card stock, the edges lined with silver. With their pen, they stated their name, assignment, location, and question, along with a short description of the demon's information.

They signed it, sealed it in an envelope, and went to their window, walking through the prisms of light from the glass. It unlatched smoothly, and they pushed both sides open, holding the letter out into the weakening autumn sun.

Within seconds, a perfectly white dove landed on the windowsill.

"Hello there, it's lovely to see you. You'll take this where it should go, won't you?" they asked softly. They brushed a finger over the dove's head, and she blinked at them slowly.

Then Heaven's messenger flapped her wings and snagged the letter from their other hand before taking flight.

She didn't go far, dissipating into nothingness as she traveled to Heaven.

They'd have an answer in a few days, probably, so for now they closed the window, shutting out the too-hot day and retreating to their desk.

It had been a while since they'd written to Heaven as well. They hoped management wouldn't be disappointed in them. Rami hoped they could share any information on the demon at all.

With a sigh, they opened their laptop and finished reading a few replies with their clients, scheduling the new appointments a couple of them had requested.

Surely a week was long enough for the demon to get back on his feet and find his own way?

As they were finishing up, Rami heard the back door open, then close, and they sat up straight, attention shifting to the open French doors.

Oh no.

"Honey, I'm home—hey, you didn't drink the coffee I reheated for you!" His voice grew louder as his steps sounded, and Rami was frozen—they should've shut and locked the doors for good measure—

There he was, appearing in Rami's line of sight and grabbing up the mug.

"Come on, now, don't be like that," he said, and sauntered right in without knocking, or asking, or—or anything.

Rami's cheeks flushed in irritation, eyes narrowing as Julian made his way to Rami's desk, setting the mug down with a click.

"Shouldn't let it go to waste, should you?" he asked, and then spun in a circle, hands on his hips. He gave a slow whistle, and paced over to the yellow couch, staring up at the bookshelves and all the books it contained.

Rami glared at the back of Julian's head. Then their gaze lifted to the visible pair of horns.

"Please tell me you weren't walking around outside like that," they said, patience wearing thin.

"Like what?" he asked, running a finger along the spines on the shelf. "You've got quite the collection here."

Rami slowly stood. "With your horns. Surely you weren't out exposing yourself to the humans—"

"Don't get your feathers crossed, I didn't show anyone," Julian said, not even bothering with more than a glance over his shoulder at Rami. "I let them out when I came in the door. This one's still aching," he admitted, and reached up to gently brush a finger over the broken end. "They're very sensitive."

At least it seemed less jagged than it had when they'd first seen it.

Rami winced in sympathy, and steeled themself. "If you wouldn't mind, this is a private study, and I'd appreciate if you—"

"Private? But this is where you listen to your clients, I'm assuming," he said, spinning in place to face them. He placed his hands on the back of the couch and leaned over. "They sit on this fancy yellow couch?"

Rami ground their teeth together. "Nothing in this room is of any concern to you, so—"

"It's a nice couch. Looks comfy. Bit bright for listening to humans drone on, though, isn't it?"

He brushed a hand over one of the pillows, before grabbing it with both and compressing it between his hands.

"Julian!" Rami snapped, placing their hands on the desk quietly. The demon dropped the pillow, which filled out again as it landed on the couch. "This room is a sacred, safe space to my clients. You do not belong in here." Rami's frustration filled out their tone, which was smooth and even, leaving no room for misinterpretation.

"Sacred, you don't say?" he asked, dripping with sarcasm as he stepped out from behind the couch.

"Quite. Now leave. I will *not* have you tainting it with your… your bad vibes," Rami bit out, waving a hand at the demon to encompass his… everything.

Julian's lips twitched. "Bad vibes?" he teased, sauntering closer, coming to the side of the desk, hair brushing his cheeks as he walked.

Rami refused to straighten up, lest the demon think they felt *uneasy.* If anything, they pressed their palms harder into the desk.

They barely graced the demon with their stare, turning their head to meet Julian's damned golden eyes.

They were filled with mirth, of all things, and something darker.

"You think I have bad vibes, angel?" he asked, voice dipping lower, smooth like Rami's coffee.

The demon leaned in, placing a palm on the corner of the desk, swaying close, closer, until their noses were only inches away.

"That's quite the compliment… coming from you," Julian murmured, gaze slipping down a few inches for just a moment.

Rami made sure the lips beneath that stare moved solidly. "*Leave.* Please," they added. Their voice did not waver.

The demon lifted his eyes, as golden as honey and just as sticky, holding Rami there in this limbo of tension that prickled across their skin.

"Alright, Feathers," he said. "Guess it's the least I could do." Julian moved first, stepping away from the desk and toward the doors. And then he was gone, broken horn and all, as the left side of the door swung softly shut behind him.

Rami swayed into their chair, hands dragging across their desk, leaving smudged prints behind.

Their hands were sweating.

"Fuck," they whispered. They wrapped their hand around their mug, stilling as no warmth met their palm.

Julian was right; it had gone cold again.

Rami narrowed their gaze, lips tight as they waved the opposite hand over the mug. A smidge of magic, like the drag of a feather through the air.

The porcelain warmed beneath their touch, and they drank the last bit of it in one go.

The smooth taste burned all the way down.

6
A LITTLE TREAT

Rami managed to avoid the demon for most of the remaining daylight hours. It wasn't until thoughts of dinner distracted them enough from the book they were reading, holed up in their office, that they finally decided they'd had enough isolation for one day.

They did not feel like ordering in, but it felt—well, it felt rather intimate to prepare a meal for someone, didn't it? They could've sworn that's how most humans courted one another. Homemade meals.

And they did not desire to give the demon any idea of the sort.

But they had this lovely wine they'd been eager to crack into, and nothing went better with that than the risotto they'd been wanting to make.

When they shut off the lights and closed the office door behind them, they paused, listening for the demon's whereabouts.

There. Upstairs, the drone of the television from their bedroom. They heard a laugh track, and beneath that, the warm chuckle of the demon.

Rami almost rolled their eyes, but resisted. Of course the

demon would be watching television. Who was Rami to judge how the demon spent his time?

Properly self-chastised, Rami trailed to the kitchen and began pulling out the ingredients they would need. They tried to be quiet, lest they draw the demon's attention, but by the time they'd flipped the shrimp, sizzling in the hot pan with the oil and spices, they heard the television go quiet.

Rami tensed, though they reminded themself to *breathe*, and attempted to relax their shoulders.

One of the stairs creaked as Julian descended to the first floor, and Rami made themself preoccupied with chopping the onion and garlic. It was already diced. What was a bit more dicing?

"Playing housewife?" Julian asked, and Rami stiffened their spine.

"You say that as if it would be an insult, but I'd like you to try to take care of half the responsibilities a *housewife* is in charge of." Nothing ruffled Rami's feathers more than the wives sitting on their yellow couch, suffering from carrying the mental workload of an entire family while the husbands waited to be told what to do.

"Aw, come on, Feathers, I meant nothing by it," Julian said, leaning against the counter to Rami's right, draping himself across it like a misplaced dishtowel.

"If you don't mean anything by it, why say it?" Rami challenged, barely glancing at the demon from the corner of their eye.

Julian's gaze on them sharpened and idled for a long moment. Rami stared at the shrimp, willing it to cook faster.

"I'm sorry I invaded the office space. It won't happen again," Julian said, standing up straighter, sprawling less over their counter space.

Rami stilled, spatula hovering over the shrimp. They sat

with their thoughts until the shrimp was pink and opaque, and then lifted the pan to scrape them onto a plate.

Then they added more oil and the garlic and onion to the pan. It sizzled upon contact, and they spoke over it.

"I forgive you."

"Well, that was easy," Julian scoffed.

Rami arched a brow, finally turning to meet the demon's eyes, managing not to peer at the broken horn first. "Are you sincere?"

Julian's brows furrowed. "I wouldn't have said it if I wasn't. Why would I lie?"

"You are literally a demon," Rami pointed out, rolling their eyes.

"Okay, you got me there," Julian said, and Rami felt the beginnings of a smile tug at their lips.

Finishing dinner up was easy, even with the demon lingering around and touching everything he could, opening cabinets to explore, sliding open drawers before shutting them with a clink of whatever was inside when it didn't strike his interest. As distracted as he was, Rami studied him when they could do it without getting caught. The horn *was* smoother along the broken edge this time—they weren't imagining it.

"Is your horn… regrowing?" Rami asked.

Julian stilled, closing a cabinet and lifting a hand up. "Yeah, probably. Does it look weird?"

Rami shrugged as if they didn't care. "It's just evening out. Does it still hurt?"

"Only a bit. Maybe once the tip smooths back out, it won't hurt at all."

Rami wanted to ask more, like who and why and how he had gotten away. But they also didn't want to make Julian relive the experience.

They can't imagine it was a pleasant one.

And maybe a tiny, smaller part of them wanted to touch it, to see if the ridges felt just as pronounced beneath their fingers.

Rami focused on the food, stirring the rice and letting the scent fill the kitchen, even though they watched the demon from the corners of their eyes.

Currently, Julian was staring at the fridge and moving all the magnets around. Their lips twitched as they watched him concentrate, the click and slide of the resin letters forming new words.

Rami frowned as they leaned forward and back on their toes, attempting to read the demon's creation.

A-N… Rami narrowed their eyes. G-E-L-S.

Well. At least the demon could—

Rami rolled their eyes as they saw the second word that began at the S, like a crossword puzzle, and ended in U-C-K.

"Rude, since I'm making you dinner and all," Rami drawled.

Out of their peripherals, the demon froze, glancing over at them, a guilty flush on his cheeks.

"Sorry, habit," Julian murmured, and then messed the letters up with obnoxious clacking noises.

"It's done, anyhow, if you'd like to collect two bowls?" they asked.

Julian nodded and went right to the cabinet containing the ceramic dishware. *He* should *know where they are, what with all his snooping around,* Rami thought to themself.

If they had to hide a small smile by the time the demon turned back to them, that was their business and no one else's.

"Thank you," Rami said, and spooned a serving of the rice and a healthy amount of shrimp into his bowl.

"Smells good," Julian said, sniffing the steam still rising.

"This is one of my favorites to make if I don't know what

I want," Rami told him. They served themself and retrieved utensils from the drawer before motioning for Julian to get out of the way.

The demon chuckled as he made room for Rami to pass, and Rami led him straight to the living room. They set their bowl down and met Julian's questioning gaze.

"Really?" Julian asked. "You seem more like the type who'd like to sit at the table, all proper and whatnot."

"Hmm. I used to be," Rami admitted, and snagged the remote from the coffee table. They passed it to the demon. "But who am I trying to impress? It's just me," they said. "Find something to watch. Would you like a glass of wine?"

"Uh, sure," Julian said. The electric hum of the television sounded as it turned on, and they gathered two glasses and the bottle from the fridge. It was a new label they'd never tried, and Rami tested it while still standing in the kitchen. They hummed in approval before filling the glasses.

"Here you go." Rami sat Julian's glass on the side table to his left.

"Thanks," Julian said, eyes never leaving the television as he scrolled through a streaming app.

Rami took their own seat in their favorite leather chair and wiggled into a comfy position before pulling their bowl close.

The click of the remote was loud in the silence as Rami waited for the demon to pick something. After a moment, they decided to eat without him.

"Gonna be honest," Julian muttered a few moments later. "Got no idea what I'm in the mood for."

Rami hummed as they finished chewing. "Close your eyes," Rami said, once they'd swallowed.

Julian narrowed his gaze before doing so, making his suspicion loud and clear.

Rami shut his eyes as well. "Go to the left three times,"

they said. After a tense second, they heard the click of the remote. "Now, right five times."

Their lips twitched as the demon obeyed. "Up ten. And finally, down two."

Click. Click.

"What'd we land on?" they asked, and blinked their eyes open.

"That's chaotic," Julian said, and stared over at them. "Just randomly picking something. What is wrong with you?"

Rami chuckled and motioned to the television. "We've picked something, though, haven't we?"

"Do you even care about old cars?" Julian muttered, and pressed the correct configuration on the remote to play the title.

"Not at all, but maybe this will be interesting," Rami said, and shrugged. "Eat your risotto, before it gets cold."

"Aye, aye, captain," Julian retorted, and Rami rolled their eyes *again*.

The demon's enthusiastic moan a handful of seconds later almost made Rami jump off the leather, it was so unexpected.

"This is fucking delicious," he groaned, and spooned up an even bigger bite.

Once Rami let the shock fade, they smiled and took a sip of wine. "Thank you, that's quite the compliment."

"Whatever," Julian drawled, mouth half full. His gaze trailed to the television while he ate, and then Rami remembered they should probably eat as well, instead of just staring at the demon.

Clearing their throat, they turned their focus toward the first episode of a show about restoring old cars, apparently. The accents were downright charming, and they couldn't help but snicker every time Julian echoed the O-sound by repeating whatever word the man on the television had said.

The risotto was one of their best creations in a while, and

they finished their bowl long after Julian finished his second serving.

"You eat slowly," the demon complained.

"I like to savor," Rami told him over the angry yelling on the television. Even though they'd been stationed on Earth for a few hundred years, food was still such a… treat. It deserved to be enjoyed as well as sustained.

"Feel free to help yourself to a second glass of wine," Rami told him.

The demon did just that, with soft steps padding into the kitchen.

Rami had been right. It *was* rather intimate, having dinner with the demon. But what was one to do?

With a sigh, they watched the man on the television rebuild a beautiful antique car, and then struggle to part with such a beauty.

"This guy's an idiot," Julian complained from the kitchen as he slid the stoppered bottle back into the fridge. "He's never going to make money that way."

"I see why he wants to keep them. She's gorgeous."

Rami supposed it might be similar to their own attachment to their Earthly possessions, like their books.

When seen in that light, Rami wouldn't want to let the car go, either.

"I guess," Julian said reluctantly.

Rami finished their food, finally setting their bowl aside and finishing off the last of their wine by the time the episode ended.

"Well, now what?" Julian asked.

He turned toward Rami on his knees and laid his head on his arm along the back of the couch, even though it clearly hurt to do so. His breath was pinched.

A lock of his hair fell in Julian's face and he blew it out of his eyes unsuccessfully. Rami swallowed, but before they could manage to reply, Julian wrinkled his nose, pressed to the fabric of his sleeve.

"I appreciated the bath last night, but I would've preferred to smell like something besides a little treat. I mean, you could've at least gone with some floral shit, but no—"

Amusement trickled through Rami. "Does that mean you think I smell like a little treat?"

Julian snatched his head up off his arm. "What? I—no, I'm just saying—why are you smiling like that—don't!"

Rami chuckled, laughing at the demon despite his protests.

"Are you saying you'd like another bath?" Rami teased, but eased their smile as they saw the demon hesitate. "You're of course welcome to it."

"Might be," Julian muttered, combing his hair back from his face with one hand, and wincing before lowering his arm. Rami noticed the sheen of his locks.

"Do you need assistance with your hair?" Rami frowned. "I should've asked last night."

"What? No, it's—" Julian lifted a hand and tugged at a piece of hair, rubbing his fingers together. "I dunked my head last night, but with my horn…"

With all of that blood in the water? Rami pursed their lips in distaste.

It wasn't exactly their problem whether Julian could keep his hair clean or not, but… well, there was something selfish in the idea of letting him suffer just because the act might make Rami a bit uncomfortable.

Something in them didn't like being selfish.

"Well, that settles it. I'll wash your hair. Should we open another bottle of wine?"

"Another?" Julian asked with an arch of his brow, before holding out his empty glass. "I like the way you think."

Rami made their way into the kitchen and pulled the

fridge open. Their fingers hovered over the different bottles beneath the light. "Go ahead and get the bath started. I'll knock before I come in."

They *felt* the demon pause before they heard hesitant steps climbing to the loft bedroom.

Rami's lips threatened to curl as they trailed into the kitchen and topped Julian's glass off with the last bit of wine from the cold bottle before opening another.

Rami was trying not to think about the fact that the demon would be *nude* when they found him.

Maybe they could drape a towel over the edges of the tub, hide his most private parts.

Oh, heavens, what had they just signed up for? Rami sipped their wine again before simply deciding to *catch up,* as the humans called it.

Then they poured themself another glass from the fresh bottle.

After selecting a rather large collectible cup from some random event in their life, Rami ascended the stairs.

The water was running, the background noise growing louder as they stopped outside the bathroom door.

They knocked softly, and held their breath.

7
AN ANGEL'S TOUCH

Julian sat up when he heard the knock, the water sloshing around him. It was full enough, surely.

"Come in," he called out, trying to pat the bubbles into place with his hands.

Yes, bubbles.

Julian had never possessed less dignity.

The door opened slowly, and Rami's head peeked in, but the angel's gaze was averted to the wall.

"Decent?" they asked.

"Not quite, Feathers. I'm literally in the bath. I'm naked," Julian answered. "But there's bubbles."

"Bubbles? Enjoying yourself, then?" Rami *teased,* and Julian had to force his last two brain cells to cooperate.

"You said I could help myself to anything—"

"Yes, yes, I know," Rami said, finally entering the bathroom. It was warm from the steam and the mirror was already fogged up.

It was oppressive, suddenly, and Julian drew in a slow breath.

"Wine?" Rami offered, and lowered a hand down to offer Julian his glass.

When Julian lifted his hand from the bath, the drip of the

water off his fingers was loud. "Thanks," he managed, barely. He took a sip to wet his suddenly parched throat.

"I brought a towel in case you were shy, but the bubbles seem to be doing their job," Rami murmured. With a foot, they pulled a stool over from the corner and nudged it into place at the back of the tub, behind Julian.

Julian sipped his wine, desperate for his brain to kick in. Why was he having such a hard time? This was no big deal. Just an angel being very… angel-like, offering to help Julian out in such a way.

Selfless of them, Julian thought with a bit of a scowl.

He let his arm rest on the edge of the tub, balancing the stem of his glass in his fingers.

He'd tucked his horns away before Rami entered the room, so at least they wouldn't be in the way. The broken one didn't hurt when it was hidden, but part of Julian feared that if it didn't get enough air time, it wouldn't heal.

Did he have any scientific knowledge to justify this paranoia? No.

But the thought of Rami's fingers on them…

He shivered, and played it off by pushing the bubbles around.

"Sadly, I don't have anything so fancy as a shower attachment, and while just now I'm realizing how handy that would be, we will have to settle for the old method."

The angel could just magic one, but Julian wasn't going to point that out. He'd much rather see what this old method entailed.

Behind him, Julian heard a plink and felt the water shift as it was disturbed before—

Julian gasped as the hot water was poured over his head, and sputtered as he moved his wine glass away. "What the— Feathers! A warning would be nice!" Julian spun a bit in the tub, the best he could, and glared.

Rami was biting down on a smile, a chuckle barely held behind those pinched lips, the wine glass balanced in the other hand, out of harm's way.

"Sorry," they said, not looking one bit sorry. "I couldn't resist."

Julian arched a brow at that. "So you could say you were tempted," he drawled.

The angel's already flushed cheeks—from the wine or the situation, he would never know—flushed a little more.

"Well, now. I wouldn't go that far, per se," Rami retorted stiffly.

Julian scoffed and turned back around, leaning his head back. "Try not to drown me," he said.

Rami huffed out a bitchy little noise, and Julian heard the cup dip back into the water. He was prepared this time, but then a soft clink sounded, and the edge of Rami's palm was cupped against his forehead as they poured the water gently. It wet his hair without getting the water in his eyes.

In fact, the water felt kind of delightful against his scalp, almost slithering through the roots. He shivered again.

"Everything alright?" Rami asked softly. Too softly.

Julians throat was dry as he answered. "Yeah. Just... feels nice."

Shut up, already!

"Good to hear," Rami murmured, and then the cup dipped. Hot water skated over his hair, soaking it to the root.

There was a long pause, and then the clink of the glass again—ah, the angel was drinking their wine as well. Julian should do that, too.

He let his eyes close and just listened to the angel move around behind him. It was intimate. Julian's skin itched and the hot water wasn't making it go away.

"Since you didn't like the scent of the body soap, you

might like this better. It *is* more of that—what did you say? 'Floral shit,'" Rami mused.

Julian's mouth popped open at the curse. It wasn't even the first time he had heard the angel swear, and yet it still surprised him, like the words didn't belong there.

He tensed as he heard the snap of the cap and then the inhale of plastic as they gathered the shampoo.

"Hands," Rami warned, before, certain enough, their hands carded through Julian's hair.

He shivered at the touch again, but thankfully Rami refrained from remarking about it.

Their hands were slow and their touch was smooth as they worked the shampoo into his locks. Julian hummed without meaning to, but the angel only faltered for a second before continuing.

Interesting.

With a sigh, Julian attempted to sip his wine, and ended up spilling a bit. Rami paused their motions for a moment while Julian managed a less messy sip.

So thoughtful. Dammit.

Then the angel's hands were back in his hair, fingers scraping along his scalp. Not only did chills break out again at the touch, but a strangled noise slipped from Julian's lips.

The angel didn't hesitate this time, continuing to scrub circles against his scalp.

Julian sank into the motions, letting the angel support his head as they worked.

"I think we might do two scrubs," Rami said after a long moment.

Julian was barely conscious. "Hm?"

"You're filthy."

He blinked an eye open at that. "Rude."

"It's simply a fact," Rami said, cupping a hand against his

forehead again as they poured water over his head. "The suds are pink from the dried blood in your hair."

Sounded like more head scratches to Julian. "Fine," he said, in fact, very okay with the situation.

"Oh, don't sound so torn up about it," Rami said, sarcasm dripping like the water down Julian's neck and shoulders.

"I'm a demon; I'll curse you and shit… hmm," he hummed, leaning back into Rami's scrubbing fingers.

The angel laughed, but Julian pretended he didn't care. Rami worked their fingers over every inch of his scalp, the back of his neck, behind his ears. Julian had never felt anything so *nice*. How did humans get anything done when *this* existed?

"I'm glad you're enjoying yourself," Rami murmured, amusement making their tone light.

"So, would you like to tell me why you showed up on my doorstep?" Rami asked softly.

Julian blinked his eyes open. The bathroom lights were softened so he didn't have to squint. "Not necessarily," he answered honestly. Was that the angel's game? Get him all relaxed and then pry?

"Would you anyway?" Rami asked.

Julian considered. He couldn't exactly explain to the angel that he was sent here to tempt them. Lying felt worse than just omitting.

"It was part of an assignment," he said quietly, the scratch of Rami's nails against his scalp the only sound.

But then the angel hummed. "Sounds like a terrible assignment," Rami said.

Julian only purred a little louder, and shivered all over again when Rami continued on to the rinse.

"It's not so bad," he told them as the angel cupped their palm over his head once more.

The warm water slid down his shoulders and he arched back into the angel's touch as the suds washed down his skin.

"And it's not like I get to choose my assignments. I just do what the boss tells me."

The angel paused for a moment, and Julian didn't think they were sipping their wine. "And who is your boss, if not Lucifer?"

Julian scoffed. "Some asshole named Carl."

Carl, the reason Julian was in this whole mess. *Want to be the first to tempt an angel?* he'd asked. *It'll be easy,* he'd said. *We're trying something new,* he'd claimed.

Bunch of bullshit.

Before he could get too worked up about it, Julian released a breath and focused on the angel's actions.

Rami's fingers sorting through Julian's long hair felt almost as nice as the scrubbing. They worked the tangles out using their fingers, and the conditioner they used made his hair soft and silky.

In Hell, Julian supposed casual touches were few and far between. With the angel's hands all up in his hair, scrubbing and touching and combing, it shouldn't have been a surprise that Julian's cock began to take interest in the proceedings. Heat rushed to his cheeks, and he glanced down, making sure the bubbles were still in place.

How embarrassing. Over an *angel?*

Just to be safe, he dragged a few more bubbles over with a hand beneath the water.

The angel would be done soon and then Julian could… deal with his problem.

He took a desperate drink of his wine, only spilling a bit out of the corner of his lips.

He was supposed to be—

Julian blinked. Right. *He* was supposed to do the tempting, not… not the other way around!

He didn't want to seduce the angel. That felt... worse. A bit unforgivable.

Did it matter if the angel forgave him?

You're a demon, that annoying voice in his head pointed out.

Yeah, but he wasn't fucking cruel.

"So you've been on Earth now for... how many years?" Julian asked lightly.

Rami's hands paused in his hair before they continued. "Several hundred years now."

"Long time," Julian murmured. "You live alone."

"You're astute," the angel drawled.

Julian rolled his eyes. "No angel buddies to hang out with?"

Rami hummed. "Not really. I was sent to observe, blend in. So that's what I've been doing."

"All by yourself," Julian mused. Even as a messenger in Hell, Julian had *friends.* Like Galen, and his new wife Maeve.

Rami hesitated, and Julian waited. "I had a very close friend once."

Close friend? A lover? "And?" Julian asked gently. He sensed the moment like a bruise, but Julian was hesitant to press.

"It didn't end well," Rami told him, voice quiet. "I learned my lesson."

Julian's chest seized at the pain in their voice, and imagined spending eternity on Earth alone. Even with everything there was to do... after several hundred years?

"You don't get bored?" Julian asked.

He winced as Rami located a particularly stubborn tangle. "Let me grab a comb," they said.

Julian made sure his lap was covered as the angel stood and walked over to the sink to rummage through a drawer.

He managed to keep his mouth from falling open. The

angel's sleeves were rolled up and pushed far past their fore-arms, to keep their sleeves from getting wet.

His cock gave another appreciative twitch, and Julian glared down at his lap.

No.

"I've made casual friends with a handful of humans over the years," Rami offered, turning with a small *aha!* and showing off their comb.

Their steps were practically silent as they took their seat behind Julian again.

"How'd that go?"

"It was sad. Humans get old and pass away. I don't. After a while, I learned it was just best to keep my distance, observe from the sidelines."

Julian frowned. "That sounds… lonely."

Rami began to pluck the comb gently through his tangles, and murmured, "It can be. But that's the job, I suppose."

"You never miss Heaven?" Julian asked.

"I suppose I do, in a way. Earth is just so… lively. Humans live with risk, with excitement, practically *daring* to do so. And they *enjoy* things shamelessly. Heaven is just… there." They paused. "That sounds terrible, doesn't it?"

Julian had to clear his throat. "Not at all."

"Heaven is peaceful. Easy. Lovely and perfect in its own beautiful way. But there's just something about Earth, and the humans and others here."

Hell was far from lovely and perfect, but Julian under-stood the sentiment. He liked Earth much better than Hell, too.

Wait. Julian held up a dripping hand. "That's what the monsters call themselves here? Others?"

"Mm, yes. The media dubbed them that when the Big Reveal was breaking news. It stuck." The Big Reveal was when all the others decided to finally come out, to expose themselves to the humans.

Julian figured he'd rather be called a monster if they were so clearly going to ostracize them from the humans.

"Well, that's unfortunate," Julian murmured.

Rami chuckled. "I agree, but what can we do?"

Julian hummed as Rami dragged the comb through his shoulder-length hair.

"So, you're a therapist. How do you keep the humans from discovering you don't age?"

"Oh, I just move away."

Julian must have made a surprised noise.

"Yes, I know. What about the books? Well, I bring them with me, that's what," Rami said. They took another sip of wine.

"Right, that's what I was worried about," Julian drawled into his own mostly empty glass. "The books."

"I've been here for about... ten years? So it's not quite time to move on yet, but it will be soon. I can stay longer when I don't befriend the locals."

"But your clients..."

"Yes. Clients do complicate things. Thankfully, with hairstyles I can give them the impression of aging without ever actually doing so. Besides, most of my clients move on before they ever have time to question it."

"Move on...?"

"They find the answers they were looking for, in therapy, and then they go live their life—you know the drill."

Right. Definitely.

"You solve all their problems for them and then they leave? That doesn't sound fair."

"No, no. I don't solve their problems," Rami corrected, the comb sliding smoothly through Julian's hair again. "I just teach them the tools so they can work through it themselves.

Empower them to live a better life." They paused. "It doesn't always work."

"What do you mean?"

Rami cleared their throat, and their voice took on that *tone* again as they said, "You can only help those that want to be helped."

Julian wanted to ask more, but Rami sounded so *sad*. "So... you're *not* preaching to them during the sessions?" Julian teased instead, cocking his head to the side.

With a touch, Rami righted his head, and Julian tried not to shiver at the gentle control the angel held.

"Of course not. I'm a therapist, not a preacher."

"Why not? You're an angel, after all. No better person to teach God's word, in my opinion."

"Well, that's very kind of you," Rami said, and before Julian could inform them that he hadn't meant it as a compliment, the moment passed. "People are always on their best behavior at church. In therapy, they reveal their true selves. It's personal, it's raw. I feel like I can help more that way, show them how to love themselves and live the best life they can, while they have it."

Julian swallowed the last of his wine, wishing for another glass. He'd need it if this conversation was going to continue.

Then he heard a plop in the water. "Shit," Rami said. "I dropped the comb. Hold on."

And then... Julian felt the distinctive brush of a hand against his side, his lower back. "Ope, pardon me," Rami said.

"What are you—"

"I can't see in the foggy water, just hold still—"

He felt the comb sink to the bottom, brushing against his ass, and Julian wondered if he should warn the angel. But then he never got the chance, because Rami located the comb.

And Julian's ass, their fingers brushing the globe of his left cheek before they caught the comb.

Julian's cock was *very* interested in these new events.

"Sorry about that," Rami said, as if they hadn't just spent about thirty seconds feeling Julian up.

"No worries," Julian choked out, full of worries, most of them horny.

"I think we're about done, anyway," Rami said. "Let's give you a rinse, then."

Julian pressed his thighs together as Rami repeated the cup motions, the now cooling water cascading down his back.

He shivered again, cursing his luck.

But then it was done, and the angel squeezed his shoulder gently. "There we go. Clean as a whistle."

"Uh—thanks, Feathers," Julian murmured.

"Done with your glass?" Rami asked, and Julian blinked at the hand filling his peripherals.

"Yeah, sure," he said, and lifted the empty glass to the angel.

"I'll leave you to it, then," Rami said, voice completely casual, and then their footsteps were retreating. Julian turned to watch them go without even a backwards glance, drying their hands on a small towel.

Were they not bothered, in *any* way, by Julian, naked and practically pliant under their touch?

Once the door shut softly, Julian leaned back against the porcelain tub and groaned.

So it's just me, then, he thought, annoyed with himself.

He could still feel their touch, fingers scraping through his hair and thumbs kneading the tense edge of his neck.

What the actual fuck?

Julian was supposed to be the one making the angel feel things, not the other way around. It was quite literally his job to tempt the angel, one way or another, before the end of the week.

How the hell was he supposed to manage that when he couldn't even sit through a bit of hair touching without getting hard?

He just needed—he had to try harder. Come up with a different plan, a new angle.

What had he expected? Angels, after all, were sexless upon creation. Julian supposed he hadn't anticipated meeting one—or being bathed by one—who stuck to it.

Now what?

Julian willed his arousal to abate and then got out of the bath, still a little slow on account of his not-as-sore knee.

The new plan only occurred to him once he'd dried, and walked into the room, seeing the empty bed.

Oh.

Of course.

Now *that* was something Julian could work with.

8
JUST ONE BED

Rami rinsed the glasses and tried to ignore the pinch of warmth that still filled their cheeks.

They hadn't *meant* to grope the demon. It was a total accident. If only the water hadn't been so foggy from his filthy hair!

And yet Rami could still feel his smooth, warm skin against their fingertips. Could still hear his soft groans that sounded downright debauched. Had he even been aware of how he sounded?

They scrubbed the wine glasses until they gleamed.

Then Rami puttered around, tidying what they could, cleaning up their mess from dinner.

Then they readied the couch for Rami's less than comfortable rest.

Eventually they heard the tub begin to drain and retrieved a fresh glass to fill with water.

As it filled, they glared over at the couch, not necessarily looking forward to another crooked-necked sleep.

With a sigh, they carried the glass up the stairs, and knocked on the wall before rounding the corner.

Rami blinked. Their steps faltered, and they tried to cover it.

Not very successfully, if the twitch to the demon's lips meant anything.

There he was, all splayed across the bed, shirtless. His horns were free once more in his clean hair, and Rami wondered if that was part of the healing process.

In the tub, even though the demon was nude, at least Rami had only a view of his back.

And what a nice back it was, a little traitorous voice said.

Yet somehow, seeing him here, in Rami's bed, bare from the waist up, felt different. Forbidden.

"Feeling better?" Rami choked out, and completed the walk to the demon's side of the bed. The glass met the side table top with a soft click.

"Thanks, Feathers," Julian said, taking the glass before Rami had even finished relinquishing it. Their fingers brushed, and Rami took a healthy step back.

It didn't stop them from staring as the demon drank, though, throat working with every swallow.

Was it warm in here?

"Alright, then," they managed. "Enjoy your sleep. I suppose I'll..." They motioned vaguely to the stairs behind them, *almost* tripping over their feet in their hurry to get away without tearing their gaze from the demon.

Julian sighed and sat the glass back down before wiggling back into a comfy position against all the pillows.

Rami only felt a small pang of annoyance, knowing the couch was waiting for them.

You know, if you really *wanted your bed back...*

Yes, yes. Rami knew they could tell the demon to go back downstairs, put him on the couch since he was capable of walking without help again.

But then Julian grimaced as he shifted into the pillows before smoothing his face into a neutral expression. His horns glinted in the light, the broken one a physical reminder to Rami of what he had gone through.

And Rami just couldn't do it, they couldn't kick him out, so they fortified themself. It wouldn't be much longer—

"I could sleep on the couch if you wanted," Julian said.

Rami blinked. The offer shocked them.

And, well. Now Rami would just feel guilty if they agreed to let the demon sleep on the couch. He was clearly still in pain, and what kind of angel were they to consider making someone suffer just for their own comfort? That was entirely selfish.

"No. No, you sleep here. I'll stay on the couch again."

The ache in their neck intensified as if in warning, and they dreaded the morning to come.

"There is… one last option," Julian said, and scooted more toward the edge of the bed.

Rami stared at him for a long moment.

Julian patted the bed, grinning like he'd just invented electricity. "You get it, right? We can share. Look how big this thing is," he said, patting the bed again to emphasize exactly which *thing* he was referring to.

Not that Rami assumed he'd be referring to anything else!

Rami was rather partial to their king-sized bed. It was an indulgence, but the loft bedroom was so large; they needed some way to fill it.

At least, that's what they'd told themself when they justified it.

"I bet we could lay on either side and not even know the other is there. What do you say?"

"Of course not," Rami said, because there was just no other answer.

An angel and a demon sharing a bed? No matter how innocently, it just didn't seem right.

"Aw, come on. Achey, bumpy couch, or cloud-soft, island-sized bed?"

Rami should walk away. Turn on their heel and ignore Julian's rather good point.

But the couch was *so* terrible. Truly.

"Come on," he encouraged. "I know your neck is sore; you've been holding it weird all day."

Rami scoffed. The demon knew them so well so soon?

They hated that Julian was right.

With a sigh, they rounded the bed and stared at the empty space. It was rather large.

But why did the demon look so pleased with himself? What was his aim here?

"You won't touch me?" Rami asked, narrowing their gaze.

Julian's lips twitched. "Won't move a muscle, Feathers."

Rami resisted rolling their eyes. Obviously, the demon wouldn't be able to control that while he was asleep. But something in his expression, his tone, made Rami believe he was telling the truth.

"Fine, alright. Fine."

"You sure? Don't sound too happy about it."

"I'm sure I'll be grateful in the morning when I wake up without an ache in my neck."

They sat on the side of the bed and almost sighed. What did humans call them? Creature comforts? Simple pleasures?

Well, anyway, Rami had missed their bed.

And now, thanks to this demon, they had it back. Though, if it wasn't for Julian in the first place, they wouldn't have lost their bed at all.

They pulled back the cover enough to make room for themself, and then took off their sweater, folding it and laying it atop the dresser. Rami usually wasn't one to wear their pants as well, but. These were particular circumstances, and Rami would most certainly not be so exposed next to a demon.

So, pants it was.

Julian turned his lamp off, casting the room into shadows, apart from the moonlight streaming in through the window above the bed.

Rami slid into the bed beneath the sheets and top cover, and scooted as close to the edge as they could.

They were pretty certain there was enough room for a whole other person between them, but Rami wasn't going to be the one to cross the invisible line.

"Well, goodnight, I suppose," Rami said, and then turned over onto their side.

"Goodnight, Feathers," Julian returned.

Several moments of silence passed. Rami could hear their pulse thumping against the pillow. Were they breathing too loudly? Could Julian hear them? Did Rami care?

They startled when the bed rustled, and something brushed against their back. They tried to turn their head, but the soreness stopped them. When no further assault occurred, they relaxed. "What is that?" they asked.

"It's a chastity pillow," the demon said. "Told you, we won't touch."

Rami settled back down with a huff. "How kind of you to protect my virtue," Rami mused, pulling the cover closer to their chin.

Julian scoffed. "No, no. I'm protecting my own virtue. Who knows what you angels are into," he drawled, another inflection in his voice that Rami couldn't recognize.

"As if I would *ever*," Rami grumbled, eyes widening on the wall across from them, cheeks flushing at just the notion.

It was then they realized the demon was trying not to laugh, shoulders shaking the mattress.

"Oh, I see, you're laughing at me," Rami stated, and rolled their eyes.

"Me? Never."

Rami ignored him and closed their eyes, willing themself to go to sleep.

Somewhere around the second hour, after counting their breaths and listening to the demon rustling around, they actually managed it.

Rami awoke slowly, sleep receding like a particularly heavy fog.

Goodness, they hadn't slept so deeply in what felt like ages. Oh, they could lay here all morning, with this comfortable heaviness to themself.

They were warm. Felt kind of like melting into the mattress.

They blinked their eyes open, the morning light shining in through the cracks in the blinds.

"Wah!" they shouted, and scrambled back from the *demon in their bed!*

Julian laughed, one hand beneath his cheek, apparently awaiting Rami's awakening, only inches away.

"Did you know you flop around in bed?"

What happened to the damned—

Rami untangled themself from the sheets and blankets, kicking a pillow off the bed in the process.

They slid their legs over the side, and grabbed the aforementioned chastity divider before tossing it back on the bed. How had it gotten over to their side, anyway?

"I don't know what you're talking about," Rami said, and

hurried over to the dresser. They grabbed themself a set of day clothes, ignoring the sound of the demon stretching luxuriously among their sheets.

"Yeah," Julian groaned. Rami turned just in time to watch him wince, lowering his arms back by his sides. But Rami also noticed the trail of hair on his stomach, leading down to—Rami averted their gaze. "Like one of those gas station chickens. That rotate," he said, and spun his finger. "You know…"

"Rotisserie chickens?" Rami couldn't help but provide.

"Yes! That," he said. "You rotisseried all night."

Rami stopped before the bathroom in indignation. "Well, you rustled around quite a bit yourself before I fell asleep," Rami said.

"How late were you up?" Julian asked.

Rami shrugged. "I'm not sure."

"Oh no, you didn't hear me masturbate, did you?" Julian asked.

Rami sputtered. "Excuse me! You did no such thing. I'm almost certain I'd know—" They caught the twitch of the demon's lip. "You're laughing at me again! Ugh!"

Rami stomped into the bathroom and barely resisted slamming the door behind themself.

"Oh, come on, Feathers, don't be like that!" Julian called out. "Besides, once you fell asleep," he continued, "I didn't have much room to do anything because you snuggled right up to m—"

Rami turned on the shower, the rush of water drowning out the demon's voice.

"I did no such thing!" they hissed to themself as they tugged their shirt and pants and underthings off. "That insufferable… *demon!*"

It wasn't until the hot water was cascading down their

back and over their shoulders that the demon's words really registered.

Touching himself! Next to Rami!

Rami's cheeks were still warm, and they couldn't blame it on the heat of the water.

Thank heavens he'd just been teasing. Joking.

Rami shook their head at the *joke*.

They still felt a little sluggish after such a deep sleep, and they looked forward to their coffee, the caffeine luring them awake instead of the jolt they'd received.

Their eyes widened as they watched the water circle the drain. Had they really cuddled up to the demon all night?

Sharing a bed was something they had done... before. Once upon a time.

They couldn't deny they had rather liked the warmth of another body next to them.

Even with those baser urges, though, they'd never even been tempted, in all their years on Earth.

Well. Aside from a little solo experimentation here or there. But those occurrences certainly didn't count. There was nothing wrong with a bit of curiosity.

And as they shifted the water to cold, they declared they weren't about to start now.

9
HEAVEN'S IMAGE

Julian snickered as he heard the water turn on in the middle of his sentence. He didn't know angels could *get* that red.

But he felt the angel might be a little upset with him, so to soften the blow, Julian slithered from the bed and down the stairs. He attempted to recreate the steps he'd watched Rami take to make their precious caffeinated beverage.

His least favorite step was the loud noise from the grinder itself, but he suffered through it. He got as far as dumping the grounds into the little paper cone above the mug before the angel made it to him.

"What are you—"

"Making you coffee!" Julian said with a grin. "Look, I ground your little beans and everything. Now I just pour the water over it, right?"

Rami's eyes, a little bluer this morning than gray, flitted from the mug to Julian's face and back again.

"…Yes," they finally said.

Julian refrained from pumping his fist in the air. Barely. Instead he reached over, calm as could be, and collected the electric kettle from its station. Steam rose between them as Rami watched Julian work.

His hand only shook a tiny bit. Could be blamed on nerves. This water was pretty hot, after all; it would probably burn. He had a right to be nervous.

The angel watched him the entire time it took to pour the water and for it to drain through the cone.

Their gaze was heavy, and Julian shuffled, uncertain as to the source of his unease.

Once he'd poured the last round of hot water, he slid the mug over the countertop to Rami's waiting form.

"See? I'm a great roommate."

Rami sputtered. "You are no such thing. In fact, you seem to be feeling quite yourself—"

Just in that moment, Julian reached up for a second mug with his left hand, grimaced, and lifted the right one instead as his side twanged. Carefully he retrieved a mug out of the high cabinet.

"I definitely feel much better than when I first showed up," he admitted into the silence Rami had left.

"Well, that's—good," Rami said stiffly. "Glad to hear it."

Julian studied the angel as he waited for the last bit of Rami's water to drain before stealing the cone from them.

"Where's your…"

Rami extended a slim finger in the direction of the trash can, by the back door. Julian cupped his hand beneath the cone to keep it from dripping as he walked it over to the trash. He dumped out the old grounds and then followed the same motions to make himself a cup.

Rami watched him the entire time. "You picked that up fast."

"Why do you sound surprised?"

"I don't know," Rami admitted with a shrug.

Julian hummed as he finished pouring his own mug, and then it was a waiting game.

"Are you going to do work again today?"

Rami shrugged. "I might check a few emails."

They looked like they wanted to say more, but more never came.

The mug was warm beneath Julian's hand as he finally completed the caffeine ritual. He lifted it, inhaled the warm, nutty scent, and sipped.

His face scrunched up. "Oh, that's…"

Rami's lip was trying not to curl, and Julian sipped it again, only to wince. "Oh no, how do you drink that? It's so…
"

"Bitter?" Rami offered.

Julian nodded, setting the offending cup down.

"Would you like me to doctor it?"

Julian arched a brow. "Sure." *I think.*

Rami nodded like they'd accepted a side quest and went about the kitchen, gathering two containers: one from the fridge, and one from the cabinet.

A creamer and a syrup.

"Are you poisoning me?" Julian asked.

Rami chuckled. "I would do no such thing. This will make it taste sweeter. Closer to one of those lattes you magicked."

Making coffee really *was* a ritual. Grinding things up, mixing different ingredients. Even steam was involved!

By the time the angel was done pouring small amounts of the other liquids into his cup, they pulled out a spoon with a long handle and stirred it together. When they handed it back, it was a paler, creamy color.

Tentatively, Julian lifted the mug and sniffed. That strong coffee scent was there, along with the sweeter notes of whatever Rami had added.

Narrowing his gaze at the angel, he tilted the mug to his lips and drank.

His brows lifted this time, the sweetness hitting his

tongue just right. In fact, it was *better* than the drink he'd magicked only the day before.

"Oh, that's *good*," Julian said.

Rami *beamed*. Like the sun through their damned shades.

They looked seconds away from performing a bow.

"Glad I could make something to your satisfaction," Rami said softly.

Julian tried not to look too closely at the swirly feeling in his chest right then.

It wasn't until they were seated in the same places as the morning before that either one of them spoke again.

Julian was on the couch, foot propped up on the short table, and the angel was in their sunlit chair once more.

"So, what about you?" Rami asked, pretending like they were looking for their place in the book, even though it was marked.

"What about me… what?" Julian questioned.

Rami's gray eyes lifted. "Do you have any… errands to run today?"

"Not really." He didn't want to admit that he'd only left the house yesterday before he said something he regretted. "I mostly wanted to snoop around. Check out this little corner of Earth." As nice as Rami's place was, Julian was hoping to see a little more of… well, Earth, while he was here.

Rami tilted their head toward Julian. "You say that like you haven't been before."

"I've visited. For, like, moments at a time, as I delivered messages," Julian admitted. He didn't have to tell Rami he didn't deliver messages any*more*. "But I've never been able to stick around to really experience it."

"How do you know so much about Earth, then?"

"The internet," Julian answered.

Rami blinked. "Hell has internet?"

"Not very good internet. It's slow as hell," Julian said with a blank face.

Rami snickered, and it was the sound of it that made Julian's lips finally twitch.

They went quiet, lost in thought for a moment, and then Rami cleared their throat.

"I could show you around a bit. Give you the full Earthly experience while you're here."

Julian's brow furrowed, surprise filling him. "You'd do that?"

"Well, I can't exactly see to my clients while you're around, so I have nothing better to do."

Ah. "Gee, thanks," Julian drawled.

"No, I just mean—since I have nothing on my plate, I might as well introduce you to some *creature comforts,* as the humans say."

Julian sipped his coffee and tried not to smile. The angel still spoke as if they hadn't been here for years and years. "I think I might like that."

Rami hummed. "Well, there is still—don't you need to lay low?"

Julian blinked at him, and Rami sighed.

"You know, to hide from whomever... hurt you," they finished, some emotion flickering in their expression before it smoothed out again.

"Nah, I'm certain they don't care where I am." *Yet,* he finished in his head. "Plus, I'm sure I could sense them, like I did all your goodness."

He still had a few days. Till the end of the week, at least.

Rami narrowed their eyes at that, but the demon refused to give any more information away, lest he accidentally tip the angel off that something was up. What Julian might be on Earth for was none of the angel's business, anyway.

"What would you like to see?" Rami asked, smoothing a thumb over the closed cover of his book.

"I don't know. What is there to see?" Julian asked.

He couldn't explain the sudden racing of his heart.

"Well. There's lots of things. Restaurants and theaters and — oh! Did you know humans have captured wild animals and sea creatures, and put them behind plexiglass so they can look at them for fun?"

Julian arched a brow. "Huh. How about that." Maybe humans *were* made in Heaven's image after all.

"Granted, I think most of the animals wouldn't do well on their own, in the wild. It's called a zoo or an aquarium, if that's something you're interested in. The otters are *very* adorable," Rami said, eyes lighting up.

"I've seen videos of those! Let's do that," Julian blurted. And if he also maybe wanted to see the angel glow like that again, he'd reflect on that later.

"You want to go to the aquarium?"

"Yes. Why not? I don't have anything else to do."

The angel sat their book aside, and Julian knew he'd won.

"I suppose it's a good place to see many of creation's creatures at once. Do you have something appropriate to wear?" Rami asked, gaze trailing Julian's form.

Julian's first instinct was to stretch out like a cat, really give the angel something to look at. But he really wanted to see these otters that made Rami sparkle just so.

"Of course I do," he said, and waved a hand down the length of his torso, pulling on a bit of the hellish magic he had free use of. His horns vanished, and his outfit shifted from the loungewear he'd borrowed from Rami to something *appropriate:* dark ripped jeans and an obscure graphic tee beneath a long-sleeved button-up. And boots, of course. On Rami's soft living room rug.

Rami's eye twitched exactly once before they spun on their heel. "I'll be just a moment."

"Well, is it appropriate?" Julian asked, standing and stretching.

The angel paused on the stairs, turning to catch him with his arms above his head. Julian felt the cool air brush against the strip of skin the action bared, and he grinned wickedly as he watched Rami's gaze trail him once more, sliding down the length of his body. Warmth stirred in its wake, and then they were trotting up the stairs. "Quite," they muttered just before they left Julian's line of sight.

Julian smirked as he heard the angel's footsteps on the floor above, the squeak of the drawer they opened to retrieve what Julian suspected was going to be a sweater, no matter how warm it was outside.

Not that Julian wasn't taking advantage of layering his own clothes. But he'd gotten that *look* out of the angel with it, so it would be worth any warmth.

Besides, Julian could handle *heat*.

As the angel joined him again after a few moments, dressed in—you guessed it—a pale collared shirt beneath a sweater with matching pants and dark dress shoes, he realized that so could Rami.

Their silver hair gleamed beneath the low lights, and Rami ruffled a hand through it as they cleared their throat and motioned to the back door. Julian extended his arm for the angel to go first.

Mostly so he could see their ass in those pants.

Also worth it.

The sun was bright and harsh as they stepped outside, and Julian followed Rami around the little walkway to the side of the small house.

He came to a stop on the concrete that made up the driveway. "What the hell is this?" Julian asked.

"A car. My car," Rami said, eying him over the top of said car, brow furrowing. "It's how humans travel long distances."

"No, I know *that*," Julian scoffed. "But this looks like a… toy."

"It is most certainly *not* a toy," Rami sputtered out. "It is a perfectly well-functioning vehicle! Do you want to come with, or—what are you doing?" Rami asked as Julian began stalking around it.

It was so square. The back window was weird, and curved around the side of the car. Three letters were on the back of it, as well as a four-letter word.

"That can't be right. No way," Julian said in disbelief.

Rami rounded the car with him and Julian let his gaze trail back to the word.

"Oh! No, that's. That's just the name of the type of car."

"You drive a Soul?" Julian questioned dryly.

Rami practically stomped their foot. "Yes, because it's *funny!* Now laugh!"

Julian actually *did* find it pretty humorous. But it was much more fun to watch the angel's face turn red again.

"Ugh! You are positively no fun. Get in the damned car," they whined, and then slammed the door as they did just that.

Julian's mouth dropped open, and as the car started he fumbled for the door handle and slid into the rather small passenger seat.

"Angel, did you just curse at me?" Julian asked.

"It's very possible," they said, and backed out of their driveway oh-so carefully. "I have been on Earth for quite some time. It would be difficult *not* to pick up on certain human mannerisms."

Not very angel-like, he thought.

"They slip out every now and then," Rami explained, and

waited until they'd come to a stop beneath a red light to turn the knobs on the dashboard.

Julian stared at all the buttons, and then watched all the different cars roll past. He knew about them, of course, had heard about them in Hell, spent some time with the creators of such things, watched compilations of dash cam videos. He just didn't remember *everything* about them.

And he'd certainly never been in one. Julian pursed his lips as he ran a hand along the smooth arm rest.

Demons had wings; they didn't need *wheels.*

"Why aren't we just flying?" Julian asked.

Rami arched a brow at him before quickly turning back to the traffic as the light turned green. "Humans don't know about angels for the same reason they don't know about demons. So we can't exactly be seen."

"Please," Julian sneered. "If they can handle dragons and werewolves and fairies, they can handle demons and angels."

Rami hummed. "Well, do you want to be the demon responsible for that? Revealing the entire race to the humans?"

Julian pursed his lips. If the higher-ups hadn't already informed humans of their existence, there must be a reason.

"Didn't think so," Rami drawled.

The road was busy and winding, and they passed all the businesses Julian had wandered around the day before, including the alley where Hell had contacted him.

Julian leaned forward and pushed some of the buttons. One turned on the radio, but there was no music playing, just a commercial. Something about cars.

I'm in a car; I don't need another one.

Julian shut the radio off with a pout and tried a few more buttons. He turned the air on, and then off. And pushed the button with a snowflake on it.

"What's that do?"

"It's super cold air conditioning. Will you please stop touching everything?" Rami asked, exasperated.

Julian pouted, and leaned back in his seat to stare out the window. To even be able to properly tempt the angel, Rami had to at least *like* Julian, so, fine. He'd try not to get on Rami's nerves.

With his focus on their surroundings, he realized they were going rather… slowly. Cars were passing them left and right. Someone went around them with the blare of a horn.

"I thought you said this was a perfectly functioning vehicle?" Julian asked.

"It is!"

"Then why are we going so slowly?"

Rami's hands tightened on the wheel before the car whirred a bit more, and then they were keeping pace with the other cars around them.

"See, was that so hard?" Julian prodded.

"I like to be cautious," Rami said. "We don't have that far to drive, anyway. My property is a hidden gem just close enough to the city so I can have privacy, and far enough to be out of the direct bustle of city life."

They were correct. Even at the slightly slower pace, it was only a handful of moments before they directed the car into a lot. A building that was all shapes and sharp blue edges stood tall, and statues of some fishy-looking creatures acted as guard.

Julian followed Rami's lead, getting out of the car and walking through the last dregs of warm air from summer's fragile hold.

He caught Rami staring, gaze inexplicably drawn up his dark form. Julian smirked.

The blast of cold air as they walked through the doors was nice, and Julian stuck to the angel closely.

Rami took care of leading him to a little booth, where they exchanged money for two wristbands.

"Capitalism. Fun," Julian teased as they walked away to make room for the next people in line.

"It was an unfortunate development, I know," Rami drawled. "Don't rub it in."

Julian stared at them as they wiggled their fingers at him. "Your wrist," they beckoned, lifting the other hand to show off the blue bands.

With a scowl, he lifted his hand, palm up. Rami's fingers curled around his wrist, and Julian wondered if the angel could feel the pulse beneath his human skin.

Was it racing? It felt a little warm in there suddenly.

The heat from outside must be catching up to him. Yeah, that was it. Totally.

Rami ripped a little piece of paper off the blue strip and then placed it evenly together.

"Now, my turn, please," Rami said, holding both their hands out now.

Julian *forced* his hand not to tremble as he slid the band from the angel's grip and then curled it beneath their wrist.

He peeled at the white sticker, and tried to place the sticky part evenly. He missed, and frowned at the little silver hairs that got stuck against it.

The angel winced and ran a finger beneath it, and Julian suddenly wanted to rip it off and demand a new one.

"Thank you very much. Now, where would you like to start?" they asked, and waved their hand out—

"Holy shit," Julian whispered, as he turned and followed the gaze of the angel.

As they walked beneath the archway, a *huge* dome of a room stretched out before them, hallways extending in multiple directions, along with a hundred different signs depicting words like *dolphins* and *penguins* and *whales*.

"I have… no clue," Julian admitted.

He vaguely recognized the words and some of the symbols, and a few images even came to mind when he tried to recall their familiarity.

"Alright, then, let's just work our way from one side to the other, yes?" Rami suggested.

Eyes wide and taking in all their blue-lit surroundings, Julian followed them absently.

They took the first hallway to the left, and Julian's attention scaled up. He gasped.

Above them was a clear shield, filled with water and all kinds of shimmery, colorful fish.

"Holy—"

"Please stop saying that," Rami bit out. "Choose another phrase, please."

"Fucking hell," he muttered as he stopped right in the middle of the walkway to stare up at the multitudes of swimming little creatures.

Rami grumbled at him, but there was a gentle smile gracing their lips, so Julian supposed it was alright.

"I take it you've never seen the ocean before?"

"I've seen glimpses of it in personal hells… downstairs. We've got a whole section of pirates, you know, from back in the day, and their worst fear is drowning, so. Can't say I've ever cared for it, myself."

"Well. That's—" Rami sputtered. "That's just plain terrible. The ocean is beautiful. If it's terrifying at all, it's only because of the awe one feels when realizing just how big it is."

Julian snorted, and Rami nudged him. "Don't be that way. This is a nice moment."

And, it was, wasn't it?

All lit up beneath the magic water tunnel with all these fish suspended above them.

"Who would've thought to collect the sea and put it in a building," Julian mused.

Rami chuckled, and Julian was so struck by the soft, amused noise from the angel that he turned to stare at them. "When you put it like that, it does sound quite silly, doesn't it?"

"Are they happy in there?" Julian asked.

Angels had always been all about the feelings, not demons. Part of their selflessness, he supposed.

"I'd say so," Rami answered.

Julian pursed his lips at that, and followed the tunnel into another room, where they looked at a few creatures in their own private tanks.

He could feel Rami's gaze, heavy and curious as it followed Julian through the smaller room until it fed them back into the larger hallway.

As far as seeing Earth went, he supposed this was a pretty good start.

But he wasn't going to tell the angel such a thing. Instead, he leaned over and read the next plaque for the fish in a small tank.

"Oh. Seahorses! I remember these guys," Julian whispered, amazement filling his voice. He lifted a hand to place it against the glass before thinking better of it, sticking his hand in his pocket and watching them flit through the water.

"You do?" Rami asked doubtfully.

"Of course I do," Julian answered, arching a brow at them before turning back to the tank. "Well, from the internet."

Rami didn't answer. When Julian shifted his gaze, he found the angel already staring at him. The water and lights were casting a blue-tinted glow over their skin. They were practically glimmering.

"You try spending a few millennia in an office and see

how much you remember," Julian told them, avoiding those silvery, too-knowing eyes.

"Sounds like hell," Rami muttered, and a laugh cracked out of Julian.

"That's exactly right, Feathers." His laugh tapered down and Rami walked ahead, motioning for him to follow.

"We can loop back through—it's hard to take everything in at once," Rami explained as they skipped past a few displays and several crowded groups of people.

They passed many hallways, and Julian didn't bother trying to keep up. He'd just have to stick close to Rami, because the aquarium seemed endless, pathways twisting into more, before a light at the end of the tunnel beckoned.

This room was crowded, but it was also fucking massive, with benches to their left as they walked in. Rami glanced over their shoulder, and their eyes were reflecting the blue shine of the giant tank that filled the room.

"Come on, you'll want to be close."

To what? Julian wondered, and then Rami grabbed him by the design on his shirt and tugged him along.

The only slot available right up against the tank was on the very left. And there was only room for one person.

"Here," Rami said, and pushed him into the spot. "I've seen them before."

"Seen what?" he asked, and then his eyes went wide as something large moved through the tank. It neared, slow and steady, and then turned right before it reached the thick glass, gliding along the side as everyone oohed and aahed over it.

Including Julian.

The creature's belly was white, but the top of him was spotted. When he swam higher up, the reflection of his spotted back was visible in the ripples of the water.

"Sharks like these," Rami said, much closer than Julian

had anticipated. The angel was just over his shoulder. In fact, once he stiffened, he felt the warmth of Rami brushing against his back. "Whale sharks. They're *the* biggest shark," they continued, unaware.

"Even bigger than great whites?"

"Even so," Rami answered.

"I think they're kind of cute," Julian admitted.

The shark was swimming out of sight again, and the people crowded against the tank shuffled.

After a quiet snap of Julian's finger, the human next to him decided he'd seen enough of this particular shark, and Rami squeezed into his spot.

His back felt a little cold, but it was nice to see Rami's expression again.

"Really?" the angel asked, low and smooth. "I think they're quite cute as well. They're just gentle giants, really."

Their gaze slid to Julian, and the demon pursed his lips under those spotlight eyes.

"That so?" he asked.

Rami nodded before turning their attention back to the tank as the shark made his way back to them.

"They eat plankton, so they're harmless. Great whites, however... humans are terrified of them," they added softly.

"Why?" Julian asked.

"There were a few cases of shark bites."

"Yep, that'd do it," Julian muttered, shaking his head.

"Quite. It spread like wildfire. There were movies and propaganda. Even today, they're blamed for something that wasn't even their fault."

"It wasn't their fault that they bit some people?" Julian clarified. Sounded like their fault.

"Well, to be fair, the humans are invading *their* space. Besides, some researchers say it was a case of mistaken identity."

When Julian stared at them in confusion, Rami huffed. "They mistook the humans for food."

Julian snorted and watched the elegant whale shark move through the water. "Well, these guys are really cute. Look at his big mouth. He's smiling."

"Maybe he has something to be happy about," Rami said.

"But these aren't your favorite? I want to see the otters," Julian told the angel.

Rami paused, gaze flitting to Julian before skittering away again. "Alright, let's go this way. I'm sure someone else would like to see the sharks, anyway."

Julian tried to keep his attention on the tanks they passed, vowing to give each of them a piece of his time on the second lap of the aquarium. More often than not, he was drawn to his unofficial tour guide. The one whose hair practically glowed beneath the lighting, reflecting the blue of the water off their silvery hair.

But if he hadn't been staring at the angel so much, he wouldn't have been able to watch them bite down on their lip to quell a smile as they entered the otter room.

Squealing kids ran around as the parents tried to corral them into paying attention; meanwhile, running water and splashing echoed in the background.

But not from the rowdy children.

The enclosure was filled with tan, rocky scenery, and a pool of clear water behind more glass, where six fuzzy, slithery little guys played.

Julian followed Rami's quickened pace to the glass, and watched their hands flutter around in excitement before they shoved them in their pockets.

"These are sea otters," the angel said, practically vibrating in place.

As Julian watched through the glass, he saw an otter swimming on his back, paws rubbing against each other as he floated. Another one dove up through the water and grabbed his tail, swimming backwards and dragging the other with him.

Beside him, Rami barely bit down on an excited noise that could only be described as a *squeak.*

Julian swallowed a laugh and elbowed the angel as both otters dove under and came up holding hands and play-fighting. "Okay, that was pretty cute."

"So that's Sylvia Plath," Rami said, pointing to the one who'd done the dragging. "And the one she's playing with is Jane Austen."

Julian narrowed his gaze, turning to watch the angel. "They have names?"

Pure, unhinged glee was lighting up their eyes; there were practically stars in them. "Yes. Each of them is named after a literary celebrity, of sorts."

"And you know them all?"

"Of course."

Julian's lips twitched as Rami pointed through the glass and gasped. "Look!"

He shifted his attention to the chunky brown figures of the otters. Something shifted in his chest as he watched one sliding on the rocky surface and down a slide, chasing a ball the whole time.

"They play with toys?" Julian asked. They were kept like pets.

"I know!" Rami hissed. "It's so cute. That one's Harper Lee."

"You come here often, then?" Julian asked, biting his cheek against the threatening smile.

"This is my favorite attraction, so I do tend to linger when I visit. *And* there's a live stream of the otters online, you can watch it at any time—" They paused suddenly, turning to Julian with an arched brow. Their cheeks were pink. "Are you laughing at me again?"

Julian lifted both hands in innocence. "Not at all." In fact, he didn't quite know how to name the feeling in his chest.

Whatever it was, it wasn't at the angel's expense.

He split his attention between the otters, one of them now rolling like a log in the middle of the exhibit, and the angel watching them. Joy radiated out of them, as bright and as pure as their pale eyes.

"Is he grooming?" Julian asked as one floated near, on his back. He was nuzzling at his fur.

Around them, adults and kids alike began giggling, and Julian tilted his head as he finally realized what was happening.

Rami's smile fell. "Oh my god," he whispered, turning around. "Give him some privacy!" they said, waving a hand in Julian's face, blocking the sight of the otter.

A human near them was snickering. "I mean, if I could reach my own, I probably would, too."

Rami's nose wrinkled, and Julian couldn't help but laugh. The otter floated on, putting on an obnoxious display of grooming, much to the embarrassment of the kids and parents around them, most of whom quickly fled the scene.

Julian thought the angel would be next, but they were so *excited,* and they clearly adored these sea critters.

Julian couldn't find it in himself to urge them to move on. "They're still pretty damned cute. Despite that one's interest in exhibitionism," he teased.

Rami shot Julian a glare that only faded by the time the next otter floated by. Rami eventually relaxed next to him, and Julian was content to watch them for a while. He let Rami introduce him to each of the otters, listening intently as Rami spilled some of the *tea,* as they called it. About the otters' complicated social structure, and the spats that had broken out recently, usually over toys or Sylvia Plath.

Their shoulders and arms kept brushing, and each touch was a bit of a marvel, the angel's warmth a surprisingly welcome comfort.

Their eyes fucking *glowed* as they rambled, and Julian couldn't bring himself to interrupt.

Eventually, he didn't have to. Rami seemed to come back to themself all at once, and only then did Julian realize they'd probably been standing there for more than an hour.

"I'm sure there are other exhibits you'd like to see," Rami offered, and glanced toward the exit.

Julian shrugged. He wasn't *not* enjoying himself, watching the otters play and slide around. Listening to the angel ramble.

"Lead the way, Feathers."

And sure enough, Julian followed.

10
ART EXHIBIT

Rami made haste as they left the otter exhibit. How long had they been droning on about *otters?*

And why hadn't Julian stopped them?

Maybe, Rami mused, just maybe, Julian enjoyed the otters as much as they did.

Wasn't that a thought?

"You're going to love this room," they said, and led Julian beneath an archway into a round, cylinder-shaped space.

"Why do you say—hol—fucking hell," he corrected himself, eyes going wide. How polite of him to do so.

The room was dark, and the only things casting light upon them were—

"Jellyfish," Julian whispered.

"Yes!" Rami said, and glanced at Julian, anticipating his reaction.

His wide eyes were quite sparkly considering the darker room around them. The jellyfish glowed, and Rami found their gaze caught on the demon. The soft blue light dabbled across his face like strokes of a brush and, well…

I thought we were at an aquarium, not an art exhibit.

Cheeks flushing hot at the thought, Rami turned their attention to the sea creatures instead.

Jellyfish fluttered through the water around them, bodies expanding and collapsing as they moved.

"Some of them are so large," Julian murmured, spinning in a circle. Rami stepped out of his way with a smile.

"Certainly."

"And they're just… glowing!"

They aren't the only ones, Rami thought as Julian turned his gaze on them.

His eyes, usually a honey gold, were darker in the lighting and yet no less captivating, sharp jaw lit by the light of the floating jellyfish.

"They do that, yes," Rami said, clearing their throat.

"I guess I see the appeal now," Julian admitted, and Rami thought it might not have been voluntarily, if he hadn't been so distracted by the jellyfish.

"Good," Rami said quietly.

Rami was practically vibrating with excitement for their last stop at the aquarium. They'd looped around to the beginning and Rami had taken their time, letting Julian ooh and aah and point at all the different creatures.

Currently, all around them, children were sticking their hands into the water at their parents' encouragement, and yet Rami didn't hesitate to lightly dip their fingers in..

"See? Softly. Just a little pet," they said, brushing the tips of their fingers over a small stingray.

"It doesn't hurt them, does it?" Julian asked.

Rami smiled down at the stingray beneath their hand. "No, it doesn't."

And how odd for a demon to be the one asking that question. Demons, evil-doers.

Julian didn't seem so evil just then, fingers lightly shaking as he swanned them over the water, testing the temperature.

"Cold," he muttered.

Rami's face was beginning to hurt from their smile. "Look, here's one," they said, and Julian lifted his hand from the water.

Julian hovered… waiting… waiting… until the stingray swam away, and Julian pulled his hand up, too, shaking it out by his side.

"Okay, wait. I can't. I can't do it. What if they're slimy?"

Rami chuckled. "They can be, yes. But it's not gross."

"It is gross, though, is the thing," Julian said, lips twitching.

Rami didn't let themself second-guess their actions as another stingray neared.

They placed their right hand on the back of Julian's, curling their fingers through the demon's and pulling his hand closer, hovering over the water.

"Here he comes, watch," Rami instructed, so intent on giving Julian the Earthly aquarium experience, they failed to notice how close they were.

The stingray slid beneath Julian's fingers, and Rami directed their hands lower, flicking through the water and over the back of the stingray.

Rami pulled their hand up as the stingray swam on.

"See? That wasn't so bad," they said, grinning as they turned to face Julian—

Who was only inches away. Their sides were pressed together, and Rami realized their opposite hand was resting on the demon's back. They were touching from hand to bicep to hips.

Rami's mouth was suddenly dry as their gaze dropped to Julian's lips, and then they realized what was occurring.

Hiding the frantic emotion that buzzed through them, they cleared their throat and stepped away. "So, you can say you touched a stingray now."

"That I can," Julian murmured. He was avoiding Rami's gaze, too.

Maybe in their mutual awkwardness they could just forget it ever happened.

Julian was the first to recover, while Rami was reliving the press of the demon's warmth against their side.

"So… what's next, Feathers?"

Rami pursed their lips at that, admitting to themself and themself only that the moniker didn't bother them quite as much as they let on.

"Well, the aquarium does close soon," they hinted. "Hungry?"

Julian averted his attention, cleared his throat. "Always. What did you have in mind?"

"I'm not sure. How do you feel about a trip to the supermarket?" Rami asked. Maybe they could find something the demon enjoyed as well, instead of just hoping he would be happy with whatever Rami decided to have.

"I don't think I have any feelings about supermarkets," Julian answered.

"Well, I need to pick up a few things. I suppose you could accompany me."

"How gracious of you," Julian drawled.

Rolling their eyes, Rami led Julian out of the aquarium and to the car outside, ready to fend off any jokes about their choice of electric chariot. But surprisingly, Julian remained quiet, though he did attempt the radio once more, only to find another commercial playing.

With a sigh, he shut it off, and Rami's lips threatened to curl into a smile, so they bit down on their cheek.

Julian rustled around in his seat, and Rami was going to shoot him a mildly annoyed glance until they realized he was just taking his button-up off. It left his arms bare, and Rami *focused* on the road like never before.

It didn't take too long to get through the light traffic and park in the lot of the supermarket. Around them, humans and others alike trailed in and out of the store, and Rami reached into the back seat to grab a set of reusable bags, gaze pointedly not lingering on Julian's arms, his muscled bicep.

Clearing their throat, they opened their car door and motioned for Julian to do the same.

To the humans they looked just the same, a pair of humans ending the day by picking up groceries.

To the others—Rami caught the gaze of a were creature as they stepped out of the car—Rami and Julian probably felt different, their energy unmistakable, despite their human skin.

But Rami reluctantly realized maybe they appreciated Julian's human skin. The sun was waning with the day's end, and the golden glow was especially lovely in Julian's dark, long hair.

The breeze picked up, blowing it askew, and Rami found themself wondering if he ever tied it up. A messy top bun was a tantalizing image.

For no reason. Of course.

They wondered how a demon would manage that with horns in the way.

Nearby, a car honked, and it tore them from their thoughts. They blinked into the evening light, shaking the thought away, and, with no small amount of mortification, vowed never to think of it again.

Julian was a demon, and definitely was not supposed to be the subject of such humanly thoughts.

"So, here we are," Rami said gratefully, smiling up at the red and blue market sign.

They walked through the glass doors, which automatically parted for them through the magic of their own electricity.

Humans—they'd thought of everything.

And Rami was thrilled to be the one showing it all to Julian.

Julian, who was… not beside them.

Spinning, Rami found the demon frozen outside the doors, staring up at them with something they hadn't seen on his face yet, not even when he'd shown up bloody and beaten.

Fear.

11
HELL ON EARTH

"Uhhh... wait. What?" Julian asked, feet stuttering to a stop in front of the big glass doors. They seemed to stretch for eternity before him.

Which was ironic, because he knew of at least three doorways in Hell that used to do the same thing.

"Have you never been in one?" Rami asked, backtracking to take Julian's wrist.

And even though it was an innocent touch, the skin-to-skin contact made his heart leap to be on the receiving end of it.

He hoped the angel couldn't feel his pulse.

Julian gulped, staring up at the grocery store. "Technically... yes. I have."

Rami cocked their head. "I'm assuming it wasn't a pleasant experience?"

"Could say that," he murmured, following the angel tentatively through the doors.

The concrete floor was silent beneath his boots as he walked alongside Rami. It was crowded, but not overly so.

"We're here at a busy time, but that's because most of the humans' work days have just ended."

"Mhm," Julian hummed, eyes darting from the line of

grocery carts to the squeaky wheels of one a lady pushed into the store, through another set of those automatic doors.

"We don't need much. I can get a basket," Rami informed him.

"Okay."

"Want to talk about why you're so tense right now? Maybe we can reason through it."

Julian scoffed. "You really are a therapist."

"Well, yes. That is my job."

Rolling his eyes, Julian let himself focus on the fond irritation as they went through the second set of doors, and Rami collected a basket from their right.

"In Hell, every person gets their own personal setup, you know."

"I've heard that," Rami said.

"You'd be surprised how many people's personal hells involve grocery stores."

"Really?" Rami asked, eyes wide as they gazed around them with a new light in their eyes. "That's very interesting."

"Some of the ones I've seen were really... overwhelming," he admitted, sticking close to Rami's side as they led him down an aisle. It looked like a candy aisle, all chocolates and nuts and crackers.

"It can get quite crazy in some places. Have you heard of Black Friday?"

"Of course I have." Now *that* had been a temptation that had gone down in history. It started with a group of CEOs, and turned into a nationwide event every year. Nothing more selfish than tricking masses of people into spending money they didn't have on things they didn't really need.

Rami's answering hum was pinched. "Well, I'd like you to know there's outstanding *good* here, too. Humans can be terrible to one another, but also incredibly... kind."

"Sure, Feathers," Julian drawled.

Rami came to a stop in the middle of the aisle without warning, and Julian bumbled himself right into them.

"What—"

"Here we are," Rami murmured, and plucked a bag of fancy-looking chocolates from the shelf.

"What're those?" Julian asked nosily as he picked it from the basket to read the packaging.

"Very lovely chocolates. They're my favorite, and this store is honestly dreadful at keeping them in stock. It must be our lucky day."

Julian arched a brow at *our*, ignoring the hitch in his chest. Carefully, he placed the bag back in the basket, not very interested in their blood orange dark chocolates.

Another one had already taken its place, and then Rami was moving down the aisle with their treats.

A smile tugged at his lips and he trailed after them. They had to maneuver around pesky children pitching a fit at the end of said aisle, and Julian grimaced as he quickened his pace to match Rami's.

The angel was wearing an amused smirk. "What are you smiling about?" Julian asked.

Rami glanced over at him. "Not a fan of kids, then?"

"They're loud and messy, so, no."

"Oh, you're a tidy fellow?" Rami teased.

Julian narrowed his eyes as Rami snagged a box of crackers from the end cap. "Might be."

These were their necessities?

Rami smoothly slid between a buggy stalled in the middle of the aisle and an oblivious man scratching his stomach as he stared at the soup cans.

Julian paused right in front of the buggy, eying the unnecessary space the man was taking up with his inconsideration.

When Rami glanced back, Julian waved his hand at the buggy and mouthed, "*Are you kidding me?*" at the angel.

Their lips twitched, then they shrugged before moving on.

Grumbling under his breath at *humans*, Julian scooted between the buggy and the shelves without assaulting the human like he wanted to.

Next Rami led them to a colder part of the store, and chills broke out beneath Julian's clothes. He crossed his arms and waited patiently as Rami hemmed and hawed in front of the cheeses.

Julian didn't even know what some of them *were*, so he tapped his foot and waited.

"Which do you think would be better?" Rami asked, pointing between two cheeses.

"You're asking the wrong guy," Julian said. "Will you hurry? It's cold over here," he complained.

Rami eyed his gooseflesh and paused for a moment before they began… shrugging off their cardigan.

Julian glanced around them to see if anyone else was shocked that the angel was suddenly stripping in the supermarket.

Once they'd unstuck the fabric from their button-up, they held out the cardigan to Julian.

Julian stared. They didn't mean for him to wear the—

"Oh, just put it on, would you? You won't catch a disease."

Rami's fingers released the sweater and Julian caught it before it could hit the ground. "That's not what—"

But Rami was already moving on, sliding between a family and an overly affectionate couple—in front of the salads, really?—and disappearing into the throng of shoppers.

Cursing, Julian pulled the cardigan on and moved to follow after the angel, but paused to grab the honey brie and the garlic and herb goat cheese.

He tried not to focus on how warm the cardigan still was from the angel's body heat. He failed.

The sleeves fell past his fingers, and the hem draped well below his hips. He was practically swimming in the fabric, and it annoyed him that he felt all warm and fuzzy about it.

Stupid angels and their stupid—

Someone knocked into his shoulder, almost spinning him completely on the slick concrete of the floor.

"Hey, watch it," a deep voice grouched, and Julian finished his turn to see who the *hell* would—

"*You* knocked into me," Julian snapped back. "Watch where *you're* going next time." He bared his teeth at the man.

"Excuse me?" the human asked.

Julian wasn't intimidated, even though that's clearly what the human was trying for, what with the brown work boots and mud-splattered jeans and bulging arm muscles beneath his sleeveless shirt.

"You heard me. I'm sure it's hard to keep your balance with all that muscle, but something tells me you can manage."

Julian's point would've probably looked and sounded tougher if he wasn't pointing at the man around the packaged cylinder of cheese.

The human's face turned beet-red. "Why, you—"

"Oh, my dear, there you are!" Rami said, swooping in beside him and the human and—*what?*

Dear?

Julian probably got whiplash from looking at the angel so quickly.

"Thought I lost you in all this mess. I told you it's busy." They looped their arm with Julian's and began pulling him away, shooting the human a glance.

"Have a good evening—pardon us," they called out to the angry man in a jovial tone.

Then they were swallowed in the crowd and Rami's arm

was warm against his and—their sleeves were rolled back, when had that happened?

Who had allowed the angel to have such attractive wrists and veins in their forearms? It was like the bath night all over again.

And Julian was *still* holding that goddamned cheese.

He dumped the packages unceremoniously in the basket. Since they'd parted, Rami had added a few vegetables to their collection. "You forgot your cheese," he muttered.

"I suppose I did, didn't I," Rami responded, and Julian glanced over but couldn't read the look in their gaze. Wasn't sure if he wanted to.

"Now, Julian, you can't go around accosting humans. If you get into a—a *brawl*—you'll end up in jail."

Julian scoffed. "As if their human prisons could hold *me*."

Rami sighed. "Good luck getting out without revealing what you are. Don't want that happening."

"Yeah, yeah," Julian grumbled. Stupid angel being right.

Rami still hadn't released his arm, and Julian wondered if it was on purpose, since they steered him right alongside them into another aisle.

"Oh, now this is more my style," Julian announced to the shelves of wine.

"Yes, I thought it might be," Rami mused with no small hint of humor. "Do you prefer red or white?"

"White," Julian answered. He only hesitated *after* the fact, when it seemed to give Rami pause.

"I don't know why that surprises me," Rami said. "You like a sweet wine, don't you?"

Julian pursed his lips. "Maybe."

"Thought so. Let's see…" They hummed as their fingers wiggled, fluttering over the bottles and their fancy-looking labels before finally plucking one free. "This should do. I'm going to get a red myself, just in case we're feeling wild."

"Wild," Julian echoed.

He felt like he was two steps behind Rami at all times. Like he could never get a grasp on what the damned angel was really thinking. What did they mean *thought so*, like they had Julian all figured out?

Their arms were still linked.

Julian didn't pull away.

And neither did Rami as they corralled Julian to the checkouts. "I find self-checkout easier, personally. But if you want the full experience…"

"No, it's fine," Julian answered.

Less interaction with damned humans.

"Alright, then, I'll be just a moment," Rami said, and unhooked their arms only to place the basket on the shelf before the scanner.

Julian watched as Rami scanned each item and bagged it in their reusable bags. The total racked up alarmingly quickly, and he narrowed his gaze. "That seems like… a lot, for these items," he said.

"Well, I did indulge in the chocolates. And cheese isn't exactly cheap."

Julian frowned. From Hell's personal punishments, he knew all about the classism that humans had created for themselves, the way some of them struggled.

He supposed an angel didn't have to worry about any of that, though.

"Worry not, however. I have this," they said, and proudly produced a plastic card from their wallet with a proud grin. "It can buy anything."

And so it did, with a simple swipe and a signature—

"Did you just dot your I with a halo?" Julian asked, warmth blooming in his chest as his lips curled.

Rami paused right before they clicked the circle button to accept the signature. "Possibly," Rami answered hesitantly.

"Of course you do," Julian murmured, something like fondness rooting in him.

He grabbed one of the reusable bags before Rami could ask, and would've grabbed the second one if they hadn't beaten him to it.

The sun was still waning as they made it out of the market alive, and Julian gave the building a backwards glance as they walked away.

"See, that wasn't so bad, was it?" Rami asked.

Julian rolled his eyes, refusing to give the angel the satisfaction, though it seemed they had it in their possession already.

It took no time at all to weave between the humans to the car, and then watch Rami drive below the speed limit, until Rami's little townhouse cottage-looking home came into view. It was rather close to the main road, but the lush gardens surrounding it gave it the illusion of privacy.

Once they were inside and Rami was pulling the items from the bag, Julian squinted at the haul, freeing his horns once more after an exaggerated groan just to grate on Rami's nerves.

"So we went to the market for… snacks?" Julian asked.

"Well, sort of," Rami said with a shrug. "This is what we'll be doing for dinner tonight."

"Oh, will we?" Julian drawled.

The angel's flushed cheeks were his new favorite sight.

…Because he liked annoying the angel, of course.

"Yes. I even have a board."

"What do we need a board for?"

"A charcuterie board. Cheeses and crackers and fruits and veggies."

"A snack platter?" Julian offered dryly.

"Yes, but *fancy*," Rami snapped. "Work with me here," they scolded.

Julian lifted his hands in a show of innocence and pulled out the bottles of wine. "Is this more of those creature comforts?" he teased. "Whatever happened to meat and potatoes?"

"Overrated. You'll like this, trust me," Rami said, and ripped open a sleeve of crackers, forearms flexing.

I think I do already, Julian thought, completely against his will.

12
ANGEL DINNER

Rami shook their head as they pulled out a wooden board. They almost hated to admit that they were rather pleased to be hosting. It wasn't often they got to, after all. The closest they ever came was with their clients, but, well, there was certainly a difference to the way they would sit on their yellow couch and hug a pillow versus what Julian was doing.

Rami arched a brow at him as he placed his hands on the counter and lifted himself up to sit beside the sink.

Well, at least he was out of the way.

But now he had a birds-eye view as Rami began arranging the board of cheeses and crackers. The plastic sleeves crinkled as they pulled the crackers free, only placing the ones that weren't cracked or broken. Then they pulled out a few tiny dishes where they added an apricot jam and a sweet pepper jelly.

"Wow, this takes some preparation," Julian mused. "Can I help with anything?"

Rami didn't know why they were surprised. They just hadn't expected the offer, but eventually, curbing their shock, they slid a knife free from the chopping block. "Do you know how to cut veggies?"

Julian scoffed. "Of course I do. Give me that," he said, and slid from the counter in one smooth, sinuous move before taking the knife from Rami's hand. Their fingers brushed and Rami pretended like it didn't affect them.

Just like they pretended they didn't notice that Julian was still wearing their cardigan, draping his lean frame and spilling over his fingers.

If Rami was appreciating the sight, they didn't get to for long, since Julian shrugged it off and draped it over the back of one of the island chairs.

His right hand curled around the handle of the knife with confidence. And now that his forearms were bare, Rami was finding it quite hard to pull their gaze away.

"You don't have to watch," Julian drawled. "I know what I'm doing."

Right. Rami shook themself out of the moment. Of course, that's why they were staring at Julian, to make sure he could do it correctly. No other reason.

It took so much strength to turn back to their own task with a soft hum.

They went about finally unpackaging the cheeses and retrieving a few more options from the fridge they had previously opened: brie, goat cheeses, some sharp cheddars.

"Technically," they said aloud to fill the silence, backed by the smooth sound of the knife against the cutting board, "a charcuterie board is strictly meats and cheeses. The word literally means 'cold cuts.'"

"So what do you call this, then?" Julian asked. "Because we have much more than that."

Rami pursed their lips. "A vegetable charcuterie board? Or... a snack platter."

The snort that came from the demon filled Rami with a new kind of delight. They enjoyed being the source of amusement for Julian.

Best not to look too closely at that, they feared.

It was domestic, sharing the kitchen with someone. Rami admitted it was kind of… nice to have someone around, sharing their space. Maybe that was the real reason why Rami hadn't kicked the demon to the curb, since he was definitely healed enough.

Why, if Rami wasn't careful, they could imagine that instead of an angel and a demon, the two of them were just … what? Acquaintances? *Friends?*

With a demon?

Rami swallowed back an unfamiliar emotion and promised to unpack it later. Maybe.

"Is there cooking in hell?" Rami asked suddenly.

"What?" Julian asked, knife scraping evenly, steadily.

"Well, I just wonder, where did you learn to use a knife like that?"

"What exactly is it that you think I do in Hell?"

Rami felt their cheeks flush and hoped they could somehow word their thoughts in a way that wouldn't offend the demon. "Well, I just—I'm not sure. Hellish things, I suppose."

Julian's laugh was thankfully free of any bitter undertones. "I was a messenger. So I delivered messages, and then waited until I was needed again."

"What did you do in the meantime?"

"Hung out at my house."

Rami turned abruptly, but was only met with the back of the demon. His muscles moved as he continued cutting. Rami pointedly didn't notice. "You have a house?"

"In Hell, yes. What did you think I did, hung from the ceiling like a bat?"

"I don't—I don't know, I've never been to Hell!"

"You should visit sometime."

Rami sputtered until they spun on their heel to continue laying out the cheese cuts. An angel in Hell! Imagine.

Julian's grin was wicked as he brought a bowl over containing the cucumbers, peppers, and carrots he'd sliced into discs and thin sticks.

"Excellent, thank you," Rami said. "I've got a compost bin right on the counter, if you would just drop the remains of the vegetables in there."

"Of course you compost," Julian grumbled.

"It's better for the environment," Rami returned.

Julian hummed and was quiet for a moment. "It's not your job to fix the Earth, you know?"

"Reduce, reuse, recycle is an important part of the human experience," Rami informed him, and carefully placed the veggies in their respective spaces on the board.

"I think humans stress too much over it. Recycling your milk jug isn't going to cancel out all the rich fuckers with private jets."

Rami nodded their head. "I do understand where you're coming from, but I still want to do my part. The Earth was made for the humans, and I'm going to treat it with care while I'm here."

Julian was quiet for a moment before he eventually offered a murmur of agreement, and then the sink turned on as—

Rami glanced over at him. He was cleaning off the cutting board and knife before placing the board in the drying rack.

"I know better than to argue with an angel," Julian muttered.

Moments later he returned to Rami's side, dish towel crumpled in his hands as he dried the board. Rami watched from the corner of their eye with a soft kind of awe as the demon handled the knife, drying it carefully before placing it back in the block. The demon folded the dish towel when he was done, and Rami felt warm at the sight.

Which was preposterous, really.

So what if the demon had manners? So what if he took care to prevent rusting on Rami's favorite knife?

"There," Rami said, and spun the board around so it could be admired from all sides. "The white wine probably isn't *very* cold yet, but…"

"It'll be fine, Feathers," Julian said.

The board was a work of art, every piece with its own place and clustered together in a tasteful manner. The crackers were fanned out around some of the jams in a perfect circle.

"This might be my best one yet," Rami said proudly. "Why, this belongs right next to some of those photos I see online. I've taken my inspiration from many videos."

"Of course you watch platter organization compilations," Julian drawled. Rami chose not to engage with that comment.

"It's certainly got a lot going on. I'm impressed," Julian said.

The sun was well past set now, and as Rami carried the board out to the living room, Julian followed behind with two wine glasses and the bottle of wine, which…

"It's chilled now," Julian said, and waggled his eyebrows.

Rami rolled his eyes, but sat back and watched Julian open it.

His arms flexed as he spun the corkscrew in, stretching the fabric of his too-tight tee shirt, and… Rami was staring again.

The cork released with a dramatic pop and Julian looked awfully proud of himself. Rami was helpless but to return his beaming smile.

Rami took a seat on their couch, relieved to relax for a bit. The day had seemed so long, for once.

First the aquarium and then the grocery store.

"I can't believe I almost had to rescue you from that large human," Rami said. They hadn't meant to say it, and flushed beneath the narrowed gaze the demon settled on them.

"You did not have to *rescue* me. And you never would have!" he… well, *whined* was the only word that came to Rami's mind. Julian filled Rami's wine glass far past polite and grinned. "If anyone, it would've been the human you'd rescued."

"I turn my back for one moment," Rami mused, waiting until Julian filled his own glass before lifting theirs.

"You don't have to babysit me; I'm a fully-matured demon," Julian said, and *floated* down to his seat.

"Maybe if you acted like it, I wouldn't have to," Rami said primly.

Julian scoffed and scooted to the edge of his seat to peer at the board. He glanced over, uncertain. "Can I just start anywhere?"

"Of course," Rami said. "There's no rules here."

But that didn't stop them from plucking up a cracker and some jam with the goat cheese. It didn't go unnoticed when Julian repeated their selection.

He popped the whole cracker in his mouth and hummed contentedly. Rami pointedly didn't stare. Not when he swallowed, the long line of his throat moving, Adam's apple bobbing. And certainly not when he sucked at the side of his thumb to clean the bit of jam from his skin.

"Everything alright, Feathers?" Julian asked.

Rami sipped their wine, gaze dipping to the board. "Peachy. Try this," Rami said, and pointed out a few different combinations.

No pairings were forbidden enough for the demon, and

Rami was plain captivated. They chuckled softly when Julian would wrinkle his nose at something he didn't like.

His pleased little noises when he *did* enjoy something were just as distracting.

"I have to confess," Julian began, and Rami snapped their attention back to him. "I thought this was a little silly. Snacks for dinner? But it's pretty good," he said.

"See? I know a few things," Rami teased, and sipped their wine, only to realize their glass was empty.

"Refill?" Julian asked, already lifting the bottle before Rami could answer.

"Please," Rami said politely and held out the dainty glass. The demon's hand curled confidently around the bottle as he poured, the veins in his hand standing out, and Rami tried not to stare. Failed, probably. But then their glass was filled to an impolite level once more, and Julian was setting the bottle down again.

Rami sipped their wine. They needed it.

They both continued to pick at the board for a while before Julian got tired of the silence and flicked the television on. "What do you watch?"

"I usually don't; I read," Rami admitted. "We should pick like we did the other night."

"Oh, come on, you never watch television? Let me guess," Julian said, turning to them on the couch and taking them in from nose to toes.

Rami tried desperately not to flush, but felt the heat rushing to their cheeks anyway. Maybe they could blame it on the wine.

"Detective shows? But, like, the British ones with the fancy hats."

Rami rolled their eyes. "They don't wear fancy hats."

"But you *do* watch them!" Julian said, leaning closer,

excitement swirling in his golden eyes. Rami stared, forgetting to reply.

Then he leaned away, turning back to the television, and Rami sought comfort in their drink once more.

"Let's see…" Julian murmured. The only sound filling the room was the click of the remote as he navigated the many streaming apps Rami never bothered with.

"How about this?" he asked, and pulled up a show Rami had never heard of.

"Sure," Rami agreed. They probably wouldn't pay much attention anyway.

And they were right. In between bouts of murder and interrogations and meddling from a red-headed character with *very* accurate instincts, Rami watched Julian instead.

They tried to piece together the different versions they'd built of him in their head. The demon, of course. Somewhere along the way they'd gotten a reputation, and no one had stopped them from inflating it over the centuries.

Then there was *this* version of Julian, the one watching the television, the same one who probably sat in his own house—in Hell—and *cooked,* apparently. He probably watched the streaming services all the time. What did *he* like to watch?

Why did it matter? Rami thought glumly. Julian was still a demon, no matter how invested he seemed to be in this gambling murder mystery. No matter how he devoured the snack platter until about halfway through the episode. He sank back contentedly into the couch with a sigh, full and pleased with what Rami had provided.

They chose to sit their wine aside at that moment, because it was becoming rather warm in the house. The alcohol, certainly.

"Have you ever?" Julian asked suddenly, and Rami lifted their head, turning to him.

"Have I ever what?"

"Gambled," he said, waving his glass at the television.

"Ah, no. No, I haven't," they answered honestly, proudly. "I don't do that kind of thing." Rami ran a hand through their hair, adjusting their seat on the couch. Though they supposed they were gambling with every moment they spent in the demon's presence.

"Do you wanna?" Julian asked, spinning to face them on the couch. He waggled his eyebrows.

Rami scoffed. "What? No! Of course not," they said. "I'm an angel."

Julian shot them a puzzled expression. "So? Come on," Julian said, leaning closer on the couch. Rami resisted the urge to scoot away.

"Absolutely not. What good is gambling money, anyway? We don't need it," they argued. "I use magic for what funds I need, and no more."

Julian was quiet for a moment longer, eying Rami far too close for comfort. "Who says we're gambling with money?" he asked.

Rami sputtered as Julian stood, sauntering toward the kitchen and plucking up something from the counter. As he spun and returned, Rami sat up a little straighter.

"No," Rami said, and held out a hand for the bag.

"Oh, come on, Feathers. Are you a sore loser? It's just a bit of chocolate," Julian taunted, and waved the bag just out of reach.

When Rami remained silent, Julian sighed and flopped down to the couch. "It'll be fun. We don't even have to play cards or anything. We can just…" A light came into his eyes and he stood, crossed to the kitchen, and grabbed Rami's sweater before returning. He held it out pointedly.

Rami glared up at him. "What are you doing?"

"*We*, Feathers, are going on a walk."

"Whatever *for?*" they asked. It was already dark out, and on a weekend, it would be crowded.

"You said there's a lot of good in humanity. Prove it," he said, shrugging.

Rami pursed their lips. How dare he dangle this opportunity out in front of Rami like that?

Humans did have good in them, and Rami loved being right about something. This would be the perfect time to show off to Julian, who seemed rather cynical when it came to humanity. Though he *did* spend the majority of his time in Hell, encountering only the worst humans.

Rami could change that.

"Oh, come on," Julian encouraged. "You'd deny me this Earthly experience? More simple pleasures in life?"

Now they *knew* they were being manipulated, but in that moment, they couldn't see what harm it would be. They were just helping the demon enjoy his time here.

They lifted their hand and curled it around the cardigan, and Julian released it into their care with a wicked smile.

"That's it," he murmured darkly, and Rami stood to hide the shiver dancing up their spine, slipping into the cardigan and adjusting it over their long sleeves.

"Fine. But only because I want to prove you wrong," Rami said stiffly.

They took another sip of their wine, finishing the second glass before meeting Julian at the door.

"Ready, Feathers?" Julian teased. "Need to preen some more?"

Rami rolled their eyes in full view of the demon, who'd at some point conjured his own sweater and melted his horns away, before reaching past Julian and pulling the door open. *Goodbye, forearms,* Rami thought forlornly.

They grabbed their keys off the hook and locked the door

behind them, aware of the demon's looming presence the entire time.

When they spun to meet him, Julian was much closer than they'd thought, his warmth chasing away the chill of the evening. Rami was almost disappointed when he swayed away and stepped back onto the path with a rustle of the bag of chocolates at his side.

"Lead the way," Rami said.

They hoped they wouldn't regret giving into the demon's whims.

13

BET

Despite the foliage surrounding Rami's home, there was no disguising just how close to the main road they lived. So it was only a matter of steps before Julian was walking side by side with Rami toward the string lights of the main strip in the little town the angel had chosen to reside in.

"Well, it used to be a little town," the angel rambled. "Now more and more businesses keep opening, and it feels a little more crowded every time I leave the house."

Julian's attention wavered between Rami and the town. It was like something out of a movie. Even the people, all dressed up in their peacoats and whatnot to brace against the cool evening.

But despite how aesthetically pleasing everything seemed on the surface, humans, by nature, were selfish creatures, just like demons. So Julian didn't worry one bit. He'd be trying Rami's precious little chocolates soon enough.

And their first opportunity presented itself on a platter.

"Look," Rami said softly, brushing Julian's arm with their hand and motioning discreetly to a group of young students. Well, everyone was young to him, but these kids must've been in their college years at least.

They were a group of four, and they were walking quickly, laughing and rubbing elbows, oblivious to the woman they were about to encounter. Rami leaned closer to Julian, making sure his attention was on them.

She was walking slowly, and Julian imagined these kids didn't have the patience for it. They'd probably cross the street, breaking the law in their self-centered hurry to continue on their way.

"They're young; they're selfish," Julian muttered, and Rami frowned before he waited patiently.

Their brow furrowed, lips parting before Julian interrupted. "No interfering," Julian warned.

"Obviously!" Rami chastised, and as if in sync, the two of them slowed as they watched the humans.

The group of young men finally realized they were approaching the woman—a witch, who was walking alone— and nudged each other to point her out. Worry filled Rami's expression for only a moment.

The woman stiffened as she heard them grow closer.

The group slowed, and two of them broke away from the pack, tugging at the others. They approached the end of the sidewalk, looking both ways, and crossed to the other side of the road.

The woman glanced over at them, shoulders relaxing as she went on with her way. Rami offered her a kind smile as she passed.

"Hah! I win," Julian said.

Rami startled. "Excuse me? You did not."

Julian frowned. "But they jaywalked to hurry around the witch," Julian pointed out, crinkling the bag of chocolates. "That's breaking the law. *And* selfish, because they could've just walked a bit slower."

Rami snagged the bag from him. "They moved to the other side of the road so they wouldn't intimidate the lone woman," they snapped. "That says much more about their character than whether they crossed an *empty road* or not."

Julian pursed his lips at that. He supposed it would be pretty selfless of them to go out of their way to avoid intimidating the woman. "Alright, fine, Feathers. You win this round. Go ahead," he said, and waved a hand at the bag.

It gave Rami pause, who clearly hadn't expected Julian to give in so easily.

Julian supposed he hadn't expected it either, but...

He watched, not even discreetly, as Rami gently opened the bag and removed a single piece of chocolate wrapped in gold foil.

They handed the bag back, and the plastic scrunched under Julian's grip as the angel peeled the foil away, revealing the chocolate beneath.

Oblivious, they popped the chocolate between their lips and hummed happily as it melted across their tongue.

Julian didn't realize he was staring until Rami's gaze landed on him, and he cleared his throat. Then his attention landed on the string lights of a bar about a block away.

"Do you go to bars?" Julian asked.

Rami frowned. "No, not usually. I'm not opposed to a pub, but I tend to go for the food, not to linger around the bar."

Sounds like something the angel would do.

"Well, I think tonight is as good a night as any, don't you? Lots of people in there," he said, pointing as they crossed the street after checking for cars.

Music spilled out the opened garage door wall of a small bar.

Rami did not do a good job hiding their grimace, and Julian studied the bar a bit more. What about it was making them dread it?

The patrons did look rather *young,* standing on the patio,

laughing with their martini glasses and beers. But to an angel and a demon, *everyone* was young.

"We don't have to stay long. Just one drink," Julian promised.

"Fine, fine," Rami conceded. "But like you said, just one."

Julian led the way through the throng of young people all the way to the bar.

It was warm and a bit crowded, and Julian couldn't help but notice the way Rami shuffled closer.

A sign reading "no outside food or drink" stared at him from above the bar, and Julian magicked a messenger bag over his shoulder, tucking away the chocolates to hide them.

It took a moment for Rami to notice the sign, but when they did, they tapped Julian's shoulder and looked worried. Julian tried not to smile.

"Don't worry," Julian said as they sidled up to the bar. It was busy and the music was just loud enough that Julian had to lean close to speak. Their chests brushed, and Julian hoped the angel couldn't hear the effect it had in his voice. "They're safe in here," he said, and patted the bag.

Rami squinted, and in the low lighting of the bar finally noticed the strap around Julian's torso.

"Thank you," Rami said, furrowed brow softening.

"Of course. Can't let our prizes get ruined or stolen," Julian told them.

Yeah, because that was the reason.

Just then the bartender moved to their corner of the bar, and before Rami could even properly greet the man, Julian was calling out drink names. When Julian turned back only to be greeted with Rami's disapproval, the demon scoffed. "It's a Saturday night, Feathers. He doesn't have time for how-are-you's."

"Well, you never know! It's kind," Rami huffed. Julian leaned closer, turning his head so Rami could speak into his ear. This close, Julian could smell them, even in the crowded bar, and he couldn't help but inhale a little deeper, that sweet cotton scent a little addicting.

"What?" Julian asked, turning back to them and pretending like he remembered what they were talking about. "Speak louder," Julian told them.

Rami's cheeks pinkened before they closed the distance between them to speak in Julian's ear. Their breath was warm against his neck, and Julian *almost* shivered. "Treating customer-facing service workers is very important in human culture," they said, louder.

Selfless angel. Julian couldn't resist teasing them. When Julian turned back to them, his grin was a little wicked. "Maybe to you, Feathers. Not to everyone."

"Well, I don't think it would hurt," Rami returned.

It was getting hot inside the bar, but Julian didn't know if that was from his own sweater, the crowd, or the proximity of the angel.

The bartender returned with their drinks momentarily, and Julian thanked him before dropping a hefty tip in the man's jar.

To offer a little kindness and make himself seem trust-worthy to the angel, that's all. Definitely not to earn that little sparkle in Rami's gaze when they met again.

Before Rami could even come up with something to say, he handed them their drink, and then took Rami's elbow. Julian's cheeks heated as he led them back through the crowd to one of the tables on the patio, accessible through the garage doors.

It was much cooler out on the patio, and Julian ignored the few glances they earned as they sidled up to the railing in a conveniently free spot. In front of them were huge planters with overgrown shrubs acting as a barrier between the patio and sidewalk.

"So. Who's next?" Julian asked, wrapping his hand around the rail and rocking forward and back.

"I'm sure we'll see someone soon," Rami answered, and stopped beside Julian.

Forced to wait, Julian tried to settle down.

It seemed Rami couldn't help but fill the silence. "How's your Earthly experience so far?"

"It'll be better once I try this fancy chocolate of yours," Julian teased.

Rami arched a brow. "So confident in your skills of deduction?"

"One hundred percent," Julian declared. And then added, "The aquarium was pretty cool, I guess."

Rami beamed, turning to him, looking so innocent in their stupid soft cream sweater. "What was your favorite part?"

Julian hummed as he debated. The jellyfish did look like something out of a movie. Something made up.

He supposed they *were* made up, by something a lot bigger than he was.

The otters had been so adorable. Even the perverted one. But Julian didn't trust that he hadn't just been enamored with Rami's own enjoyment.

"I think the jellyfish," Julian finally answered, though it had only been a few seconds. "Pretty magical, if you ask me."

"I guess, in a way, they are," Rami said, echoing Julian's very thoughts. Their shoulder swayed into Julian's before they stiffened and scooted away.

He glanced over at them in surprise, and found their gaze already locked on Julian. Heat dusted his cheeks, though he couldn't imagine why, and he sipped his martini to cover it.

The night passed in a blur of chocolates and fruity drinks. Through a bit of magic, their corner of the patio stayed quiet.

The humans might have felt uneasy when they spied the two odd balls, and avoided them altogether.

Privacy, after all, was extremely important.

Julian chuckled as the angel won yet again, looking pleased as a peach to reward themself with a chocolate.

"Who returns lost money these days?" Julian muttered. "I would've kept that twenty."

"Money does run the entire world here, so you weren't *wrong* to assume he'd keep it."

"And yet I *was* wrong."

"You were," Rami agreed, not looking the least bit sorry.

Their shoulders swayed together again around the third drink, but this time they didn't separate. Rami's arm was warm against Julian and he soaked it in, wondering when the angel would notice and hoping they wouldn't.

"He's going to offer them his jacket," Rami said, and tilted their head at a couple on the sidewalk.

Julian considered it, feeling the nip of the cold air through his own sweater. It'd be stupid not to offer one to a date, and very selfish. So he said, "Nah, no way."

"Might as well go ahead and hand me my chocolate," Rami teased.

Julian scoffed at their confidence, glancing over to find the angel practically sparkling, leaning against the rail, drink balanced in deft fingers as they tried to casually watch the couple without seeming obvious.

A moment later, the two humans paused, and the taller one rubbed a hand down the other's arm. They exchanged words, and then he was pulling off his jacket and offering it to his companion.

Julian already had the chocolate balanced in his palm for the angel to take by the time Rami turned to him with a triumphant expression.

"Told you," they said.

"You sure did," Julian agreed, and watched Rami eat their treat.

They ate each one like it was their first, humming and smiling and pleased as could be. Their throat worked as they swallowed and Julian wished he was strong enough to look elsewhere, but instead he was staring as Rami licked their lips.

Julian finally tore his gaze away, shifting his attention anywhere but the angel.

He supposed the angel couldn't win them all. They'd catch onto him before then.

"Hah, told you so. My chocolate," Julian teased a few minutes later, dangling the gold-wrapped treat in front of the angel before snatching it back after his victory.

He sat his drink down to unwrap it, and studied the logo stamped into the top of it before he unceremoniously popped it between his lips.

It melted on his tongue, the tang of the orange and the bitter sweetness of the chocolate making his jaw tingle. He swallowed, mouth watering at the citrus. After pressing the chocolate to the inside of his cheek so he could talk while it continued melting, he turned to the angel to—

Well, he was going to comment on how delicious it was, but found Rami's stare caught on Julian's lips.

He swallowed once more and their gaze tracked it. At the last second their sky-blue eyes darted up, darkening to a deeper gray, a storm of appreciation.

"It's really nice," Julian choked out.

"I have good tastes," Rami muttered. "In chocolate," they added a moment later.

"Chocolate, right," Julian agreed, and swallowed the last bit of buttery softness.

Silence wedged its way between them, but their arms

were still touching. Julian lifted his drink, taking a sip, and cleared his throat.

"So. You curse. You drink. You indulge. And now you gamble," Julian pointed out, and turned to glance at Rami. "Not very angel-like, if you ask me." Selfish motivations for an *angel*.

Rami's face flushed, mouth dropping open a bit in response. "Well! I find that rather rude, just so you know," they huffed.

Julian choked down a laugh, lips twitching.

But then Rami stood up straighter, hands gripping the rail. "Very rude, actually. You can't just barge into my life—an angel's—and pass judgment on *me*. You're a demon, so you have no room to talk whatsoever."

Julian's smile faltered. This wasn't what he'd intended. "I'm a demon; I can do what I want," he argued, defensive at the angel's shift in tone.

Rami's expression shuttered suddenly, and they leaned further into the railing, away from Julian. "You also lie, because that's not true at all. Else you wouldn't have turned up on my step in this state." Their gaze flicked over him disapprovingly. "Someone didn't want you doing whatever it was you were doing."

Julian shifted away, too, ignoring the chill against that arm. "Is that what you think it was? A punishment?"

"Was it not?"

Julian supposed he should be relieved that the angel was so far off the trail. Instead, it rankled that the angel naturally assumed Julian was a no-good demon who'd done something to deserve getting the shit kicked out of him.

"Guess you don't think very highly of me, do you?" Julian guessed, tone coming out sharper than he'd intended.

Rami stiffened, stared at him, genuine confusion in their expression.

"Am I supposed to?" they asked.

And Julian knew they were an angel, and Julian a demon. He also knew that he hadn't exactly given the angel a lot of reason to trust him thus far. But he'd thought…

What, exactly, had he thought?

Annoyed with himself, Julian downed the rest of his drink and sat it gently on the table beside them.

"I suppose not. After all, I'm just a demon," he answered bitterly.

Rami frowned at that, and Julian glanced over his shoulder at the bar still in full swing.

"I think I'm ready to get out of here," he said, and pushed the chocolate across the table to Rami. "Won enough chocolates to satisfy yourself?"

Rami finished their drink and sat it beside Julian's. "Yes, I think so," they said, squinting at Julian as if trying to see through him.

"Great. Let's call it a night," he said, and led the way out of the bar.

Rami stayed close behind him, the bag of plastic crinkling as they wormed their way through the crowd and onto the street outside.

The silence was a canyon between them, and Julian, for once, let it lie.

He might have been pouting. Maybe even a little brooding. So what?

So what if his feelings were a little hurt? He *was* a demon, sent here to do demonly things, and yet the idea that Rami saw nothing but what Julian technically should've *wanted* them to see… hurt.

Now he just had to figure out what to do with this information.

14
APOLOGIES

Julian was upset.

It was clear. The demon wasn't doing a very good job of hiding it, if he was trying to hide it at all.

Not only was he avoiding Rami's gaze, but he was walking faster, arms tucked tight into his sides, hands in his pockets, and Rami doubted it was because the breeze was chillier than it had been a few hours ago.

At least they wouldn't have to worry about their chocolate melting. They gripped the plastic in hand and wondered what Julian had done with the cross body bag he'd magicked just for the bar.

Had he hand-waved it back out of existence? Left it behind?

Squinting against the cold, Rami stared at the back of the demon's head as they walked.

Rami must have said something to upset the demon. There was no other explanation.

His body language clearly read: *fuck off.*

And the demon stuck to that as they entered the house. Rami headed for the stairs, anticipating the end of the night and sleeping in their bed once more.

But Julian did not follow.

"Everything alright?" Rami asked, knowing the answer already.

"Yeah, of course. I'm just not tired yet, so, uh, why don't you read, or whatever you do. I'll be up later."

Rami peered at him, but Julian was averting his gaze.

Maybe they could make more headway into the book they've been reading. "Okay," Rami told him, and then made their way up the stairs.

As they readied for bed, they were hyper-aware of every sound from the lower floor. Before long, the murmur of the television filtered up the stairs, and Rami sighed as they sat on the bed.

Fine. If the demon wanted to pout instead of talk about his feelings, that wasn't Rami's problem.

He'd come to bed eventually.

The demon did not come to bed.

Rami blinked themself awake, unsure how long they'd been asleep. The moonlight was streaming in through the window above the bed, casting a soft glow on the empty side where Julian should be sleeping.

Rami rolled over and faced the unruffled expanse of the bed, knocking their book off their chest as they did so.

Why did Rami want the demon here, anyway? It didn't matter where he slept.

Rami narrowed their gaze. If he was feeling so much better, he didn't even *need* to sleep in Rami's bed.

So, technically... technically, the demon was basically

healed. Sure, he probably couldn't stretch for the top shelf in Rami's cabinet, but he was well enough to stand on his own two feet. And it wasn't Rami's business what trouble he got into once he left.

At this rate, Rami could honestly throw Julian out the very next morning and no one would blame them for it.

But what if the demon got into a predicament, and got hurt again, or even… what if he did something stupid and exposed them all?

If demons were accidentally exposed, it would only make sense that angels would be exposed, too. Two sides of the same coin, or something like that.

With a sigh, they rolled over, staring at the ceiling instead of the empty side of the bed.

Something was all tangled up inside them, and Rami needed to unravel it.

It was hypocritical of them to accuse Julian of pouting instead of talking when Rami was doing the very same thing.

Below, on the lower level where the demon was no doubt avoiding Rami altogether, it was silent. Not even the television was droning.

The demon wasn't even *snooping*. Rami would know if he was; he'd be making noise.

So. Rami needed to take advantage of this time they had to themselves, and figure out what this *feeling* was in their chest.

Rami puffed out a breath, closed their eyes, and imagined kicking the demon out come morning. Never seeing the demon again.

They shuffled in the bed, so uncomfortable with even the suggestion that they couldn't lie still. The make-believe scenario bothered them more than it should.

They blinked their eyes open at the ceiling.

Maybe it was time to admit to themself that they didn't want the demon to leave.

They maybe even liked having him around, no matter how annoying he was.

Am I really that lonely? Rami thought.

Maybe they were.

Or maybe the demon wasn't as bad as they were so intent to believe.

Guess you don't think very highly of me, do you? Julian had asked.

It dawned on Rami, then, laying in the bed alone. They'd hurt Julian's feelings.

Of course.

Sure, Julian was a demon. But. He also respected Rami's boundaries, like with the office. He was kind, even if he didn't want to admit it, protecting their chocolates, heating their coffee.

Rami's frown deepened. Oh no. Did they… *like* the demon?

They huffed. At the very least, they no longer… *actively disliked* the demon.

What did that even mean?

Rami sighed. "I guess I could start with an apology."

That was ultimately what pulled Rami out of bed, wrapping themself in a cozy robe and sliding into their slippers.

They crept down the stairs, suspicious of the silence and yet hesitant anyway.

They paused as soon as they reached the bottom landing.

There, on the couch and buried under a heavy blanket pulled up to his chin, was Julian. The television was frozen on the *are you still watching?* screen.

He'd fallen asleep watching television.

Rami didn't know why that made their chest ache.

Rami trailed a little closer, steps quiet and careful.

Julian didn't stir.

Like this, asleep and still, he looked… soft. Innocent.

His head was crooked to accommodate the length of his horns, and up close, Rami could tell the short one was smoothing out beautifully.

Their heart clenched at the reminder of what he'd been through.

Rami struggled to merge their own bitterness toward demons with the image of the man in front of them.

It was like trying to force the same ends of two magnets together: it just didn't fit.

Rami watched him for a moment longer, the steady rise and fall of his chest, the ease of the lines around his eyes.

Eyes that were… open?

Rami stumbled back with a shout.

"Watching me sleep, Feathers?" Julian croaked out, voice raspy from sleep.

Heat rushed to Rami's face and they steadied themself on the arm of the couch.

"Not on purpose," they admitted. "Actually, I think I'm having a revelation."

Julian began to sit up. "Well, that's never good. What are you—"

"I'm sorry," Rami blurted.

Julian paused, arms bent to push himself to a seated position, and then continued until he slumped against the back of the couch, staring up at them. "What for?"

He rubbed sleep from his eyes and Rami felt their chest cave in.

"I've treated you unfairly, I think is the case."

"I'm listening," Julian said, leaning back against the couch. He pulled the blanket closer, and Rami had no choice but to see it as a protection barrier.

"I want to offer some context for my… thoughts, if you'd be open to that," Rami said.

Julian squinted, suspicion in the line of his lips, but eventually, he nodded.

"Go ahead," he said, and patted the couch next to him.

Rami sat after only a moment's hesitation. Then, under Julian's curious gaze, Rami drew in a deep breath. "As much as I preach to my clients about communicating their feelings, I am beginning to learn it's not so easy, is it?" They chuckled, but Julian did not return the sentiment.

Clearing their throat, Rami began. "I've been here for… a *long* time," Rami said. "On Earth, around humans."

"You're old as dirt, yes, I know," Julian drawled.

A smile twitched at Rami's lips. That's more like the demon they've come to know.

"And as I'm sure you're aware, there's a lot of… *bad* in this world."

"Being selfish doesn't *always* have to be—" Julian stopped himself as Rami leveled him with a dry stare. "Right, this is your context. Shutting up."

He mimed zipping his lips and throwing it away before retreating his arm back beneath the plush blanket.

"I haven't even heard from Heaven in a long time. So I've just been here, studying humans, getting to know them, taking my notes and sending what I can back to Heaven. To angels, they're just another jellyfish to watch through the glass. To *them*," they said, motioning vaguely to the windows, "it's very real. Humans experience such *tragedies*, Julian," Rami said, begging him to understand, remembering the wars they'd seen, the stories they'd heard from their clients. "Atrocities committed for nothing more than one's own… selfishness." They paused, hung up on the word, something ringing in the back of their mind, but they couldn't put their finger on why. "But according to Heaven, it's all natural. *That's just the way of things,* they'd say."

Before Julian could speak, Rami lifted their hand. "I know it's not up to us to police them. That is precisely my point. A single human can suffer so much and receive no good in return. I've seen so much of it down here. Where things are real, where *real* people are having to live day after day and bear witness to evil, bad things."

Julian was silent.

Rami was, too, attempting to funnel their jumbled thoughts into coherent words. "I think somewhere along the way, I began to resent the bad. No matter what my job is, it doesn't feel *right.* It's a broken system, and I thought I was above it. Turns out, I think I've fallen into its trap all the same." Their lips twisted, disappointment welling up. Disappointment in themself.

"Because somewhere in all that, I began to blame demons for it. Demons became a target for all the unfairness, all the darkness I'd witnessed. And logically, I know that's not true. So. I'm sorry," Rami said, sitting up a little straighter. They caught Julian's attention and held it. "I'm sorry I've been judging you so harshly against a narrative of my own making. I shouldn't have said what I did at the bar."

Their speech through, Rami sat and waited.

Julian stared at them, head cocked to the side. They could practically hear the gears turning behind those golden eyes.

"Gonna be honest, Feathers, I don't really know what to say," Julian finally muttered. His gaze trailed away before snapping back.

"Well, that's—"

"No one's ever apologized so thoroughly before."

Rami blinked at that, and realized distantly that Julian was leaning closer.

"You… forgive me?" Rami asked, swaying forward, caught in the orbit of this demon.

Unbidden, Rami's gaze dipped to his lips, quirked in a bit of a smile.

Julian waved his hand back and forth, and Rami's heart fell before the demon winked. *Winked.*

It was devastating.

"Yeah, I forgive you," he said softly, and then—

And then.

A kiss. So gentle, barely a brush of their lips, and oh, this was a terrible idea, of that Rami was certain. But Julian was so close, and so warm.

He was from Hell, wasn't he? He probably ran a little warmer than others.

How did he smell like that? All… deep, velvety cocoa, not dissimilar to the very chocolates Rami loved. Or their morning coffee, the slightest hints of that heat.

And his lips were softer than Rami would've thought.

It was chaste, a press of mouths, and then Julian pulled back and Rami was yanked from the moment, back to reality.

Their cheeks *flamed,* and they pulled away. Julian's expression was unreadable.

They would just… pretend that this never happened. *Yep. Yes, that. Okay.*

Rami cleared their throat. "How is the couch treating you?"

Julian turned his head to the side, a grotesque noise cracking.

Rami must have contorted their face into a displeased facade, because the demon took one look at them and snorted.

"That answer enough for you?"

"I suppose it is. So you'll come upstairs, then?"

"Did you miss me?" Julian teased, and Rami caught the twinkle in his eye *before* getting flustered.

"I wouldn't go that far," Rami said in return.

And yet they stood, waiting for Julian to throw the blanket to the side and follow them up the stairs.

The chastity pillow still went in place. Rami still told Julian to be sure not to touch them.

Julian still had a half smile on his lips as he agreed.

And Rami fell asleep much easier that time, knowing Julian was near.

15
EDUCATION

Julian woke before the angel did, and smirked as he recognized the snoring weight on his chest.

In the last twelve hours, Julian thought he'd experienced every emotion on the spectrum. Upset, anger, annoyance, shifting into disappointment as the television droned and the clock ticked by.

Even his temporary sleep had been uneasy. The cycle continued when he'd woken with the angel standing over him. Confusion, hesitation, then understanding and a little awe. Maybe even a little affection.

Julian stared down at the angel on his chest, cheek smushed against Julian's pec, mouth slightly parted with each deep breath. He knew what that mouth felt like now.

Maybe more than a little affection...

Their silvery hair was askew, out of place, and his fingers itched to feel it.

But Julian was good, so he kept his hands to himself. The sun rose, streaking the room in golden light, and Julian was... content.

He'd been getting ahead of himself last night, in his hurt. He thought back on the whole day and cringed at himself for allowing the angel to...

To be kind?

Julian winced, rolled his eyes. Even still, part of him wondered, who did the angel think they were? Taking Julian to the aquarium like he was some... some child to entertain?

But. But Julian had *enjoyed* their little excursion. He'd even enjoyed the grocery store, in a way. Or maybe he'd just enjoyed how Rami had come to the human's rescue. Or how they'd given Julian their sweater.

He scowled up at the ceiling, ignoring the pinch in his chest.

He replayed Rami's apology over and over in his head, again and again.

Julian felt... sad for the angel. Here on Earth, all alone, their own faith faltering amongst all the bad in the world. His chest ached for them. It had to be so lonely.

Gross. Feelings.

And yet, despite how Julian had forgiven the angel, the whole situation had only reminded him why he was here. He still needed to tempt them.

Nothing had worked so far, because Julian was still *here.* That's how it worked. As soon as the temptation was successful, as soon as the angel did something irreparably selfish, Julian would materialize back in Hell for a debrief.

And *then* he'd be allowed free reign on Earth, tempting humans and others alike to be a little more selfish.

As if they could sense his oppressive thoughts, Rami shifted, and eventually rolled away from Julian with a smack of their lips, pulling the blanket close.

Julian was left bare to the cool air of the apartment, and couldn't help the twitch of his lips as he watched the angel bundle up in their blankets.

It made it all the easier for Julian to slip from the bed, and magic himself a new set of clothes and hair that wasn't flattened by the pillows.

The angel didn't stir, not even as Julian tiptoed out of the room and down to the bottom floor.

He followed the angel's ritual and made himself coffee, sipping it with a scowl before opening the fridge to search for the containers the angel had used to sweeten it the day before.

He felt a bit like a witch as he added, stirred, and tasted until it was to his liking. A morning potion.

Snickering at the thought, he took a seat at the counter and soaked in the silence.

But his thoughts soon turned serious once again. Julian sighed.

He wasn't here to have *fun* and play around with the angel in human establishments. To experience creature comforts or simple pleasures. He was here to complete an assignment. Frolicking with Rami beneath the shiny fish and eating fancy, rich chocolate was not it.

Julian would just have to… what, exactly? Continue to tempt the angel?

It hadn't exactly worked so far, or Julian would already be back in Hell.

The angel cursed, though infrequently, more than Julian assumed was polite for *angels*.

Rami enjoyed their little treats and pleasures. They indulged, even. Now, thanks to Julian, the angel even gambled, but it wasn't enough.

Julian rolled his eyes. Short of, what, robbing a bank just for the hell of it—and the demon knew better than to expect such a thing—he wasn't too certain how much else to tempt the angel.

Unbidden, he felt a ghost of the angel's touch on the back of his hand, felt their fingers squeeze around his own. The warmth of their body pressed up against Julian's. Their lips soft against his.

There was always…

He shook his head. No. That felt cheap, predictable. Cruel, for some reason.

His head tilted to the side with the weight of a new idea.

Something told Julian that the angel hadn't exactly experienced the *simple pleasures* that happened between the sheets. However, if he was just to simply educate the angel on matters of sex, and then let the pieces fall where they may…

After all, it wasn't sex itself that would complete the temptation. It would be the selfish desire, the need to sate their own pleasure that would do it.

And yet somehow, this revelation didn't make Julian feel better.

"Oh! Good morning," Rami offered in their chipper little voice as they appeared at the bottom of the stairs. Julian hadn't even heard them up and about, and snapped his head up.

That's what he got for letting his guard down around this angel. And he'd get a lot worse, too, if Julian didn't see this damned assignment through.

"There you are, Feathers," Julian called out. It came out softer than he'd intended, and he dropped his head, scowling down at his still steaming coffee.

"Looking for me, were you?" Rami asked. Julian recognized the tease in their voice, and he was helpless but to meet their gaze with a quirking smile despite his frustration.

Julian felt… spiky. Unsure and uncertain and mixed up, and he wasn't sure how to handle all of it at once.

"Wouldn't go that far," Julian returned, mimicking the angel's words from the night before.

They smiled softly—so fucking softly—and trailed to the counter to make their own coffee.

Today they were dressed as usual: pants and a collared

shirt and a fluffy cardigan. They were still wearing their slippers.

"Thank you for listening to me ramble last night," they said, busying themself with the beans and the grinder. "It was very kind of you to listen even after I'd said something so callous."

Kind, Julian thought with an ache in his chest. Sure.

"No worries, Feathers." Julian swallowed. "In fact, I know just how you can make it up to me."

Rami sputtered. "Make it up to you? Was the apology not enough?"

"This will be fun. Come on," Julian coaxed. "I went to the aquarium. We had a snack platter. I think it's time for me to show you something."

"Might I inquire where this something is?" they asked, slippers hushing across the floor as they pulled the kettle off the stove.

"You could. But I want it to be a surprise," Julian said.

Rami stilled, arm stretched above them to the shelf of mugs, and Julian stared at them, wishing he could see the expression on Rami's face.

"Well, that's kind of you," Rami said, and placed a mug on the counter top with a ceramic clink.

There it was again. That word.

Soft. Sweet. Gentle. *Kind.*

All the things Julian wasn't allowed to be. The spikes he felt were tensing, as if eager to burst or fend off all the very things Rami *was,* and was accusing Julian of being.

"Wait until you see where we're going before you say that," Julian told them, and pushed away from the counter to take a seat on the couch.

Rami did not reply, and it was a tense silence that passed agonizingly slow before the angel walked past Julian… to also take a seat on the couch.

Julian glanced over at them, then to the chair—that Julian only just then realized he had begun to think of as *Rami's* chair.

"I don't get any hints as to where we're going?" Rami asked.

"Nope," Julian bit out, and sipped his too-hot coffee. The burn was good. The taste was better.

Rami hummed. "I suppose I'll just have to wait and see. Is there a dress code for this sort of destination?"

Julian snorted. "No, not at all. It's just a shop."

"Oh, a shop? I love shopping," Rami said, sipping from their mug with a stupidly cute little smile on their face.

"Of course you do," Julian muttered.

Rami didn't offer him a reply, which was just as well.

His spikes were still spiking, and he drank his coffee and sat his mug on the table with a clack.

"Why aren't you in your chair?" he finally snapped.

Rami turned to meet Julian's gaze. "My chair?"

"Yes," he said simply, and motioned to the chair to their right. "You sit there every morning. Why are you on the couch?"

"I suppose I felt like sitting here this morning. Is that so bad?" they asked, a single brow arched in a challenge.

Julian deflated, his spikes receding. "No. I guess not," he grumbled.

Rami hummed again, and what the fuck was that about?

There was little else to describe what Julian did for the rest of the morning besides *pout*.

So he pouted, and waited for the angel to drink their coffee while they flipped through the pages of yet another book. Julian couldn't remember if it was a new book or if it was the one they'd been reading every morning. Something told him it was new.

Julian stewed as the sunlight slid across the wall across from him, marking the passage of the day.

To occupy himself, he magicked a phone and pretended there was anything of interest on it. Julian had gotten his fill of the internet when he was in Hell, after all, and watched the time tick away achingly slow.

When the hour was polite enough, Julian stood. "Alright, are you ready?"

Rami dragged themself from the pages with a slow blink. "Oh, for the surprise! Yes, certainly."

Gently, the angel placed their bookmark inside the pages before shutting it and setting it so carefully on the side table.

"We don't have to drive; it's within walking distance," Julian said.

"Oh, it's close by? Lovely."

Julian almost rolled his eyes. He contained himself—and his horns—somehow.

Doing so became increasingly more difficult as they stepped outside to begin their walk, and Rami instantly grabbed hold of Julian's arm to pull him close. He sputtered at first before the rhythmic clicking of a wheel caught his attention, and a bicycler sped by the two of them in a blur.

"Humans are particularly ruthless on the sidewalks—be careful," Rami told him.

Warmth rushed to Julian's cheeks. His chest went all tight. The angel was soft and warm against him. They smelled like cotton and that sweet scent of the soap they used.

Julian took a comfortable step away, his spikes flaring again to puncture any of the softness offered.

"This way," Julian said, and directed the angel down the sidewalk.

"Yes, I'll follow your lead," Rami said, and Julian gritted his teeth.

What the hell is wrong with you? This is your job.

This is what you want, isn't it? Easier to tempt the angel if they're soft *for you.*

Julian didn't *like* this softness, or maybe he liked it too much. He was particularly frustrated that Rami was trusting him so easily, treating him so kindly when he didn't deserve it.

This *fucking* angel was just so *understanding* and *nice* and *kind* and Julian was decidedly *not*. In fact, Julian was being an asshole this morning, and the angel was *not* giving him the fight he wanted.

So he scowled and pouted his way to the shop, knowing the angel was following closely, viscerally aware of all the *goodness* emanating from behind him.

"Oh," the angel said softly when they realized where Julian had stopped.

"Yep. It's exactly what you think it is," Julian drawled, and pulled open the door of the sex shop.

"You've been showing me simple pleasures. Maybe it's time I show you a different kind of pleasure," Julian said.

Never one to shirk their manners, Rami swallowed, their smile tight but pleasant as they stepped through the door.

"Hey there, let me know if you need help with anything." The voice belonged to the clerk behind the counter with dyed hair and piercings galore, and Julian grinned fiercely at them.

"I know my way around, but thanks anyway," he said, if only to get a reaction out of the angel.

And oh, what a reaction it was. The angel stiffened, sliding to the side and making way for Julian to step further into the store. Their cheeks were already pink, and growing warmer by the moment.

"By all means, lead the way then, expert," Rami said, practically whispering. It came out like a hiss, and Julian wanted to *glow* with the victory.

Finally. He'd flustered the angel.

Julian would've given up if he hadn't been able to get *some* emotion out of them, what with all the silicone dicks and vibrators hanging on the walls.

"No, I think you should take the lead," Julian said to them, lowering his voice. "What are you curious about? I'm happy to answer any questions you might have, Feathers."

Rami's gaze was pointedly sharp, their cheeks still red, hands fluttering at their side and over their pristine clothes before finally shoving them in their pockets.

"No, no. I *insist.* Please take the lead," Rami said through gritted teeth and a forced smile.

Poor angel—they seemed so distraught.

Julian turned to the selection, wondering where to start. He took confident steps to the dildo wall, a rainbow of silicone toys stretching out before them.

He snickered quietly at his own word choice.

"Do you even know what these are for?" he teased.

Rami's face was all pinched when Julian glanced over. "Of course I do," they snapped. "I am rather well-read, you know."

Julian arched a brow at that, his gaze turning to the toys for a split second as he walked down the wall a bit before snapping back to the angel, studying them closer. Rami owned rows and rows of books.

"Well, sure," Julian agreed. "But, I mean. You know of it outside of books, too, yeah?"

The angel was quiet, and Julian slowly turned to them, reading the purposefully blank expression easier than he was sure the angel wished him to.

"Feathers," Julian hissed. "Never?"

Rami shook their head, lips thinned, eyes pointedly avoiding the wall of phallic objects.

"How have you—" He lowered his voice. "How have you been on Earth this whole time and never had sex?"

Julian's skin itched. He knew the angel was holy, but *holy hell.*

Rami was looking increasingly uncomfortable, and Julian was too shocked to cull his reaction.

"Why would I?" they asked.

Julian's mouth dropped open, and it took him a moment to work through his surprise. "What do you mean, *why?* You're on Earth! Sex is, like, humans' favorite thing. They start wars over it!"

"Had it not occurred to you that is the exact reason I have no interest in it?"

Julian arched a brow at that. "No interest? Really?" he asked, recalling the pause at the aquarium, the particularly sinful way the angel's lips had wrapped around the chocolate just the night before. The kiss. Julian stepped closer. "Not even a little?" he asked, softer, slower.

It worked, drawing the angel's attention to his lips. Julian watched as they floundered, dragging their silvery gaze back up, the memory playing behind those eyes.

"No, not even a little," they lied.

Hmm. Julian smirked. "Then it won't bother you if I look around a bit more, then?" he asked jovially.

Rami's lips opened and closed twice before they shook their head. "That's your discretion."

Did their voice sound strained? Julian resisted the urge to let a victorious smile slither over his lips.

He grabbed the angel's belt loop as they turned away, stopping them in their tracks. "Oh, no, you don't," he said. "You're shopping with me."

Oh, he should've done this from the *beginning.*

Their cheeks were flushed as Julian dragged them along. It wasn't as if Julian planned to use any of the items, but subjecting Rami to the uncomfortable topic was too good to pass up.

"Who knows," he asked. "You might learn something you didn't know."

"I'm certain I know plenty," Rami said lowly.

"So that's what you're always reading? Porn books?" Julian teased, and leaned forward to grab a far-too-large tentacle dildo, reading the package as if he cared exactly what was in the silicone.

Rami sputtered, eyes going wide at the sight of the item in the box. "I—I do not read *porn* books, and even if I did, I'd have nothing to be ashamed of. Not when you're here… fondling *that* thing!" they hissed.

"Romance, then, I bet," Julian needled. "Yeah, you seem like the type."

"I beg your pardon. What type is that?"

"A hopeless romantic. You do tend to romanticize the human experience. Bet that's not all you romanticize," he said, waggling his eyebrows and rubbing a thumb over the silicone suckers on the tentacle through the *Try Me* hole in the plastic.

"I'm an angel," Rami said, gaze sliding to the clerk who couldn't care less what they were whispering about in the corner, flipping a magazine and chewing gum obnoxiously.

"So?" Julian asked. "Doesn't mean you're not allowed to be a *little* selfish."

It would be a gateway drug.

Julian didn't find as much humor in the thought as he probably should have, being a selfish temptation demon, after all.

"Sex isn't *bad*," Julian said, lowering his voice. "It's self-care. It improves your mood, just like those little truffles you love so much. And that's science."

The plan was revealing itself. Rami would get a taste of

pleasures of the flesh, and they'd want more, and never having had it before, after all these years? They'd probably be selfish about it.

That seemed to shut Rami up, and their lips thinned into a tight line. They swallowed, gaze flicking once to the box in Julian's hand before snapping away again.

Julian hung the box back on the wall and ignored the choked noise in Rami's throat.

"What else can we find around here?" he murmured, and caught Rami's wrist to pull them along.

Julian came to a stop only a few feet later, the tamer silicone calling to him. If he was selling this whole situation to a naive angel, he didn't want to give them the wrong idea.

"Maybe something smaller to start with," Julian murmured, just loud enough to reach Rami's ears. "What do you think?" he asked, tapping the different box.

"Do you plan to take these back to hell, then?" Rami asked him instead of offering any thoughts.

"Aw, roomie, don't be like that," Julian whined quietly.

"We are *not* roommates."

"Why not?" Julian pouted. "Is it rent? I can pay rent."

"No rent required. You're only staying for a bit," Rami said, as if they didn't believe their own words.

Julian smiled. "Right. Just for a bit."

Rami visibly relaxed, and Julian rolled his eyes. "You never answered me. Which one?" he asked, and pointed to the two boxes in question.

"I don't have an opinion," Rami said, head lifted as if all this was below them.

Julian hummed and let his stare trail over the wall, pausing on a totally different item. He grinned wickedly as he reached up, only wincing a bit at the stretch of his ribs before Rami made that choking noise again.

Then warmth covered his back, and an arm stretched

above his, effortless and smooth, knocking the box he was after loose before a thick hand clasped it.

"Here," Rami hissed, cheeks redder than they'd been so far as they shoved the box into Julian's chest. "You're insufferable."

"Aren't I just?" Julian asked. "Aw, come on, you like me," Julian teased.

Rami scoffed and averted their gaze, but nowhere was safe, and it returned to the floor seconds later.

"So now the question is," Julian continued, "do I want to be fucked or do the fucking?" he mused, holding up the tentacle and the fleshlight.

Rami's wide, gray eyes snapped up to his, their mouth a little slack.

"W-well," Rami began. "I suppose it depends on what you prefer."

"Eh, moods change, you know," Julian said, shrugging.

Rami was quiet at that, but the moment passed before Julian could question them about it.

"Oh, pretty!" Rami said, and darted away from the wall toward the side room with the lingerie.

"Oh my *word*," they hissed only a moment later, pointing at the crotchless lace on the mannequins. "They have no shame."

"Well, it's a mannequin, so. They don't have anything at all, really."

Rami visibly relaxed in the absence of phallic-shaped objects, running their hands over some of the fabric as they walked slowly past.

Julian watched the angel feel the textures. Some cheap, some not.

As he saw the angel double-take at a set of hot pants, Julian's lips twitched. they'd never seen such things before.

Which was ridiculous.

Right?

Had the angel really spent the last however many centuries with only their romance books for company?

Even in Hell, Julian had managed to find another demon or three or four to hook up with. Have temporary fun with.

Julian frowned. Rami never let themself grow close to the humans, outside of their clients. So who the hell would they have been intimate with?

His chest ached, and he rubbed at the spot. Was Rami lonely?

Julian would be, if he were in their position.

Running a hand through his hair, Julian sighed.

He had a job to do. But he'd have to find another way to do it.

Because Julian wasn't going to use sex to tempt this angel. He *couldn't*. And if that meant he was waitlisted at the end of the week for another few centuries…

Julian resisted the urge to groan aloud, and cursed as Rami trailed down another aisle.

Grumbling, he followed after the angel.

He'd have to find another opportunity. But how was he supposed to tempt someone so selfless?

And why was it becoming harder to want to?

16
PASTRY CASE

Rami was past the point of wondering if they were going to pass out from the amount of blood rushing to their cheeks.

They'd simply accepted their fate, and watched as Julian touched all the little silicone toys.

Well, maybe *little* wasn't quite the right word for some of them.

When they agreed to this venture with the demon, they hadn't quite expected *this*.

To escape, they'd darted into the adjoining room, which seemed much safer. They could look at lingerie. Maybe even appreciate the fabric and shapes.

Even if they didn't quite understand the purpose of them. From what they'd read, weren't you just supposed to take them off, to get to the… sex?

He grimaced at another set of crotchless panties on a mannequin. Ah. Well, humans certainly solved that problem, didn't they?

Rami's eyes widened as they caught sight of fishnets with a tentacle pattern. The mannequin wearing them was also proudly displaying the very same silicone toy Julian had been fondling.

Rami glanced around the room. Julian's head was bent as he examined something on another aisle.

The curiosity was too much.

Rami poked a finger into the appendage, feeling one of the silicone suckers. It was cool and smooth to the touch, and they cocked their head to the side.

Hm.

They'd of course heard and read about these toys, but Rami had never ventured out to properly investigate. The books they read were close enough to the real thing, surely.

"Whatcha doin'?" Julian asked suddenly, and close by.

Rami jumped a foot in the air and spun, clasping their hands behind their back. "Nothing!"

"Didn't look like nothing," Julian drawled, and peered around their back. "You know, if you have any questions, we can treat this like an… educational trip."

Rami pursed their lips in thought.

"Yeah!" Julian said, clearly enthused by his own idea. "I meant what I said. You've introduced me to the simple pleasures, like how you showed me the sea creatures at the aquarium and that little snack platter and the chocolates. And I'll show you all… this," he said, and waved a hand to encompass the room.

"I doubt you'll show me anything I don't readily know," Rami retorted.

Julian arched a brow at that. "Reading about it in your little books is a whole lot different than *experiencing* it."

Rami's cheeks flushed at the thought of Julian *experiencing* anything of the like.

But. Education was very important.

And it wasn't like Rami had anyone else to ask.

Actually, thinking of this as an educational experience really quite helped. They were learning, and nothing more.

Face aflame, they turned away from the demon. If they

were going to ask questions, they couldn't very well look him in the eyes while doing so.

"Do… do people actually like this?" they asked, poking their finger into the silicone of the toy to feel the suckers again. It wobbled when they removed their touch.

Julian made a choking noise, and Rami glanced over their shoulder at him before averting their attention. "Is everything alright?"

"Yeah… yep. Peachy. Tons of people like this kind of thing. That's why it exists," he said, motioning to their surroundings. "That's why all of this exists."

Rami's brow furrowed and their gaze lifted, drifting from the… *dildo* to the demon and back again.

"Do *you* like this kind of thing?"

Julian coughed a bit, and shrugged. "I mean, I'm not… opposed," he said, voice strained.

"Right," Rami said, dragging the word out. "So you, and other humans into this kind of thing—why… tentacles? I mean, what does this have to do with the octopus?"

The noise Julian made was more in line with a laugh that time. "M'not attracted to a fucking sea creature. It's just a fun texture. Something a little different than the plain ol' penis, you know? It feels… nice."

Rami's cheeks flushed at the idea of Julian enjoying this… toy.

Inside him.

Clearing their throat, Rami pushed the thoughts away. "So what's with all this, then?"

Julian hummed, and Rami watched his deft fingers stroke a mesh covering. Not that it would actually cover anything, since it was see-through.

"It's just… dressing up. Like… okay, don't you wear your best sweater for your clients?"

Rami gasped. "I am *not* sexually attracted to my—"

"No, no. I know, that's not what I'm implying. Let me finish explaining," Julian grumbled, frowning over at them.

Rami thinned their lips and nodded.

"I'm just saying, you want to impress them, look good for them, professional. Some people like to dress up for their partners, play around. These clothes make them feel good, powerful, just like your fancy little loafers and sweaters do. It's supposed to be fun."

"Fun," Rami repeated, glancing around the room at all the colorful fabrics. The fuzzy necklines and the flowing gowns. "I suppose, to some, these things could be considered fun."

The characters in their books certainly seemed to enjoy it.

"See? Now you're getting it," Julian encouraged.

Rami couldn't look directly at his smile. It was a little too close to the sun.

As they averted their gaze, their attention caught on a red and white display across the room.

"Julian," Rami said suddenly.

"Yeah, Feathers?"

Rami pointed across the room. "Is that what I think it is?"

Julian followed the direction of his finger, and snorted as he finally saw the display. With a bark of laughter he crossed the room and tugged Rami with him.

"That is exactly what you think it is."

Before them, two mannequins with voluptuous breasts were dressed: one in a white sheer number with feathers, and one in red. The white one had a matching feathery halo suspended over the shoulders with a pair of wings visible behind it, and the other had a pair of horns and a tail.

Rami turned a dead stare to Julian, who lifted his hands. "Hey, I didn't make the display."

"How dare they," Rami muttered, glaring at the sexualized version of what humans thought angels were. Sure, they'd seen adverts for this kind of thing during America's Halloween, but they'd thought it was just that. An advert. "This is… so silly."

"Exactly. But it's also sexy," Julian countered.

Rami arched a brow at that, forgetting to be embarrassed in their surprise. "If this is the type of angel you think is sexy, you do not think angels are sexy," Rami told him.

"Well, I mean." Julian waved a hand at the mannequins. "Do you not?"

Rami made a doubtful noise. "No! Angels don't even have —" They waved a hand at the exaggerated breasts of the mannequin. *"That!"* Angels certainly didn't have nipples, for heaven's sake. "And as for the demon? Well, your horns and wings don't look like that."

"What does that have to do with anything?"

Rami shrugged. "Surely you're not asking me to judge the attractiveness of these plastic horns? Because the answer is no. I think this is a cheap imitation. Besides, we all know demons aren't *red.* They're gold. Which is much prettier than whatever this is." They waved a dismissive hand.

"Tell me how you really feel, Feathers."

Rami sighed. "I just *did*—oh, I see."

Julian's lips twitched before he nodded and turned away from the angel and demon costumes.

As they left the room, a stand caught Rami's eye. "Ooh, jewelry?" Rami asked, pausing by the display. They spun the wheel, watching the twinkle of the jewels reflect back at them. As it came to a stop, Rami squinted at the text and the crude image of where the jewelry supposedly went.

Rami dropped their hand, aghast. "You mean it goes… there?" Rami asked.

Julian nodded, looking particularly proud of himself. "Sure does."

"Does it not hurt?" Rami hissed. Why would humans do such a thing?

"Of course it hurts. It's a needle going through your—"

"That's enough! I don't need to hear anymore," Rami cut him off, shaking their head.

"Well, come on, that was kind of a silly question—*does it hurt?*" he mocked. "Of course it hurts, dicks are sensitive, y'know?" he drawled, waving a hand at Rami.

Impossibly, Rami's cheeks flushed even more, and they turned away. In their embarrassment, they didn't even consider that the question might have been rhetorical. "I think I've seen quite enough. Are you done here?"

The pause was extremely telling, and Rami hastened their steps on the way out of the store, not even bothering to wave to the clerk, who wasn't paying attention anyway, smacking on their bubblegum.

Surely Julian knew that angels don't—that they aren't—

"Wait, wait, wait," Julian chanted as he pushed through the glass door, steps quickening to keep pace with Rami. "What are you running off for? What was that about?"

The cold air did little to cool their cheeks, and they walked in a hurry down the sidewalk.

Rami's fretting must have been enough to clue Julian in, because his steps disappeared for a moment before he caught back up.

"Did I say something wrong? I didn't mean to make you uncomfortable—"

Rami stared at him, wild eyed, considering where they'd just come from.

"—Okay, I see now that sounds hypocritical, but I mean it. I do! Uh, where are we going?"

"To a bakery. I need something sweet to make up for the trauma you just subjected me to."

"A bakery?" Julian asked, interest coloring his tone. "Sign me up."

The topic of sex dropped altogether, and Rami was relieved. They walked to the bakery, and Rami greeted the clerk behind the bar by name, staring through the glass and attempting to narrow down their favorites while he busied himself behind the counter.

"What do you like?" Rami asked Julian.

"Well, I'm not sure," Julian replied.

"Do you like chocolate? Citrus? Powdered sugar?" they questioned. "Little cakes, or donuts or croissants or brownies?"

Julian paused, staring at the selection beneath the glass. Rami startled a moment later when Julian nudged their arm. "I like *every*thing."

Rami's eyes widened under Julian's gaze locked on them, intent and purposeful.

Rami swallowed and flicked his attention to the multiple pastries. "Everything?"

"It's true. No preference. Jelly-filled donuts. Long johns. Bonbons," he tilted his head, eyes twinkling in the bakery lighting.

Was he saying…?

Rami resisted a scoff in front of the waiting clerk. It shouldn't *matter* what Julian thought, or the kind of person he was attracted to, and whether Rami fit into that mold, and yet… it did.

Rami pursed their lips. "And what if—what if I said neither filled donuts nor long johns felt… right? To me."

"Meaning…?" Julian hedged.

Rami stuck their hands in their pockets and rocked back on their heels. "Meaning… the pastry case is just a case."

Julian blinked at them, then cocked his head to the side. "Still?"

Rami nodded. Julian shrugged.

"Well, Feathers, to that I'd say… alright. No big deal. But I do have a lot more questions than I can ask right here," he said. His golden eyes were light, the smile he offered reaching them. Rami stared back, unsure how to answer, and unsure of this light, fizzy feeling in their chest—

"Uh, so, what do you guys want?" the clerk asked.

Rami stiffened, having momentarily forgotten just where they were, what they were doing.

The clerk glanced between the two of them uncertainly, but gathered the pastries as Rami pointed through the glass and called them off.

Once Rami paid with their magic card, Julian led the way out of the bakery and even held the door open for them.

"Thank you," Rami said, white box balanced in their palms.

"So, can we talk about it?" Julian asked.

Rami sighed, warmth threatening to color their cheeks.

"Fine. If you must." The street was mostly empty for a cloudy afternoon, and Rami pulled their cardigan closer, just to have something to do with their hands.

"First: why'd you run off? What did I say?"

Rami frowned, recalling why they'd run out of the sex shop in the first place. "I was just… surprised, I think. You talked as if you assumed that I knew what having a—long john was like," they said, and waved the box at Julian.

His brows furrowed, and Rami watched him run the conversation in his head, at the same time Rami did.

"No, I—okay, wait," Julian said, waving a hand in a sharp angle through the air. "You've been on Earth for *how long* and you don't know the difference between 'y'know,'" he said casually, "and '*you* know?'"

Rami's lips thinned as they replayed the inflection in Julian's voice a bit better. "That might have been my error,"

Rami admitted. "I was flustered. It's something I'm a little... sensitive about."

"Understandably," Julian offered with a contrite twist to his lips. Then he brightened. "And seriously, everyone knows angels don't have *pastries in their cases*," Julian said with a wink. "But I know it doesn't have to be that way. So. Why'd you never choose?"

Rami shrugged. "Nothing felt right. We—" Rami glanced around, then leaned closer and lowered their voice. "Angels were made without a gender. Why should I have to pick just because the humans did?"

"Okay, point. But, like, sex?"

Rami arched a brow—being very brave, they thought, having this conversation—and stood up straight once more. "Yes. What about it?"

"You never got curious?"

Rami's gaze flicked back to him before it skittered away. "Of course I did. I said nothing *felt* right, didn't I?"

Julian *tripped,* and Rami stuttered to a stop as the demon gathered his feet beneath him. "*Oh,*" he choked out.

Amusement curled through Rami. "Yes, *oh.*"

"So you did try them out, take them for a test drive. Did you enjoy it?"

Their cheeks were as red as the stop sign they approached.

"I don't see what business it is of yours."

"It's not. Doesn't mean I'm not curious," he retorted.

"If you must know, I didn't really care for... the solo act, whether I tried out a... a donut or a long john."

Julian snickered, and Rami shot a glare in his direction just as he straightened up, wiping his smile away with a hand across that strong jaw.

"My experiences were... fine. Nothing to write home about."

Julian's lips twitched. "Well, I'd hope not. Heaven probably wouldn't care about your sexcapades," Julian drawled.

Rami sniffed haughtily. "You know that's not what I meant. It's a human expression."

"I know, I know. Don't get your feathers all ruffled. Have you tried it with other people? It's more fun that way."

Julian spoke as if he had experience. Which, of course he had. Naturally.

And Rami felt totally normal about this information.

Rami moved ahead as they rounded the corner to their home so Julian couldn't see their face as they said, "No. There was never anyone who would've been a suitable partner."

Julian paused at that. "Really? So you haven't—with anyone?"

Rami shrugged, fiddling with a flap on the white box. "I try not to get close to humans, what with their fleeting life spans and all. So I've never really had the chance to, I suppose."

"That sounds… lonely," Julian finally settled on, and pushed the gate open for Rami.

He even locked it back.

Rami swallowed as they thought of Julian's statement. "It can be, I suppose," Rami said, and unlocked the front door, letting themself in. Julian followed close behind, and as they shut the door behind them, the walls felt large and oppressive, looming.

Julian was staring at them when they turned to take the box to the kitchen.

"What is it?" Rami asked.

"You've never befriended a human? Ever? In all the years you've been here?"

A pang of hurt lanced through Rami's chest. "I wouldn't say that," they said softly.

Julian's expression cracked, and in those golden eyes Rami found genuine sympathy. "I see."

Rami cleared their throat, and placed the box on the kitchen island silently. They untucked the flaps and the scent of fresh baked goods wafted into the air.

"I can't help myself sometimes," Rami told him. "I find myself drawn to them – humans. The goodness and light they can exude. And sometimes the darkness, too. I just wanted to help," they recalled, frowning down at the pastries. "But time is a mortal's greatest enemy, and unfortunately, they are destined to lose."

"Do you want to tell me about them?" Julian asked. He was closer now, pulling open a cabinet to remove two plates.

Rami tapped their fingers against the countertop. They hadn't talked to anyone about this kind of thing… ever.

Julian was the first to ask.

Rami stared at him, eying the now visible horns. The smooth, short length of the broken horn haunted Rami. It made them want to take care of Julian.

But what reason did Julian have to stick around?

"Why are you still here?" Rami asked suddenly.

Julian sat the plates down gently, tilting his head and gazing at Rami. "What do you mean?"

"You're healed. So why are you still here?" Rami realized he could've left by now, to do whatever it was that demons did.

And yet Julian hadn't left.

And no one had come knocking on Rami's door to look for Julian, either.

"What can I say? Annoying you has been the most fun I've had in a while," he said, and there was a soft note to his voice, a casualness in the way he shrugged.

And. Well, that was alright, wasn't it?

Rami smiled.

17
STRESS RELIEF

Rami hummed as they placed pastries on two different plates.

"It took a while for it to kick in—the realization that they'd die every time," they began. "I don't want to tell you what year it was; that'll give away my age," Rami drawled.

Julian snorted. "Was that a joke, feathers?"

With a shrug, Rami pushed Julian's plate toward him.

"Now, if only we had…"

"Oh, look," Julian said, pulling a hand from behind his back. "Wine to pair."

Rami didn't bother hiding the grin threatening to curl their lips. "How convenient."

After the wine was poured and they migrated to the living room, Rami took a seat on the couch before pausing and turning toward the leather chair they usually sat in for the morning.

"Unless you'd like me to sit in the leather chair," Rami poked.

Julian rolled his eyes and shook his head. "Shut up," he said, and if Rami wasn't mistaken, he even sounded a little… fond.

"We're having wine and pastries for dinner," Julian pointed out.

Rami waved a hand at him. "We're an angel and a demon —I think we'll be alright."

Julian took a sip of his wine before humming and motioning a hand at them. "Okay, so. Story time. Continue."

Rami inhaled deeply before nodding. "Right. So, where to start?"

"The beginning, usually," Julian teased, plucking a half of a cinnamon roll from his plate.

"Yes, thank you, that hadn't occurred to me," Rami responded dryly, then took a deep breath before beginning. "I've always quite enjoyed the sweet things in life. Pastries and breads and the like. So, to no one's surprise, my favorite places to visit were bakeries."

"Of course," Julian mumbled around a sticky bite. Rami pointedly wasn't watching as he collected the extra icing at the corners of his mouth with his tongue.

"One of the shops I frequented had this young man who worked in the kitchen. Atticus. His father ran the front counter."

Julian nodded to show he was paying attention, and Rami sipped their wine before continuing.

"Sometimes, if I was lucky, I'd manage to catch the baker outside, on his break."

Julian arched a brow at that.

"We'd talk," Rami clarified. "He'd vent about his father, and I'd listen. Sometimes he would sneak me an extra pastry even though I promised him it wasn't necessary, risking his father's wrath like that." Rami tried to keep their tone light, breezy. But the story was not a light one, and Julian must have sensed that.

Rami took another sip of their drink. "He worked... a lot.

He was at that bakery more often than he was at home. Part of me thinks that was on purpose."

Rami picked a layer off their chocolate croissant as they considered the best way to dive into the hard part of the story. Their stomach was tight with the memory, the anxiety.

Even after all this time, Rami knew the feel of the cobblestone beneath their feet, the scent of the baked breads in the air. The smell of flour on Atticus's skin.

"He tried to run one night. Showed up on my doorstep, hurt." They chuckled, but it wasn't from humor. No wonder they'd felt compelled to help Julian. It was the past repeating itself. "I bandaged him up, and spent the whole night wondering what kind of person could hurt their own son." Rami had shared their bed with Atticus that night. At that time, Rami hadn't quite got the hang of sleeping yet, but they'd pretended, instead keeping vigil for any sign of Atticus's father.

"Despite my concerns, Atticus returned to the bakery the next morning. I don't know what happened, but after that, Atticus wouldn't talk much to me. I was still… relatively new to being on Earth. So it didn't feel like my place to intervene, even though I knew it was wrong, what was happening." Bitterness leaked into Rami's tone.

"Atticus didn't come outside for his breaks anymore, and his father sneered at me every time I came in, no matter how much coin I spent on their baked goods."

"Ungrateful bastard," Julian muttered, scowling.

"I managed to see Atticus a handful of times after that, on days his father wasn't in the shop. Each time he seemed… darker. His light was dimmed. I don't know what was going on behind those closed doors, but I knew it wasn't good. I knew I was also forbidden from interfering."

"Fuckin' rules," Julian cursed.

Rami drew in a deep breath, fortifying themself for the

next part. "I could have saved him, but I didn't. And then there was the fire," Rami continued.

"Oh no."

Rami's fingers tightened around the stem of the glass, heart heavy and throat stuck. "Yeah. I don't know what happened—only that Atticus was the only casualty. His father wasn't even in the shop that day. So, after a lifetime of fear and abuse, Atticus burned to death. His abuser was left to pick up the pieces, but he was *alive.*"

"Shit, Rami," Julian said, and leaned back into the couch, staring down at his wine.

Rami nodded, remembering the smell of the ash, the soot that fell from the sky. "I didn't learn my lesson that time. As the years went by, I befriended several humans, actually. I never grew as close to them as I had to Atticus, but the result was the same. They all died. That's the only future humans have: death. Eventually, I quit trying to befriend them, and moved around plenty so no one would notice I aged. Too many years passed, and here I am," they said, waving their hand holding the wine glass around slowly, motioning to the bookshelves and television.

"You're still a therapist—you're still listening and connecting with humans, though."

"Yes, I am," Rami agreed. "After Atticus, I told myself that I wouldn't be a bystander again. I still can't interfere, but I can listen, and try to help. Try to empower them however I can. And one day, when they start noticing that I don't age, I'll refer them to another therapist, and move on."

Alone, they added silently.

Julian's lips were pursed, a bit of icing still dotting the corner of one.

Rami smiled and pointed at their own lip to indicate it to Julian, who made a show of licking the icing away to make them laugh.

"So how do you deal with it?" Julian asked.

Rami cocked their head to the side. "What do you mean?"

"How do you get past it? Move on? Deal with the stress?"

"Oh, I just… carry on, I suppose."

Julian arched a brow at that. "So you're repressing it. Doesn't sound very healthy to me."

Rami sputtered, turning toward him on the couch. "I do not repress; I dealt with my sorrows and mourning when the time called for it. Now I just do my best not to think about it."

Julian's expression didn't change and Rami replayed their words in their head. "Okay, I see what you mean."

"It's gotta be stressful, right? Being up here, dealing with all these humans, hiding what you are. What's your coping method?"

"Well. I guess we're doing it right now," Rami said, lifting a pastry. "Sweets, wine, and books. Hot baths." Though it had been a while since they'd indulged in that particular luxury.

Julian stood, clapping his hands together and startling Rami in the process.

"Bring your treats. We're running you one of those fancy baths."

Rami's cheeks flushed.

…From the wine, of course, definitely not the implication Julian was making.

"What?" Rami asked, eloquent as ever.

"Come on, let's go," Julian said, and motioned for Rami to follow him.

Julian made it all the way to the kitchen to grab the bottle of wine and the box of remaining pastries before he stood by the stairs.

"Well? What are you just sitting there for?"

"I—you." Rami paused, blinked. They met Julian's gaze and held it for a moment as their thoughts raced. They were curious enough to see where this would go. "Okay, then," they finally said.

Rami stood and followed Julian, abandoning their empty plate to the table and making a note to take care of it later.

They were only a little wary as they followed Julian up the stairs.

He headed straight for the bathroom, and sat the box and wine on the counter.

Rami leaned against the doorjamb of the bathroom, watching as he stoppered the tub and turned on the water.

Then he spun toward the cabinets and pulled a door open, only to find extra towels and toilet paper and cleaning supplies.

"It's the—" Rami began, but Julian interrupted them.

"No, no, Feathers, I've got this," he said, holding a hand out. The next cabinet revealed the bath items he was clearly in search of, judging by the little triumphant noise he let out.

Rami's lips twitched, and a swell of something like affection bloomed in their chest.

The bottles of bubble bath soap clinked together as Julian pulled one out, opening it and sniffing.

He wrinkled his nose, which Rami found hopelessly adorable, and placed the bottle back on the shelf before trying the next one.

"You have a lot of choices here," Julian mused aloud, as he sniffed the third bottle.

"Well, I enjoy them all. A little variety is nice."

Julian hummed at the scent of the fourth and—

It occurred to Rami suddenly that Julian was picking a scent *he* liked, only for Rami to be the one to bathe in it.

Their cheeks flushed, and they averted their gaze as Julian leaned over the tub to pour some of the bubble bath in.

"Don't use so much," Rami whined, and stepped away from the doorframe to peer over Julian's shoulder.

"Well, I assume you want enough in there to cover your delicate bits," Julian retorted. "Or where your delicate bits *would* be," he added, tipping the bottle for one last drizzle into the water before closing it and moving around Rami to place it back in the cabinet.

The only reason Rami would need to cover their *delicate bits* would be if Julian planned to stay—

"Venting is a proper step in the relaxation process, didn't you know? It requires two people."

Rami didn't quite know what to say.

"Don't worry," continued Julian, who clearly wasn't having the same problem. "I'll step out and then you can just call me in when you get settled. Sound good?"

"But I'll be *naked*," Rami finally managed to hiss.

Julian paused halfway through the door, one hand on the frame and the other on the knob, ready to pull it closed.

"I won't peek, promise. I'll even sit with my back to the tub. Shout when you're ready!" he said with a smile, and then the door was shut and Rami was alone.

The bathroom was already warm from the steam of the hot water, and the mountain of bubbles was slowly growing.

Rami pursed their lips, gaze bouncing between the door and the bath.

Julian was right. The bubbles *would* cover Rami's body. And if he did sit with his back against the side of the tub, there's no chance that he'd be able to see through the water.

And if they just ate pastries and drank wine and vented about their lives, what harm could it do?

Rami cocked their head to the side. Maybe they could finally learn a bit more about Julian.

This was their chance.

With a sigh, Rami gave in, and grabbed the hem of their sweater before pulling it off. Their collared shirt followed and chills erupted across their skin in the air of the bathroom.

They shivered, and hurried to push their pants and boxers off their hips. With deft movements they opened the closet and tossed their clothes in the hamper before shutting it quietly and turning toward the bath.

They knew Julian would wait for their signal, but they still moved quickly to slide into the hot water and hide beneath the bubbles.

The heap of bubbles was up to their flat chest, and they chuckled softly before shutting the water off. With such a thick layer, they felt completely protected from the wandering gaze of any demon. So with a confidence they were hesitant to feel, they called out.

"I'm settled!"

There was a thump against the door before they heard Julian's throat clear. "Awesome. Coming in," he said.

The door pushed inward and Rami glanced over, met with… Julian's back.

"Told you, I won't peek. Let me just grab— you left your wine! Can't have that," he rambled, and gathered the pastry box and both their wine glasses before he attempted to walk backwards again.

Rami covered their mouth with a hand, stifling more laughter at Julian's stiff movements.

"Please don't fall," Rami asked.

"I won't, I won't," Julian muttered, and stopped about two feet away from the tub. He held a hand out behind him, Rami's wine glass lopsided in his grip.

With an exasperated sigh, Rami took the glass.

"Hurry up and sit down," Rami told him, smothering a laugh.

"I'm going, I'm going, jeez," Julian retorted.

With a single deft move, he bent his knees and lowered himself to the floor as he crossed his legs.

Rami was staring right at the back of his head, horns—well, one of them—tall and proud, and unless Julian *really* cranked his neck around, he wouldn't be able to see Rami very well at all.

They relaxed a bit more and sipped their wine, feeling the warmth of the glass and a half they'd already had working through them.

Their face was flushed from the steam and they leaned their head back against the lip of the tub.

"How is it?" Julian asked.

Rami gazed down at the tub full of bubbles and back to the demon on their right.

"It's lovely, actually," Rami murmured.

"See? I have good ideas."

"You had *one* good idea," Rami pointed out.

"The wine and pastries was part of that, too."

Their lips curled around the edge of their wine glass. "Okay, so three good ideas."

"That's basically a pattern," Julian argued.

Rami rolled their eyes, amusement curling through them more than any kind of annoyance.

"So, now what?" Rami asked.

"Are you feeling relaxed?" Julian asked. The cardboard of the pastry box scraped as he opened it once more. "Which one do you want?"

"Pick for me," Rami said, and wiped their hand on the towel Julian offered before he lifted a danish out. "Will you tear it in half?" Rami asked, and bit down on their lower lip as Julian sighed like it was such a chore.

"At least if I drop it you'll still have the other half to try," Rami explained.

They accepted the pastry from Julian when he handed it over blindly, and…

It felt really rather divine to eat a pastry from one hand and sip wine from another all while they soaked in the hot water, bubbles popping and whispering around them. Very indulgent.

Meanwhile, Julian wiggled his fingers over the box before plucking free an eclair.

"Be careful with that," Rami warned. "You'll need a bath after me."

"Maybe I like things a little messy," Julian said, and just barely turned his head to the right and winked.

Their cheeks flushed even more, and they considered the fact that it might not be the heat of the water after all.

But instead of facing the facts like a reasonable being, Rami took a bite of the danish.

A loud moan cut through the room, and Rami startled, wine sloshing within its glass, water lapping at the edge of the tub.

"What in the—" Rami began.

"This is so good," Julian groaned. "I'm a genius." He spoke around his mouthful, and Rami wrinkled their nose before they bit into their own danish again.

The blueberry was tart on their tongue and the glaze of the danish was sweet. A perfect balance.

And surprisingly, the wine Julian had magicked paired well with the sweets, too.

They finished their tarts and chatted about nothing of importance, certainly nothing so heavy as Rami's lonely existence.

"Tell me about your house in Hell," Rami said. "What's it look like?"

Julian hummed, and Rami watched his side profile as he

sipped wine, lips curling over the edge of the glass, horns glinting in the low light.

"It's not very big. A bit smaller than your place. Hell is a corporation, an office. And the living areas are much the same. All sleek, sharp lines and cold steel. Surprisingly modern and minimalistic." He glanced around the bathroom. "It's nothing like your place."

"You must miss it, then," Rami said.

"Not as much as you might think," Julian admitted. He swirled the wine in his glass and Rami sipped their own, waiting for an explanation. "It gets lonely, too."

"No demon… fraternities to hang out with?"

Julian's nose wrinkled, and Rami felt it like a shot through the heart. "Not so much. I mean, sure, I have acquaintances, but Hell is all about looking out for yourself. Trying to get up the ladder to have more freedom. Not too much time for palling around."

"But then how—" Rami snapped their mouth closed, realizing their question was severely nosey and a little too casual.

"What?"

"No, no. Nevermind. It's none of my business."

"Oh, come on. I'm far too curious now. Ask me."

Rami gulped, cheeks already heating. "Well, if it's too personal, you don't have to answer—keep that in mind."

"Yes, yes, go on."

"I was just wondering, if demons aren't very… friendly with one another, how did you become so versed in things of the, ahem, sexual nature?" Rami winced through the whole question, and finished off their glass of wine to wash down the taste of the awkwardness.

"I'll put it like this: you take your fancy bubble baths and eat yummy pastries to de-stress, and I look for more… physical relief," he said. "And Hell is *very* stressful, so I'm not the only one."

"Ah, so you… with other demons?"

"Yeah. I didn't exactly have the time while delivering messages to try and seduce a human."

"And does it… work?" Rami asked, while they held out their glass, arm balanced on the side of the tub.

Julian picked up the bottle and refilled without even being asked.

"De-stressing with sex? Yeah, I'd say it works," he said, voice softening. There wasn't a hint of a tease in his tone.

Rami swallowed, trying to imagine Julian with someone else. Anyone else.

They found they didn't want to.

"You interested, Feathers?" Julian asked, and there was that light note in his voice, an out, room for Rami to get flustered and deny and scold.

Instead they… considered.

Julian was experienced. Rami was more than a little curious. And it wasn't like, as an angel, Rami would ever find someone more understanding of their situation than a demon.

"And what if I was?" Rami asked softly.

Julian stilled, glass lifted to his lips, mid-sip.

His throat clicked with the action, and leaned away from the tub, half turning to see Rami's expression.

"I'd want to know exactly what it was you were interested in, so I'm not misunderstanding."

Rami took a fortifying breath, ignoring the warmth rushing to their cheeks under Julian's stare. "You said it was *better* with another person. What if I wanted… what if I wanted you to tell me what to do?"

"You mean, how to touch yourself?"

"Yes," Rami answered.

"I thought you were a pastry case," Julian said, brow

furrowing but head cocked in a way that made sure Rami knew Julian didn't mean anything about pastries.

"I can still try out a long john, if I wanted. Or a jelly donut. Whatever feels right in the moment, I suppose."

"And what feels right in this moment?" Julian asked.

Rami considered.

They didn't think they were ready to have anything inside them yet. And if Julian was going to… guide them through this expedition, then it made sense if Rami tried out the one Julian would be most familiar with.

"A long john," Rami answered, lifting their gaze to Julian.

His cheeks were flushed for once, and Rami hoped it wasn't from the steam. "I could help with that. If you really wanted."

Rami lifted their gaze when they said, "I think I do want."

Julian's nostrils flared as he sucked in a silent breath and turned his head back around, pressing his mid-back into the tub.

"Okay. Let me know when you're ready to begin."

This was happening.

Rami could always put a stop to this. They could tell Julian to get out, and never broach this subject with him again.

But Rami… was more than a little curious. More than a little seduced by Julian's company. They'd been alone for so long—what *would* it be like to try such a thing with another person? Even if they never touched, only talked.

With a hint of magic, not even enough to ruffle the air, Rami changed their body to match that of which they were curious.

A bit of a tingle below their waist and at their chest—they wanted the full experience, nipples included—accompanied the shift, and Rami shivered before settling back against the porcelain wall of the tub.

"Okay, I'm ready," they said.

Julian's head tilted to the side. "Really? It was that easy?"

Rami's cheeks flamed. Were they too eager?

"It's as easy as any magic."

"Huh. I guess that makes sense," Julian mused. "How do you feel?"

The hot water was still surrounding them, lapping at their skin. "Warm."

Julian's swallow was audible in the quiet bathroom. "Give me your glass," Julian said, and Rami didn't even question it, just laid their forearm over the edge of the tub, empty glass balanced in their fingers.

Their hands brushed as Julian took the glass and Rami wondered if they'd imagined the spark. Maybe that happened normally?

Rami considered. It certainly hadn't happened when Melissa had hugged them just a few days ago.

Maybe it was a Julian thing?

Or maybe it's a You And Julian *thing.*

Rami would have scoffed if they hadn't had a modicum of self-control. This was simple curiosity. Student and teacher, if anything.

A bit more warmth stirred in them at the suggestion.

"Close your eyes and lay your head back."

Rami laid their head back, and flattened their lips, giving Julian a droll stare that he probably wouldn't even—

He turned his head and caught Rami's glare. "How did I know you'd be making that face?" Julian asked, chuckling, the sound deep and lovely. "I'm not going to peek, just—do it. I'll do it, too."

Rami glanced down at the bubbles, which were still piled high. Impossibly high.

Was Julian magicking the bubbles to stay in place?

Rami softened even more as their gaze flitted back to the

demon, whose eyes were closed, head resting against the lip of the tub, mismatched horns seeming to glimmer in the low lighting.

Rami finally let their eyes drift shut. "Fine."

"Alright. So. You're warm. What else?"

They felt as if this was a test.

"There's no wrong answer," Julian said, voice gentler. "Where are your feet?"

Rami's brow furrowed. "Pressing against the foot of the tub."

"Hands?"

Oh. "Beneath the water," Rami answered. "On my thighs." Their fingers flexed against their own skin in response.

"Okay," Julian murmured. "Where's the water touching you at?"

Rami was so close to opening their eyes, but they didn't. "It's up to my sternum. The bubbles are higher."

Now that they thought about it, the bubbles kind of tickled where they popped against Rami's skin, against their nipples.

"They… tickle," Rami said bravely, like they might earn a gold star if they gave Julian the right information.

"Good," Julian murmured so gently. "You're on the right track. Keep going."

What do I feel?

"The air is cool against my skin, when the water isn't touching it. I can feel the hair on my thighs, against my palms," they admitted.

"And what's it like saying it out loud?" Julian asked.

"Embarrassing," Rami confessed. "I can tell my face is probably red."

Rami heard Julian shift, and blinked their eyes open to catch him looking at them.

His lips were curled. "It's red, alright."

"You said you wouldn't look."

"Not at anything scandalous," Julian added.

Rami rolled their eyes.

It was so… intimate, sharing these things with Julian, in the same room, only inches away.

The warmth in their cheeks was stirring lower as they met Julian's gaze.

After a long moment filled with a tension Rami was too hesitant to name, Julian turned back around and closed his eyes. Rami mirrored him.

"How do all those books you read describe arousal?" Julian asked.

Rami exhaled sharply. Even though they knew the conversation would eventually lead to such topics, they floundered.

"They used words like, uhm—warmth," Rami admitted. "Lots of… tension, and building waves. Sparks."

Their voice cracked on the last word, and they realized they'd already felt that spark, and the tension and warmth.

"Does any of that sound familiar?" Julian asked, something *knowing* in his voice.

The idea that Julian knew, was going to be here, would likely be talking to them while they touched themself was…

Rami swallowed loudly, feeling a pinch in their gut, an echoing heat in their groin. "Maybe," they whispered.

Rami heard him shuffle again, and peeked one eye open only to find him settling back down, eyes still closed, full lips parted, the longest strands of his wild hair brushing his cheeks and that sharp jaw.

Rami drew in a breath, fingers digging into their thighs before they averted their gaze. The bubbles were still chest-high, popping against their skin and yet going nowhere.

With a silent start, Rami realized the slowly growing warmth within them had settled between their legs.

Feeling *very* brave, and eager to chase this delicate moment, Rami slid their hand up their thigh, closer to the thickening—

"Focus on it, that feeling," Julian murmured.

Rami flinched, water splashing as they jerked their hand away.

"Sorry, didn't mean to startle you," Julian said.

Rami glanced at him and found his lips curling.

"Don't laugh at me," Rami warned, stomach flipping at the thought.

Julian's lips turned down at that, and then he was looking at Rami. "I would never laugh at you. Not like this, at least."

His tone, his words, and the heavy stare they were delivered under were so serious. Rami knew he meant it.

"Do you wanna stop?" Julian asked.

Rami considered it. Imagined Julian nodding and getting up and leaving without a backwards glance, protecting Rami's sensibilities or something.

But this… heat beneath their skin was new and exciting, and it had been so very long since anything exciting had happened to Rami.

"No," they finally said.

Julian's gaze darkened at that, and Rami swallowed. They couldn't look away, caught in his sticky honey depths.

"Good," Julian said, soft and low.

Then he closed his eyes again and leaned his head back on the tub.

"Where were we?" Julian asked.

Rami suspected he already knew the answer to that question.

18
UNDER INSTRUCTION

Julian's eyes may have been closed, but Rami was under no such obligation.

So they stared.

Watched Julian's lips move as he spoke, watched as he swallowed.

Let the sight of this demon alone build the warmth inside them until…

Until Rami skated their hand beneath the water again, knuckles bushing against the hard length between their legs.

They sucked in a breath, and it was audible. Julian stopped mid-sentence.

He shuffled, rocking from side to side as he tugged at the fabric of his pants stretched across his thighs.

A lightbulb went off in Rami's head.

"Are you aroused?" Rami asked suddenly.

Julian paused, then settled down. He cleared his throat before saying, "Well, yeah. You're inches away from me, touching yourself while I talk, so. I'm not unaffected."

Another bolt of heat struck through them. "Oh," Rami said eloquently.

"Does that make you uncomfortable?"

"No," Rami breathed, surprised with just *how* comfortable

they were, not alone in their feelings. "Quite the opposite, I think."

Julian tilted his head back, and if his eyes were open Rami suspected they would've been pointing up, pleading for patience.

The irony was not lost on them. And maybe in that moment, the reminder of who Julian was—a demon—should've provided clarity, snapping Rami out of their aroused trance, but it didn't.

"That's... good," Julian choked out, and leveled his head again. He rubbed his palms across his thighs, and Rami's lips twitched.

They liked the idea of Julian being aroused by *them*.

What was the saying? "All hot and bothered?"

Julian said this... *act* could be *fun*.

Rami was having fun flustering Julian—did that count?

It lit something within them, the idea that Julian wouldn't touch himself, all while Rami got to—

Their hand brushed against their hard length and they sucked in a tight breath.

"Tell me what you're doing, Feathers. You're killing me here," Julian said, his voice a rumble.

They weren't sure how having to say it all out loud was better than Julian just turning around to look, but Rami found it... titillating.

Rami swallowed, wetting their suddenly dry throat and staring at Julian's side profile as they said, "I'm... touching myself."

Their cheeks were warm to the touch. This was so embarrassing, and somehow that made it all the better, building the heat in them.

"Do you want me to—I can tell you what to do now, if you'd like," Julian murmured.

Rami nodded before they realized Julian wouldn't see it,

and had to find their voice enough to say, "Yes, I think I'd like that."

"Okay," Julian breathed, and then gulped.

It was audible in the room, and Rami watched his throat work through the action.

"Wrap your fingers around yourself, not too tight," Julian directed, and Rami obliged.

At the full contact of their hand, Rami shivered, the water sloshing with their movements, their skin pebbling with gooseflesh and nipples beading.

Well, that's new, they thought.

They *had* done this before, but at the time, it hadn't felt anything like this. *This* was sending sparks barreling through them, making their stomach clench and the length in their hand pulse.

"Slide your hand up," Julian choked out, voice softer.

Rami did, and they bit their lip against the small noise that wanted to escape.

"And down," Julian practically whispered.

Rami could see his hands gripping his thighs tightly, and wondered if he was hard beneath his jeans just like Rami was beneath the water.

"Tighten your grip on the upstroke this time," Julian told them.

Rami swallowed down a moan as they did so, and Julian's head whipped toward them.

Rami paused, caught. "You said you wouldn't look."

His eyes were dark and wide and Rami wanted to melt into them. But then Julian snapped his eyes closed and swallowed again.

"Sorry. You sound—"

"What?" Rami asked, fist tightening around their length. "What do I sound like?"

"Like you're enjoying it. Is it… different? From when you did it by yourself?"

Rami tilted their head back, collecting their thoughts. "Yes. It's—I know the mechanics. It just never—I never was able to… come," Rami admitted. They'd never been quite this turned on when they were doing it alone, either.

"Oh," Julian breathed, cocking his head to the side. "Do you want to try?"

"What if I can't? Isn't that—people on Earth are rather sensitive about such things."

"You don't have to be embarrassed," Julian said, and then threw his head back with a groan. "I want to show you."

"Do you want to touch yourself?" Rami asked, surprised the words slipped out so easily.

In the shocked silence that followed, they realized they wanted exactly that—they wanted Julian to touch himself. To find pleasure at his own touch while thinking of Rami.

"Can I?" Julian asked, breath tight in what Rami hoped was anticipation.

Another shiver went through them as Julian asked for *permission.*

It was heady.

"Yes," Rami answered. "You can touch yourself." *Because I said so.*

A noise slipped out of Julian, and the sound rocked through Rami.

Rami stared, watching Julian's hands slide up his thighs and work at the button. The hiss of the zipper seemed loud in the silence, and then Julian was pulling himself out, hand wrapping around his length with no shame whatsoever.

"Just—just do what I do," Julian told them.

Rami nodded, eyes wide, mouth dry, and watched as Julian slid his hand up and down. The head of his cock was flushed and peeked out from his grip on every stroke.

Rami mimicked him, the water sloshing with each move of their hand.

They squeezed their fist just like Julian did as they dragged their hand up, and a shaky breath slid out.

His rhythm was slow, and Rami kept pace easily.

Something swelled in them, making their lower back tight and their stomach clench. This felt more similar to what they'd read in books, and they chased that feeling, eyes locked on Julian's every movement.

But as the moments passed and Julian's muttered directions grew high and tight, Rami wanted… more.

They cleared their throat. "You did say it was better… *with* someone," Rami said carefully. "Is that still the case?"

"*Yes,*" Julian blurted, head tilting back. His eyes slid open before he slowly turned to face Rami. His cheeks were flushed, horns glinting in the light, and Rami decided they enjoyed the sight quite a lot. "I would love that. Please let me touch you."

Please.

The request cut through Rami's sensibilities like a knife.

"Since you asked so nicely," Rami breathed, legs shifting beneath the hot water.

Julian sat up on his knees, turning toward the bath, and Rami's breath caught, watching his slim fingers curve over the tub's edge.

"I'll go slow," Julian promised.

And then he was pushing up his sleeves and slipping his hand into the water.

Rami startled at the first brush of his hand against their skin, his palm flattening against their thigh. He squeezed, just lightly, and it made Rami's stomach tighten.

"Okay?" Julian asked, his eyes locked on Rami's face.

They couldn't hide like this. They were completely exposed, no matter how much the bubbles tried to cover.

"Yes," Rami said, their voice no stronger than a whisper.

They met Julian's gaze, watched him watch them as his hand moved, sliding up their thigh, grasping once before—

A sound slipped out, their breath escaping as Julian's deft fingers curled around their length.

"How's that?" Julian asked, voice deeper now.

"That's—certainly different," they managed to say, attention sliding to the slowly popping bubbles, revealing more of Julian's wrist and knuckles as he worked.

Julian kept his word, hand moving slowly up their cock and back down. On the next upstroke, he tightened his fist and Rami's hips shifted instinctively.

Heat coiled in their belly, corkscrewing tighter with each stroke.

"That's right," Julian murmured, head tilted to the side as he watched Rami. "It feels good—let it."

Rami huffed an annoyed breath and lifted their gaze. "I'm trying."

"There's your problem. Don't try. Just let it happen," he said.

Rami groaned, more out of frustration, but when Julian's thumb brushed over the tip of their cock, they gasped.

Julian studied them like they'd give him a pop quiz at the end of the class. He watched them pant and moan and tsked when they bit their lip to stifle any noise at all.

"How is your partner supposed to know they're doing a good job if they can't hear you?"

And, well, Julian did have a point there.

So Rami was a little freer with their noises, especially as Julian slid his hand lower, cupping their balls, brushing the pad of his finger just behind them.

Their hips jerked again, sloshing water up and wetting the edge of Julian's sleeve.

"You look… very good like this," Julian whispered. "Flushed and panting and *wanting.*"

Yes, Rami did *want.* They wanted the swirling pleasure in their gut to strike. They wanted to come, but there was just something missing.

Their arms were laying along either side of the tub, gripping the porcelain edges tightly. Julian's sternum pressed into their forearm with each stroke and it took them only a moment to realize he was practically rutting against the side of the tub.

His cheeks were also flushed, and his lips were red from where he kept biting them, which Rami found rather hypocritical, but now wasn't the time for that.

Their attention was caught on the shine of his mouth, his full bottom lip just—

Let it happen, he'd said.

"Is kissing out of the question?" Rami heard themself ask, blood rushing in their ears as bliss pierced through them.

Julian groaned and shook his head. Then Rami was lifting their right hand and sliding it into Julian's hair as he leaned up to Rami.

Their lips pressed together hesitantly. Rami still wasn't completely sure what they were doing, but they'd seen enough movies, read enough books.

They knew this was different.

This wasn't the chaste brush of lips they'd exchanged the day before.

Rami tilted their head, slotting their lips against Julian's, and, well.

Julian moved his lips first, and Rami followed. The soft glide was like a spark, fine and hot, and as Julian's rhythm sped up, they gasped.

Oh, Rami thought as Julian's tongue dipped out to slide along Rami's lower lip.

They tightened their grip in Julian's hair and felt him smile at their eagerness, and even *that* was something that added another bolt of heat to the spiral inside them.

He stroked them and kissed them and their tongues twined.

It was a *real* kiss, like something torn right from the pages of their books.

Elation filled them alongside the pleasure, slowly cresting, growing sharper and scarier as they gasped into the kiss.

He cursed, and Rami tasted it from his lips.

Rami's other hand lifted to fist in Julian's shirt instead of over the edge of the tub.

"It's—" they began, cut off with another shiver of electric delight.

"I know, I know," Julian said, kissing them again and again. "It's okay. Come on. Just let go," Julian said, so softly it made Rami's heart pound.

They moaned into Julian's mouth, felt their cock pulse in Julian's fist. Their lower back tightened, stomach tensing, and—

Release. A wave crashing. Fireworks exploding. White light.

None of the ways their books had described orgasms came even close to what Rami felt, burying their head into Julian's shoulder, gripping him tight.

His strokes slowed as Rami spilled over his fist, and they wanted to look but couldn't quite work up the courage, letting the waves of pleasure wash over them.

Rami went limp, not realizing how tense they'd been until they relaxed, their fist easing its grip on Julian's clothes, untangling from the dark strands of his hair.

"Sor—"

They didn't even get a chance to finish their apology before Julian was kissing them again.

The sound they let out was muffled, and their tongues twined again as Julian's hand finally released their cock. He laid his palm on Rami's thigh once more before squeezing.

When he pulled back, his gaze was dark and half-lidded, eyes dancing over Rami's expression.

"How was that?"

Rami swallowed. "I can safely say I never experienced *that* by myself," they said.

Julian grinned, and it was positively calamitous.

He's so handsome.

Their lips curled at the thought, the ease with which it came, the way it settled, and they… let it.

"Glad I could help," Julian said, eyes twinkling.

Rami really did release him this time, clearing their throat, their blush making a return.

"Don't get shy on me now," Julian teased.

Rami rolled their eyes, and suddenly, viscerally, remembered Julian's own orgasm.

"Oh!" they said, and sat up a bit, uncaring where the bubbles ended up. "Did you—"

"Don't worry about it—I, ah, managed."

Awe filled them, pulling their lips into a slow smile. "Without even touching yourself?"

"Don't sound so surprised," Julian said. "You were quite the spectacle."

"Oh," Rami breathed. "Well, thank you, I think."

Julian snorted a little laugh, and brushed his dry hand through Rami's hair. "It was definitely a compliment. Now," he said, and leaned back. "Why don't I leave you to get actually cleaned up, and I'll be waiting."

"Okay," Rami agreed.

They tried not to stare, but Julian was just so *smooth* with the way he stood, shifting so Rami couldn't quite see him tuck himself away.

And then he gathered the box and the wine glasses and slipped out the door with a wink.

Rami collapsed against the back of the tub with a sigh, unstopping the tub with their toes.

Without Julian's interference, the bubbles disappeared almost completely, and Rami stood before switching the shower on.

Once they were *actually clean,* they shut off the water and stepped out, toweling off and—oh. They didn't have any clothes—

A knock on the door, followed by Julian's voice. "I've got one of your little plaid numbers here," Julian said. "I'll set them outside the door."

Rami smiled, chest expanding with something as easy as a breath but much heavier. They retrieved their sleep clothes and tugged them on before finally opening the door and escaping the warmth of the bathroom.

Julian was already seated on the bed, the television turned on and the pastry box placed in the center on a pillow.

"You're not freaking out, are you?" Julian asked, sipping his wine with a pointed glance.

Rami chuckled. "No, for once," they said. Their mind was blissfully free of their general anxiety.

"Well, what a surprise," Julian murmured, and patted the bed. "Come sit. Fancy a cuddle?"

Rami arched a brow at that, cheeks flushing. A cuddle?

"Oh, come on," Julian urged.

Rami sat, pulled the covers over their lap, and scooted closer to Julian, who was practically sitting in the middle of the bed.

Their shoulders brushed before they leaned close together, the press of Julian against them warm and lovely. Not quite a cuddle in the way Rami had envisioned it, but a safer option.

It struck them that they might have enjoyed the not-so-safe option, too.

The two of them ate their pastries and drank their wine that Julian re-chilled, and each time a modicum of space dared to separate them, Julian was quick to eliminate it.

Rami began to wonder if this whole cuddle business was for their own sake, or Julian's.

They found they didn't mind even if it was.

As the night wound down and they shut the lights off, Rami couldn't help but wonder, in the safety of the darkness, if Julian wouldn't be interested in showing them a few other things.

19

THE EXCHANGE

Julian slept soundly. His favorite part of Rami's entire home was this bed.

It was soft, pulling him in deep and refusing to release him until the early morning sun threatened to blind him.

Distantly, he noticed the ache in his broken horn was finally, blissfully gone. It might not grow back, but at least it didn't hurt anymore.

He floated in half-sleep, more positive thoughts washing over him.

Like the events of the night before.

Julian found his lips curling. He couldn't believe it had happened. Not now, or after the fact, and hardly during the act, too. Julian hadn't expected Rami to take him up on the offer, but he'd apparently underestimated the curiosity of a virgin angel.

He could still feel them in his hand, feel their lips against his. It was better than he could remember his past hookups ever being, and Rami hadn't even touched him back.

When he blinked his eyes open, he frowned at the absence of Rami's weight atop his chest.

Instead, he found the angel inches away, watching him sleep.

He stretched beneath that gaze and groaned just for show. "Like what you see?" he teased.

Rami pursed their lips as if they were considering agreeing and, well. Julian felt a little warm at that.

"I've been thinking," Rami said.

Unease slithered through him, and for a moment he imagined this was it. Last night had gone too far, and Rami was kicking Julian out for crossing a line.

"Oh? That can't be good," Julian mused, and pushed himself to sit up a bit.

He rubbed sleep from his eye to stall, and Rami blinked at him before seeming to shake themself.

"You're well versed in the nature of... sexual matters," Rami began.

Julian just about choked on his next breath. "Okay," he said slowly. Where was this going?

"And I'm... well, I know in theory, but not in practice."

"Sure..." Julian hedged, daring to hope.

"And I've been thinking about what you said. About how I've shown you the simple pleasures of humanity, and how you could possibly show me the *other* pleasures."

Julian blinked. "Okay."

"And, well, after last night..." Rami cleared their throat. "Would you maybe be interested in showing me a few... other things?"

Julian resisted the urge to smile, biting the inside of his cheek as he tried to stay cool.

"I think I'd be amenable to that."

Rami's eyes widened. "Really?"

Julian shrugged. "Yes. Why are you so surprised?"

"I don't know," they answered.

Julian grinned, unable to curb the desire to tease the angel just a little. "Was it that good, then?" he purred.

Rami rolled their eyes and climbed from the bed. "You're insufferable."

"It's only because you're paying me such a huge compliment," Julian retorted. "I mean, one little handy and you're ready to learn—"

"If you're going to be crass, I'll rescind my offer," they said, crossing their arms and staring at him from the edge of the bed.

Julian snapped his mouth shut, lifting his hands in a show of innocence. "I'll be good."

Rami narrowed their eyes and stepped away. "That's what I thought."

Julian rolled over onto his stomach and leaned toward Rami, a hand outstretched. "You mean you didn't want to start now?"

"It's so early!" Rami cried, spinning around.

Pausing.

"It is called 'morning sex'." Julian teased.

"So. That is a… *done* thing, then? Morning sex?"

"Of course, Feathers. It has a name for a reason."

Rami pursed their lips, and Julian wanted to cheer, knowing he'd already convinced the angel.

He *itched* to feel Rami's skin against his. To teach them more about… anything. Everything.

Julian sat up, pushed the covers aside, and scooted to the edge of the bed. He spread his legs, an invitation in nothing but boxer shorts, and Rami's gaze slid lower to take in all Julian's bare skin.

"What do you wanna learn?" Julian asked.

Rami's cheeks were glowing, the color deepening the longer they stared. They shuffled, turning toward Julian directly.

"I've read—" They stopped themself, glancing away, clearing their throat.

Julian didn't want them to be embarrassed, and he held out a hand. "Come here," he said softly.

Rami hesitated for only a split second before closing the distance between them. They stood a few inches away, plaid pants swaying to brush Julian's knee.

"You're not uncomfortable, right?" Julian asked.

"Not in the way you're thinking. I'm just… uncertain."

"That's okay," he promised. Even his cheeks were heating as he said, "Wanna come back to bed and kiss some more?"

Rami's lips twitched, a small smile making itself known as they nodded. "I think I'd like that."

"Good," Julian purred before taking their hand and pulling them down.

With an "oof," they fell into him, and naturally straddled his lap. Their hands pressed into his chest, pushing away. "What are you—"

"Comfy?" Julian asked, holding their hips to steady them.

"Yeah, yes, sure," Rami rambled, hands sliding up to grasp Julian's shoulders.

He scooted back on the bed a bit to give them more room and tilted his head up to Rami, who now sat a few inches higher.

They stared down at him, and behind the wall of uncertainty Julian could feel in the grip of their hands and see in the pinch of their lips, he recognized that they wanted this, or else they'd be pushing him away.

"Okay?" he asked anyway.

"Okay," Rami said.

Julian slid a hand up to cup the back of their neck and gently tugged them down.

Their eyes slid closed by the time they would've crossed to meet Julian's gaze, and then their lips were meeting.

It was *tender* and pleasant and the angel knew enough to magic away their morning breath, just like Julian did. So they tasted of nothing but the sweetness Julian had come to associate the angel with.

The coffee and the pastries and the wine, and now the gentle hand in Julian's dark hair that he could only describe as sweet, too.

Their mouths moved against each other, meeting again and again in the softest of motions.

Julian parted his lips a bit, and Rami followed his lead. But then they surprised him by being the first to drag their tongue along his lower lip. His breath caught and he opened for them, letting them lead so long as they wanted to.

They wanted to, that much was clear, as they smoothly slid their tongue into Julian's mouth, replicating the movements Julian had shown them the night before.

They were eager, and knowing they were eager for *him* was doing something to Julian's head. His cock was taking interest in the proceedings, thickening beneath the press of Rami in his lap.

They were learning.

I'm teaching them.

I'm their… first.

A shiver went through him with the realization, and Rami leaned away to meet his gaze.

Their lips were red and full from the kisses, eyes half-lidded. "Okay?" they echoed.

"Okay," he croaked.

They leaned back down without hesitation, crushing their lips to Julian's, sinking deeper into his lap.

His breath caught as Rami shifted against him, Julian's hard length pressing against them through his boxers.

Then they deepened the kiss, pulling Julian even closer.

He swayed into them, arms wrapping around them until they were chest to chest, melting into one.

Heat surged through Julian at the way Rami led the kiss, their hands framing Julian's face, tangling in his hair, cupping the back of his neck. They even tilted his head, and Julian moaned in the back of his throat.

They paused, pulling back to stare at Julian, and both of their chests were rising and falling with hurried breaths.

"What do you want?" Julian asked.

Rami's pupils were blown wide, their silvery iris only a thin circle.

"I want..." They swallowed. "I want to feel good like I did last night."

Julian's chest swelled to bursting, and he nodded. "I can make you feel good again."

"But I want, with the—" They shut their eyes and sighed, and Julian squeezed his hands around their hips, supportive.

Julian thought he knew what they were asking, but he wanted them to say it, even if their cheeks were bright red.

"I want you to show me how it feels with—when I have a..."

"Cunt?" Julian suggested.

Their nose scrunched up in prim disapproval before they smoothed their expression and nodded. "Yes, that," they finally said.

The way Julian's blood pressure skyrocketed at just the thought, he felt a tad faint.

This angel was so... endearing. *Fuck.* Julian couldn't wait to show Rami everything he knew, to make them so comfortable they wouldn't care about the verbiage.

He groaned and leaned forward, knocking their lips into another kiss. "Fuck yes. I'd love to." There would be time for easing Rami into the dirtier words later.

Rami relaxed at his words, sinking into him even more,

their knees taking less and less of their weight in favor of sitting on Julian. He loved the feel of them across his thighs, pressing into him.

Julian let himself lean back, pulling Rami with him. Their hands planted on either side of Julian's head, and they inhaled a small breath.

"I've been wanting to feel you like this," Julian said, hands sliding up the outside of their thighs, squeezing them.

"W-why's that?" they asked.

"Just—feeling you against me. Knowing you're there." Julian attempted to shrug. "It's nice."

"Nice," they echoed.

Julian continued their touches over Rami's clothes, up their hips and sides and over their shoulders before cupping the back of their neck and angling their mouths together.

Rami softened against him, into him, until Julian was pressed flat to the mattress, the weight of Rami solid and perfect.

Their thighs were spread over Julian's lap, and his bulge was between their legs, hardly hiding beneath the thin fabric of his boxers.

"We have options," Julian said into the kiss. "I can use my hands on you. My mouth."

Rami's nostrils flared at that, and their lips parted, brushing against Julian's.

"Do I have to choose?"

Julian hummed. "No, I suppose I can choose if you really want, but—"

"I mean, both. Do both," Rami clarified.

A smile curled his lips and he groaned. "Feathers, you don't know what you're doing to me."

"Tell me," Rami challenged, and it gave Julian pause. "While I kiss you some more," they added.

Julian's heart thundered as they dropped a kiss to the

corner of his mouth, and then continued on down the sharp edge of his jaw to his throat.

Could they feel his pulse against their lips?

"I think you are quite possibly the hottest thing I've ever seen," Julian admitted quietly.

Rami paused with their lips at his throat and glanced up. "Oh?" they asked.

This wasn't fair. Julian felt like the tables had been turned, and he could do nothing but let Rami explore.

"I would let you do anything you wanted to me," he continued. "I'd do anything to you that you wanted me to."

Above him, Rami shivered, sliding their lips lower onto his collarbones. They nipped, their teeth a tad sharper than the situation called for, but Julian *liked* that and this angel was already far too good at reading him.

Chills broke over his skin, tightening his nipples, making his cock throb against where Rami's belly pressed into him.

Their hands were warm and soft, one pressed into the bed and the other dragging down his side.

"Go on," they said, breath hot against Julian's skin.

This was supposed to be about Rami, and instead Julian was the one threatening to fall to pieces.

"I'm glad it's me. That I'm the one teaching you these things," he confessed.

"Are these sensitive?" Rami asked, pausing above Julian's chest.

He swallowed. "They can be."

And just like he'd thought, Rami lowered their head, tongue swiping over the small, stiff peak of Julian's nipple. He shuddered beneath them, arching into it.

Everything felt new with Rami, and he didn't know why. Maybe it was because everything was new *to* Rami, and Julian was struggling to separate the two.

Either way, pleasure slid through him from Rami's

mouth, and their hand splayed across his stomach, his abs jumping beneath their touch.

His cock throbbed, trapped in the boxers, and he groaned, head tilted back.

"You're pretty," Rami said suddenly.

Julian groaned again, exasperated, and pressed a foot into the bed, throwing his other leg up and over Rami to flip them, pushing them down into the mattress this time.

"What—"

"It's my turn," he said, and silenced Rami with a kiss.

Then he copied Rami's own movements, kissing along their jaw and throat, and nipping at the space he hoped was sensitive behind their ear.

Rami's breathy little gasp told him he'd guessed right.

Before he could move lower, their shirt needed to go, so Julian trailed his fingers along the hem of it, glancing down at them in question.

They nodded, and then lifted their arms when Julian shoved the shirt up, dragging it off their arms.

Sure, Julian could have magicked it away, but this was more personal, more fun. More tantalizing, to strip Rami himself, to bare all their skin.

They were pale and lovely, unblemished, chills rushing in a wave over their skin, beading their nipples.

He dared to stroke a thumb over one. "You always have these?" he asked.

Rami shook their head. "Angels have no need for breasts. Or nipples."

Julian arched a brow, stroking a hand over their flat pec. "Would you ever try breasts?"

Rami's cheeks glowed red at the thought. "Maybe one day. For now, one thing at a time."

Julian's blink was slow, as if he was imagining, and then

he lowered his lips back to their skin, starting at their hip this time.

A choked noise was cut off before it could be born, and Julian smiled against their skin, nipping once before continuing north. Over their stomach, between their pecs, and up to their collarbones.

Rami's hands were framed on Julian's hips, their grip tightening with each press of his lips.

Julian hummed, lifting his gaze, mouth hovering over Rami's chest. "Want to find out if yours are sensitive?" Julian asked.

Rami's cheeks were flushed, and they nodded, apparently unable to produce more of a sound.

I did that to them.

Julian defied the urge to grind into them, not wanting to push them too far too fast, and instead shifted his hips away as he lowered his mouth.

A brush of his lips over the peak sent more chills down Rami's spine. They shivered beneath him.

Their hands squeezed tighter around Julian's hips, and they repeated the action just so he could feel all ten fingers biting into his skin.

When he closed his lips around the peak to suck, it pulled a gasp from them. He flicked his tongue over it next, until Rami was positively shaking beneath him.

"I think it's safe to say they're sensitive," Rami breathed a moment later.

Julian lifted up with an obscene pop. "You think?" he teased, pressing a kiss to their sternum to soften the blow.

"I'm not one to rush things, usually. However—"

"You want me to hurry up?" Julian asked, attempting and failing to resist the smirk on his lips.

"Oh, don't look so proud of yourself," Rami drawled, and

gripped his hips snugly. "You think I can't tell how this excites you, too?"

Julian swallowed, the smirk slipping away under the darkening gaze of the angel.

"Are you excited, too, then?" Julian asked, pressing his hands into the bed to slide down Rami's body.

He slipped his hands beneath the waistband of their plaid pants and underwear, waiting for their nod before Julian tugged them down.

He didn't bother trying to avoid any of the awkwardness of having to straddle one thigh and then the other as he wiggled their pants down.

They both chuckled at the antics, relieved when Julian shoved them off their feet and let the fabric slip to the floor.

Julian sobered as he caught a glimpse of them, all silvery hair and glistening pink, shiny and flushed.

"Killing me, Feathers," Julian whispered.

He settled back between their spread thighs, and the moment turned into something serious once again.

Julian was hard, pressing into the bed beneath him. Splaying his hands across the tops of their thighs, he squeezed. He loved how their flesh spilled around his fingers, and wondered if it would be inappropriate to leave bruises.

That might be a little advanced, he decided, and glanced up at the angel he feared wouldn't leave his mind anytime soon.

Their eyes were wide as they stared down at him, reclining on their forearms for a direct view.

"Alright up there?" he asked, breath skating across the skin of their stomach.

They nodded, the movement jerky, uncoordinated.

Every touch was new to them, Julian reminded himself. *Easy. Gentle.*

"I'm... anticipatory," they murmured.

Those dorky words shouldn't have flared such heat through him, and yet he swallowed and dropped his gaze to their skin, unable to stand the desire blazing from their eyes.

Julian slowly pressed a kiss to their hip. "Wouldn't want —" Another to the junction of their torso and thigh. "—to keep you—" A final kiss to the sensitive, practically translucent flesh of the inside of their thigh. "—waiting," he said.

Finally Julian lowered his mouth to them in a wet, open-mouthed kiss. They jolted at the contact despite watching it happen, and their taste hit Julian's tongue. He wrapped his lips around them, offering a short, quick suck.

Their hips lifted off the bed as they gasped. Julian peeked up at them and saw their hands gripped into the bedspread, their eyes still wide and locked directly on Julian.

"You're—you're quite a vision down there," Rami breathed.

Julian hummed, drawing lower and swiping his tongue through their folds until he reached the well of arousal, dipping inside to coax more.

They moaned, and Julian squeezed their thighs in encouragement before sliding his hands closer, spreading them apart so he could flatten his tongue to them, dragging it up, up over their clit.

Rami let themself go lax, falling to the bed and covering their eyes with an arm.

"Do you mind what I call this?" he asked.

They lowered their arm, picking their head up, brow furrowed in confusion. "What?"

"This," Julian said, and brushed his thumb alongside them, stroking their arousal.

"I-I don't know," Rami said, shaking their head, cheeks flushing as their thighs tightened around Julian's body from the pleasure. "I don't think I care—whatever's appropriate."

"Just let me know if I say something you don't like," Julian told them.

They nodded, collapsing back down to the bed, boneless.

Julian tried not to feel too smug about that.

It didn't work.

He dragged one of his thumbs down the center of them, dipping into their core to spread the slick of them, nipping at their thigh, slowly digging his teeth into their skin.

"You're so wet," he remarked, no more than a breath.

Rami threw that arm back over their eyes, hips rolling into Julian's touch, breath short.

As Julian swiped his thumb back up, swiping over them, they moaned, and he repeated the action only to hear the noises they'd make.

"Do you like when I stroke your clit?" Julian asked.

They agreed not with words but with a hand fluttering over Julian before settling on squeezing his shoulder.

They were so flustered and cute, Julian couldn't stand it, and he gently circled their wrist. He pulled it to the top of his head and glanced up at them.

"I don't mind a little tug," he said. He liked his horns touched as well, but Julian was taking it one thing at a time, like Rami had said.

Rami gulped, and then their fingers were gliding through Julian's hair, gentle and smooth, avoiding his horns.

The touch spread chills over Julian's scalp and down to his shoulders.

He swallowed a groan and dipped his head back down to Rami, lapping at them as if he couldn't get enough.

He couldn't.

Nothing could've prepared him for their taste, or the ease with which they gave themself over to the pleasure, rocking against Julian's face, gripping his hair, moaning with abandon.

When their breath caught and their thighs tensed, Julian pulled back.

Rami huffed, snapping their head up. "Why'd you stop?" they asked, lips bitten red and parted with their breath.

"Didn't want you to come yet," Julian answered honestly, nuzzling against the junction of their thigh. "There's so much I still have to show you."

Rami grumbled at that, letting their head fall back onto the bed. "I'm not gonna survive it," they said, dramatic as ever.

Julian chuckled, something light and bubbly popping in his chest, filling him with hot air.

It wasn't what he was used to feeling, not while his dick was rock hard, and he was resisting the urge to grind into the mattress, the taste of an angel on his tongue.

"You'll be fine. Just as long as I keep my mouth on you, right?" Julian drawled suggestively, dropping his mouth where it belonged.

The angel groaned, hand tightening in Julian's hair, their hips lifting at the same time to press their cunt against him.

He dragged his tongue through their folds, lower, lapping at their entrance just to taste more of them before replacing it with a finger.

Julian nipped at Rami's thigh as they released a shaky breath.

"I'm still going slow, promise," Julian said, and they nodded, the movement jerky.

Their hand softened in Julian's hair and he rubbed his cheek against their warm thigh, a forgotten housecat who wanted attention. It worked, and they tightened their hold again.

"I'm not going anywhere," he said, and wrapped his lips around their clit as he pressed that first finger inside.

Rami gasped, squeezing around the digit, and Julian shuddered as his cock leaked against the boxers he still wore.

Julian was the one making them feel good, shuddering as he stroked into them, achingly slow.

They opened for him beautifully as he added another finger, felt them clench around him. He sucked at their clit, laving his tongue between their folds. He crooked his fingers, searching, searching—

Rami cried out, hips jolting as Julian found their sweet spot, brushing the pads of his fingers over it again and again.

Rami was completely unapologetic about what they liked, unafraid to tell Julian when he needed to—

"Stop saying that, this is not a cheap porno," they drawled, tugging at his hair after Julian asked them, "You like that?"

It was entirely surprising and unbelievably endearing. It left no question whether Julian was pleasing them or not, and as he stayed between their thighs, he learned exactly what made them moan and twitch the most.

He craved that moment when their hand tightened in his hair, dragging him closer for more, more, more.

Julian added a third finger, and they moaned for it. Moaned for *him*, his name falling from their lips, and Julian finally knew what it was to worship.

He'd pulled them to the edge only to deny them at the last second three times. But at the sound of their lips forming his name—*Julian*, in that soft, almost whimpering tone—he melted. Caved. Rolled over, belly-up.

He'd give this angel anything they wanted.

Their fingers scratched at his scalp and Julian rutted into the bed as he sucked at them, as he fucked them with his fingers—

Their grip tightened, almost painful, and he let them drag him away, stilling his movements.

"Don't come," they panted, face and chest flushed, sweat glistening on their skin like diamonds.

Christ, I'm a goner.

"Why not?" Julian asked, the edge so close and yet so far now that he'd stopped moving his hips upon their command.

"Because I want to see it happen," they said, and Julian—

Groaned, dropped his head to their thigh, and cursed. "Okay," he agreed, and their grip in his hair turned gentle again, at least until they dragged him back between their thighs.

"This—this is better than anything I've ever read on a page," Rami said, voice shaky as Julian lowered his mouth to their clit again. "It feels so good, Julian—" they moaned, and Julian's cock twitched, but he held his hips back from the mattress, waiting like they'd told him to.

A shiver went down his spine at the suggestion, and he crooked his fingers again, feeling them tremble.

"Yes, yes, that's so good," they panted.

Their other hand tangled in his hair as well, almost as if they were holding him between their legs.

The notion of it went right to Julian's head and sizzled down his spine and he groaned, the vibrations of it centered around the clit.

They shook beneath him, more sounds slipping from their throat, whines and pleas and also… commands.

"Come on, I'm so close, please—" they begged, fingers tangling in his hair, scalp tingling from the tugs. "Don't you dare stop," they snapped, and Julian wouldn't have dreamed of it, not with that edge to their voice, sharp with pleasure and desperation.

Julian suctioned his lips around them, fucking them on his fingers, the sounds of it downright filthy as he slid in and out them.

"Julian!" Rami cried.

He felt it happen, the split second of their entire body stiffening before their cunt clasped tight around his fingers, fluttering as they cried out.

Across his tongue their clit pulsed with each thrust of his fingers as he worked them through it, felt the wetness around his fingers grow. He slowed his thrusts and pulled away when they tensed in oversensitivity.

Their hands slid from his hair and he removed his fingers, the noise slick in the silence of the room, no other sound besides their own breaths.

Julian sucked their taste from his fingers, swallowing them down before resting his head against their thigh, letting his legs hang off the bed.

His own cock gave a sad twitch, still eager and extremely jealous of Rami's release.

He gripped their thighs and resisted the urge to grind into the bed, desperate to know exactly what Rami meant by *watch*.

Life came back to them slowly, and Julian chuckled softly at their dramatic antics. They groaned, throwing an arm over their face.

"I've died; that's the only explanation."

"La petit mort, and all that," Julian offered.

"I see why it's called that, now," Rami said. They sighed heavily. "Only one thing can resurrect me, I think."

"What's that?" Julian drawled.

Rami sat up, eyes suddenly clear even when half-lidded.

"You."

20
GIVE AND RECEIVE

Rami was still flushed, still felt smooth and liquidy from their orgasm—

They shivered. It was even better than the one the night before, and Julian's fingers were still glistening from their arousal and his spit.

He'd licked them clean, which sent a whole new flare of heat through them.

But Julian—poor Julian was still unsatisfied.

Well, not completely unsatisfied. He clearly took some pleasure from having his mouth on them, his fingers inside them.

"You," Rami declared, and pulled Julian up their body with gentle hands before repeating his move from earlier and flipping them.

Rami sat astride his lap and felt the bulge of him between their legs. It was decidedly suggestive, and that now-familiar warmth licked through them, but this was about Julian. About making Julian feel good.

And it was Rami's turn to do so.

"I want to put my mouth on you," Rami said.

They felt quite validated at the way Julian whined.

"Fea—Rami, I won't last long at all that way."

Rami inched down his thighs, hands splayed against his flat stomach. "Do you see me complaining?"

"No, but—" His brows furrowed, mouth opening and closing as he tried to find words.

"I want to make you feel good, too," Rami told him, softer.

His face went through a set of emotions too quickly for Rami to discern before it settled on a fond acceptance.

"Okay," he finally said.

Rami slid their hands lower, tugging at the waistband of his boxers.

Julian wiggled his hips to help Rami free him and their breath caught at the first unimpeded sight of him.

He was still hard, cock flushed, the head shiny with his own arousal. Once Rami wrangled the boxers off his feet, they climbed back up him and settled between his legs much the same way Julian had.

They eagerly wrapped a hand around him, gazing up at Julian, his head tilted back against the bed, one hand tangled in his own hair.

"I'm not the only one who's wet," Rami remarked, and Julian's breath caught in his throat, a strangled noise escaping.

Julian's cock pulsed in their grip and they stroked him, slow and easy, watching the bead of precum appear at the head, glistening like a pearl.

"Can't say things like that," Julian croaked.

Rami tilted their head to the side, pausing with their lips parted just above Julian's cock. "Why not? You liked it," Rami inferred, and then went with their instincts and lapped at the bead.

He was salty on their tongue and it made their mouth water for more.

Rami barely heard his moan, but felt the way his hips twitched up into them.

With the hand not occupied, they flattened their palm against his hip and held him down.

"Sorry I made you suffer for so long," Rami said, not sounding sorry at all. Mostly they were excited, curious, wondrous at the opportunity to explore with someone as kind and open and accepting as Julian had been.

Honestly, this was the least they could do, they thought magnanimously as they stroked him slowly.

Who else would understand Rami's predicament? Who else would Rami get to be so honest and open with?

When the next bead appeared, Rami lowered their mouth and sucked the head of his cock between their lips.

"Christ—Rami," Julian moaned.

They watched his hands tighten in the blankets, head going lax against the bed.

He pulsed in Rami's grip, and it emboldened them to take him a little deeper.

It was powerful, this position, having someone—Julian—a demon!—weak at their touch.

For once, the thought of Julian as a demon didn't bother them.

They couldn't find it in them to care, not with his taste on their tongue and his moans finding their way to Rami's ears.

Warmth buzzed through their head and their body, arousal pooling low just from this action.

They knew to wrap their lips around their teeth, to suction them around the head, to let their saliva spill out to ease the glide of their hand as they tried to figure out the rhythm.

It was sloppy, most likely, but Julian gave no indication that he cared or that it felt any less good because of it.

They remembered with crystal clarity what Julian had done to them, and slid their hand away from his hip with a warning squeeze. They cupped his balls, feeling them drawn up and tight, and even mimicked the same motion of brushing a finger just behind them.

Julian groaned and shouted a warning—

"Rami, I'm close," he panted.

Rami gave no sign of slowing down, finally figuring out the rhythm, moving their hand in time with their mouth.

They glanced up and found Julian's jaw slack as he stared down at them. Maybe they should've been embarrassed to be perceived in such a way, mouth full and unable to close, messy. Instead, beneath the heat and the disbelief in that gaze, they only felt warmer.

They pulled off, making quite a show of it, spit even clinging to their lip that Julian watched pop with wide eyes.

"Are you going to come for me?" Rami asked, voice raspier than usual, and lowered their head again.

"Y-yes," Julian whispered after taking a moment to absorb the filthy question.

Rami really liked bringing Julian to stunned silence.

They took even more of him, hand sliding lower on his cock with every pass as they let him slide past their lips.

He tensed in their hand and over their tongue, and Rami pressed it to his length as they pulled up, rubbing at the underside of the head, taken with the texture of him.

"Close," Julian muttered. "So close," he warned.

Rami was eager for it and took him even deeper, until he brushed the back of their throat. They'd read about the gag reflex in books, and knew it could be a problem for some. And decidedly made it *not* a problem for themself.

Still, it was an odd feeling, having something so far in their mouth in this way. They swallowed around him, heard his answering croak, and figured they'd done something right.

"I'm—oh, fuck," Julian gasped.

Rami squeezed their hand, stroking him only once, twice

more before he shouted and threaded his hand through their hair, tightening. It sent chills down their spine and then he was pulsing across their tongue, his release spilling into Rami's mouth.

They swallowed him, the taste salty and a little bitter but all Julian. With their lips suctioned around the head, they took every drop and gently stroked him until there was nothing left. The whole time Julian moaned and twitched against the bed, and Rami finally released him when Julian went limp.

Rami crawled up next to him and collapsed against the bed alongside Julian. They were touching from shoulder to thigh and even though they'd just done *so* much touching, it still delighted them. Like they couldn't get enough.

Julian groaned, lifting a hand to place it against Rami's thigh, squeezing in what they felt might be affection.

"So was that… alright?" Rami asked, a smile twitching at their lips.

Julian huffed, rolling his head to the side to eye Rami. "'Alright?' You just sucked my soul out through my cock."

"I don't think that's how that works," Rami teased, amused despite the flush on their cheeks. A beat passed while they caught their breaths. "I think I'd like to try that with a cock of my own one day," they admitted.

Julian whined, and Rami tried to push away the blush of pride.

"Can I kiss you?" Julian asked.

Rami shrugged. "Is that a done thing? After that act? I've read that some—mmph!"

Julian cut off their worries with a kiss. A filthy one. Where he didn't hesitate to slide his tongue against Rami's, collecting the remnants of his own taste. His hand slid up their cheek to tangle in their hair and hold them to him.

Something in Rami's chest burst at the tenderness, the

intimacy, of laying naked alongside someone and simply kissing.

It was downright romantic, and they tried not to read too far into it, fearing it might be a little late for that.

Instead they let themself sink into the molasses of the moment.

They finally broke apart, breathless and staring at one another. Rami tried to gauge if Julian was having the same revelation.

"A-plus, Feathers," Julian said eventually, voice crackly and warm.

Rami didn't even bother pretending the praise didn't go straight to their head. "What do we do now?"

Julian shrugged and stretched, and Rami appreciated the long line of his body. "Are you hungry?"

"I could eat," Rami mused.

"You pick. Do you wanna go somewhere or stay here?"

Rami pursed their lips. Leaving the house highly diminished their chances of experimenting some more.

"We can order in," Rami decided.

Julian's lips twitched as if he knew what Rami was thinking, and could it be that he was having the same thoughts?

They crawled from the bed and hand-waved some clothes on. Usually Rami would've showered to start their day, but they couldn't find it in themself to wash Julian's scent from their skin.

Rami realized it was late morning by the time they made it downstairs, and it felt… good to break their routine a little.

Maybe Julian was influencing them a little too much.

And they found they didn't quite mind. Not when Julian shared the kitchen with them, grinding the beans while they prepped the kettle. Not when he magicked a second pour over for his own mug and not as he hovered, literally, with his head on Rami's shoulder and arms around their waist while they poured the hot water over the grinds.

This must be what humans called *the honeymoon phase.*

Rami supposed they understood now why it was so good. Why humans constantly chased companionship.

Rami'd forgotten how nice it could be. And even then… had it ever been quite *this* nice? Certainly never this intimate.

"How do you want to spend the day?" Rami asked him. "What simple pleasures are you interested in?"

Even though *this* was the nicest of humanity's simple pleasures, they decided.

Julian's hands squeezed their sides, and he turned his head to lay his lips on Rami's throat, just over their pulse.

"I can think of a few things."

Rami chuckled, a giddy zing of happiness—and the threat of arousal—tingling through them.

"There's not an Earthly experience you want to see today?"

Julian hummed, lips buzzing against Rami's neck, ticklish. "Hmm. Well, what local events are going on?"

Rami tugged out their phone and went to the town's group on a social media app before handing it to Julian. "You know, you could go anywhere in the world and see things. The Eiffel Tower, Niagara Falls. I'm sure all of that would be much more entertaining than whatever we find on here."

"But you're right here," Julian pointed out.

Rami's breath caught, and their heart gave a fateful thump. They continued pouring the coffee, and sat the kettle aside before doctoring Julian's coffee appropriately.

"Ooh, look at this, Feathers," Julian said, and held the phone out to them, oblivious to the too-big feelings he inspired in them.

They read the screen and arched a brow. "You want to go to a pride event at this bar?"

"Yeah, why not? There's going to be drag!"

Rami wouldn't mind indulging him. "Alright, let's do it. But what are we going to do until—" They glanced at the graphic again. "9 PM. Goodness, that's awfully late."

Julian chuckled softly before unwrapping himself from them and grabbing his mug. "Well, we have all day. What do *you* suggest?"

Rami pursed their lips, trying not to give their thoughts away.

"We could go out for lunch," Rami suggested, but they did not do a good job selling the suggestion.

Julian shot them a look before setting his coffee aside and sliding up onto the kitchen island.

In nothing more than an oversized shirt and his boxers, he looked quite… ravishing.

Rami swayed towards him, finally giving up the ruse and setting their coffee aside, too, abandoning it for the moment to settle between Julian's thighs.

"You're right," Rami murmured. "This is a much better idea."

21
ANGELIC AUDACITY

I*'ve created a monster*, Julian thought as Rami nestled between his legs.

Their hands slipped around Julian's waist, pulling him to the very edge of the counter so they could grind together.

He hummed into the kiss, Rami's lips twitching against the vibrations. Their hands trailed up his hips, over the planes of his chest and shoulders to cup his face, tilting him back. His horns knocked into the cabinets with a soft scrape.

They broke the kiss, and Julian's eyes fluttered open to stare at them.

"I've always wondered…" they began.

Julian was well on his way to thickening up again, eager to show Rami whatever they wanted to experience.

"What?" he rasped. *Tell me, I'll do it, anything you want,* he almost rambled, but he squashed the words between his teeth.

"Are your horns… sensitive?" Rami asked.

Julian groaned, tipping forward to rest his forehead against Rami's shoulder.

"Wanna find out?" Julian questioned softly, teasing and already knowing the answer.

"I very much do," Rami breathed, the words hot against the skin of Julian's cheek and neck.

"Let's go upstairs," Julian said, lifting his head.

Rami's eyes were stormy and dark and *heated,* and Julian got a little lost in their warmth for a second. Then he wiggled closer to the edge of the counter, intending to drop to his feet and lead Rami upstairs.

Instead, it seemed the angel had other plans, as Rami scooped Julian closer, tucked their hands under his ass and thighs, and lifted.

Julian gasped, wrapping his legs around Rami's waist and his arms around their neck, holding on.

"You're strong," Julian managed.

"Might be," they said with a smirk, their confidence new and brilliant and blinding.

Julian was well and truly fucked.

Or I'm about to be, at least.

Going up the stairs was a challenge for even Rami, and Julian guided them. Their chuckles filled the stairwell until they got to the top and Rami spilled him onto the bed.

"Does the broken one hurt?"

"Not anymore," Julian answered, and brushed a finger over the smoothed out tip.

His horns had always stood straight off his temples, curved a bit backward and then forward. He'd always been envious of Galen's horns for having a fancy swoop that went with his hair. Julian's were impossible to hide.

And now, Julian would always be reminded of what had happened. Before his ever-present worry could bully its way to the forefront of his mind, he glanced up at Rami.

Julian decided just maybe he'd find a new appreciation for them, like the kind alighting Rami's gaze.

"They're shiny," Rami murmured as they settled across Julian's thighs.

They reached out a hand, pausing just inches away, and with a single tilt of Julian's chin they closed the distance, a finger brushing up the curved length.

Julian bit down on the inside of his cheek to silence the noise that wanted to slip out, eyes drifting closed.

"What's it like?" Rami asked before they touched the other with the same slow drag of their digit.

Chills broke out over his skin, shimmering down his spine and back up, yet Julian forced himself to remain still. "It's very fucking similar to stroking my cock," Julian admitted.

Rami's hand paused, finger barely touching the very tip of Julian's right horn, the long one. "Is that so?" they asked.

Julian hoped the strangled noise in his throat translated enough of a confirmation.

"Come on, now, you know I like to hear you," Rami said.

Julian had taught them that, hadn't he?

"This one's long," Rami observed, and wrapped their whole hand around his horn, stroking from base to tip. "About a foot in length, I'd say."

He swallowed a groan, mostly to see just what Rami would do if he kept testing them. Julian inhaled slowly, the heat in his chest all fuzzy and hard to breathe around. Rami was sitting right over his hips, and he grabbed on, letting his fingers dig into their skin through the clothes they'd magicked on. He was entirely aroused, and pulled them down into him as he bucked his hips, careening them together. If he wasn't imagining it, he felt Rami's own hardness, and he rocked into them again.

Rami's breath caught, and their gaze flicked down from his horns to his lips. "Impatient?"

"Maybe a little," Julian croaked out.

Rami stroked his left horn, the short one, with their entire hand. "Does that help?"

Julian couldn't nod in Rami's hold, and instead panted, "Yeah, yes. Keep doing that."

He rolled his hips up, and the pressure of Rami in his lap and their hand around his horn was almost too much. He tightened his grip on them, the soft give of their skin beneath his fingers enticing as ever.

"This is going to sound quite blunt," Rami began, hand squeezing around the tip of his horn before sliding away completely.

Julian's eyes snapped up to them. "What is it?"

"I have an idea."

"I'm learning to love your ideas, Feathers. Tell me."

"You seem determined to remain quiet. So how would you like to put that mouth of yours to good use?" they said.

Said mouth dropped open at the audacity of the angel, whose cheeks turned red. Julian watched the panic spread across their expression, lips parting to babble on about how inappropriate a request it was.

Before they could get there, Julian lifted his hands to the button on their pants and slipped it free before yanking at the material.

Rami stopped his hands in place, before Julian could reveal them, and Julian glanced up at the angel.

"This time, I want to try it with a cock," they clarified.

"I am more than okay with that," Julian said, nodding eagerly, and Rami let go of his hands after a short search of his expression. Hopefully they saw how genuine he felt, how fucking turned on he was by them.

Julian finished stripping them, and they even chuckled at the urgency to his movements.

Once Rami was naked, Julian caught the sway of them between their thighs and didn't bother holding back his groan that time.

Julian had never been someone's first anything before,

and here was yet another first that Rami was willing to experience with him. Julian was struck for a moment, completely clothed while Rami's skin was bared, sitting atop him like it was nothing. Like it wasn't the highest honor anyone had ever bestowed upon Julian.

Thank you didn't seem an appropriate offering, so instead Julian tugged Rami closer, up across his chest, because if nothing else, he'd offer himself to them. To take and to experience and to… use.

"Will you be able to breathe?" Rami asked.

Julian gripped the back of their thighs and moaned as they shuffled closer.

"I don't even care," Julian mumbled, nipping at the sensitive skin of the pale flesh he could reach.

Rami huffed, and grabbed a horn to force Julian's head to the mattress. Warmth spiraled through him at the possessive motion, and he stilled, lips parting.

"At the very least, I want you to tap my thigh twice if you need a break," they said.

"I will," Julian promised. "Now get up here."

Rami sighed like it was some great feat, but shuffled into place, thighs sliding on either side of Julian's head, the white noise of skin on skin amplifying the sizzling embers in his own body.

He heard their hand meet the wall for balance, the other still curled around his horn.

They were sitting up, but Julian was surrounded by them, their scent and warm thighs, their length dangling close but out of reach.

A strike of heat flickered down his spine. Fuck, he loved this, and grasped at their thighs for restraint, not wanting to rush.

At least, not too much.

Rami's hand was still tight around his horn, so he couldn't

exactly lift his head to taste them. Instead he had to wait, gaze trailing up their soft body to meet Rami's eyes.

Julian laid his hands over their hips, thumbs digging into the crease, ever closer to their length and attempting to pull them down to him.

Rami nodded once, and that was all the permission Julian needed.

He wrapped his palm around them, bicep resting along their thigh so he could begin to stroke them. They gasped at the touch, arching into it, and finally tilted correctly, so Julian could point them between his lips.

They curved over him, hand sliding against his horn, and Julian's hips jolted into the air of their own accord. With a groan, he parted his lips and tasted Rami, their flavor spilling across his palate as he lapped at their head.

Rami released a moan as Julian dragged his tongue along their length, their hand tightening around his horn.

"Oh, that's—" Their observation melted into a hum of pleasure.

Julian's cock throbbed, trapped beneath his clothes, while Rami was completely nude above him, thighs tensing under Julian's hand.

He dug his fingers in, squeezing and kneading with one hand while he stroked Rami with the other, lips curled around them, cheeks hollowing.

"Julian—" Rami breathed.

He lifted his gaze, finding Rami flushed and lips slack and eyes as dark as anything as they stared down at Julian.

His lips were stretched around their cock, hard and hot and resting against his tongue. Julian sucked them like a starved man, taking them deeper, urging them to tilt their hips.

They surged against his face, a cry slipping out before

they bit their lip. Then slowly, Rami began to rock against his face, far too gently.

Julian grabbed onto them harder, fingers pressing in, hoping to leave marks, and tugged them against him in the beginnings of a rhythm.

"Oh god, that's—" Rami began, and cut off as they rolled their hips. It slid their cock deeper into his mouth, pulsing against his tongue. He flattened it, giving them something to grind against.

They had all the power here, and something about that made Julian want to melt into the sheets. They gripped his horn and held him in place as their thighs tensed with each movement, growing braver by the minute.

Their touch alternated between a tight grasp around the girth of his horn and lazy strokes that made Julian whimper around them. He hoped they could feel the vibrations.

He felt them press deeper, finally relaxing into it, trusting that they wouldn't hurt Julian. He swallowed around them, chasing the taste of their arousal until they were finally tilting their hips and sinking deep.

Gag reflex? Julian didn't know her.

"You're— oh fuck," Rami panted, and the heat beneath Julian's skin *flamed* at the sound of the curse falling off Rami's lips.

He was the one that made them say that.

His hands tightened, yanking them lower, closer, deeper. He knew he was messy, lips and chin and cheeks coated in saliva and their precum and yet he still wanted more. Part of him wanted to talk, to coax them to the edge, but the other part was loath to remove his mouth, even for a second.

So instead he carried on, arms flexing as he offered them support, guiding them to fuck his face, his tongue.

He lifted his gaze to watch their belly tighten as they held him down, using him for their own pleasure, hips rocking with abandon.

"So good," they breathed, and while Julian knew they were likely referring to the *act,* in his head, they were telling Julian *he* was good, and his cock twitched.

He was still trapped beneath his clothes, but knew by now there had to be a wet spot on his pants. Julian was weak for this angel, and even weaker for making them feel good, for bringing them pleasure. All it would take was a single glance and the angel would know just how close Julian was. From tasting them, feeling them, watching them. From the way their hands swapped places, their left wrapping around his short horn.

It was healed, so their hand stroked smoothly over from root to tip. Julian anticipated it would feel like it always did, but somehow it felt even *more* intense than normal.

He groaned around the length in his mouth.

"I'm close," Rami announced, hips falling out of rhythm before they found it again. "Fuck, I think—you—" They huffed an annoyed sound, abandoning whatever they wanted to say in favor of gripping his horn, pulling Julian up into them at the same time they rolled their hips down.

He swallowed around them, and knew they felt the cinch of his throat from the way they groaned.

They began a quick, even stroke against Julian's horn, and he moaned, the sound nothing more than a vibration, lost around the length of them.

Rami felt it, an answering noise spilling out, hips rocking against Julian's face.

They were desperate, he knew. It was in the grip around his horn, the hitch of their breath, the tensing of their body. They were doing nothing more than chasing their own pleasure, and Julian was just a tool to help them reach it.

The thought made Julian's gaze flutter shut, warmth corkscrewing through him, right down his spine.

One of their hands slapped against the wall, and Julian's eyes snapped open to find them staring down at him. "Keep looking at me," they said, and Julian did just that.

He watched their fingers curl against the wall, head falling back as they rocked their hips, sliding their cock into him again and again. He saw it come over them, felt their thighs shake around his ears and beneath his fingers. He felt them pulse over his tongue and grind themself against his face.

They let out a filthy, needy whine when it happened, and Julian tried to swallow them just that much deeper as they rode him. They stroked Julian's horns and then he felt the kick of their cock across his tongue. They came down his throat, and he swallowed dutifully. Only a bit escaped, slicking his lips and chin.

They squeezed the base of his horn and in return Julian's cock twitched, a warning flare at the base of his spine. As their thighs and grip tightened again, he let it burn through him.

He groaned into them, felt the answering shake of them above him, but Julian was too far gone, spilling in his pants like an overeager teenager.

Rami pulled away, their softening cock slipping over Julian's lip. Once he was released, he turned his head as much as he could to nip at the sensitive skin of their thigh.

Their hands slid away from Julian's horn with a last stroke, making Julian shake beneath them.

They untangled, Rami retracting a leg from one side of Julian's face to collapse beside him on the bed.

Julian tilted his head, wiping his face on the shoulder of his shirt, and wrapped an arm around them, dragging them close.

"That was something… new," Rami mused, voice lazy and drawling as they relaxed against Julian.

"Certainly one way to pass the time," Julian answered.

"What do you call those? Horn jobs?" Rami asked.

Julian snorted, barely shaking the angel who lay on his chest. "Sure, let's go with that."

Rami nosed at his collarbones, tugging the neck of his shirt down. "I think I'd like to do that again."

Julian's cock gave a pitiful, mournful kick.

"Not right now," Rami clarified, and Julian sighed. "But soon. I want to be able to see you better while I touch your horns."

Julian realized, right then, that he was an idiot for ever even considering tempting this angel with sex. *The selfishness of their desire would do them in,* he'd thought. But of course, for someone who was so good at taking what they wanted and chasing their own pleasure, Rami sure was so fucking *selfless* about it.

Julian shivered. "Whatever you want, Feathers."

Rami hummed, the sound a buzz against his skin. "I like the sound of that."

And the thing was, Julian did, too.

22
INTENTIONS

No matter how infinitely Julian's existence stretched on, he imagined he'd never forget how it felt to walk into a queer bar, on Earth, with Rami.

It was low lit with multicolored lights, and rainbows were plastered *everywhere*. But even more colorful were the patrons already nursing pretty drinks, awaiting the start of the show.

And following the theme was Rami themself. Julian had only seen the angel in their muted grays and whites and navy blues. Now, though, they were stunning in much their usual style, but with a bit of color. Sure, they hadn't strayed too far, still sporting a pair of navy pants and a gray sweater, but the difference was the rainbow threaded through each stitch.

Julian had dressed as usual, layered in black, horns tucked away so as not to scare the humans.

Julian nudged Rami, and pointed at the string hanging from the ceiling with pronoun tags, waiting for anyone to take them.

Julian snagged a he/him tag while Rami plucked a they/them tag, and then Julian ushered them to the bar.

"This is delightful," Rami told him, leaning close to speak into his ear.

The atmosphere was so open. No one was staring, and everyone seemed so happy and excited to be there, broken off into loud groups cackling with laughter.

It was everything Julian had heard and seen in the media from his little television in Hell, brought to life.

He reached down and squeezed Rami's hand, unable to take his eyes from some of the more extravagantly dressed patrons.

"First time?" the bartender asked them, wearing a he/him pin. His eye makeup sparkled beneath the rainbow lighting.

"How could you tell?" Julian drawled.

He smirked and took their drink orders, and when he plopped their glasses down in front of them, confirmed. "Show starts in thirty. I'd go grab seats while you can."

Julian grabbed his drink and waited for Rami to do the same before leading them toward the more crowded part of the bar, where everyone was seated at low tables in front of the event stage.

Figuring Rami wouldn't want to be front and center, Julian stopped at a high-top table off to the side and arched a brow.

"Perfect," Rami said, and slid onto their seat.

Julian pushed his chair up right beside them. He didn't even bother trying to excuse it by saying he wanted to be able to see the stage better.

They both knew it was because Julian wanted to be close to the angel.

And here, in this bar, the angel didn't shy away from him; instead, they took his hand and squeezed it.

"I haven't felt this much joy from a group of people in a long time," Rami said.

"I take it you don't come to these often?" Julian asked. It was a shame that Rami had all this time on Earth and yet had never experienced so many things. Whereas Julian *wanted* to be here, to see and do it all, and yet couldn't.

The irony was not lost on him.

"These places are usually all about community. It's... not easy to linger in the corner, separate from such open, welcoming people."

Julian could see that.

Especially as someone in a bright pink cowgirl outfit approached their table.

"Howdy, y'all. Been here before?" she asked. Her pronoun tag was situated right next to a trans pin.

"First time," Rami answered, smiling.

"Well, I was practically dared to come introduce myself to the new cute couple, so here I am! Don't be shy—you can come sit with us, if you'd like. I'm Jesse," she said, and held out a manicured hand.

Rami took it with a grin, and introduced them.

Julian didn't bother correcting her on their relationship status. Neither did Rami, Julian noted with a patter of his heart.

Rami turned to him, the question in their expression, and Julian shrugged.

"Might as well get the full experience," he said, and grabbed both their drinks.

"That's the spirit," Jesse encouraged, and then led them to a small round table housing a group.

"Hell yeah, you got them!" one of them cheered, and scooted their chair over.

Jesse unapologetically stole two chairs from another table and shoved them toward Rami and Julian.

Rami grabbed the chairs before pushing them into place and motioning for Julian to take a seat.

"So chivalrous," Julian murmured in their ear, just to see them blush.

"God, you're both so cute together," someone at the table said. "I can't believe we haven't seen you around before. Are you new to the area?"

"I am," Julian said, and raised his hand.

"But I've been here a while. This is just my first time venturing out, I suppose," Rami offered.

Julian was pleased to see Rami actually talking to other people. Surprisingly being open.

Beneath the table, he squeezed their thigh, and they glanced over at them with a grin.

Their cheeks were flushed, either from the already almost empty glass of their cocktail, or the attention, or the atmosphere itself.

Whatever it was, it was a good look on them.

Julian's heart did that *thing* again, where he temporarily felt like there was no room in his chest for another breath.

"So are there often such exciting events on a Thursday evening?" Rami asked.

The group chuckled and nodded. "A few times a week, actually," they shared, and Rami's eyes lit up.

Julian had a feeling they'd be checking out these different events.

Assuming I can stick around for that long.

The lights dimmed and a spotlight came on, and Rami's expression was one of absolute awe and disbelief as the drag queen entered the stage.

Their jaw dropped open, and they shared an amazed glance with Julian.

I'm in trouble, he thought.

By the time the stage lights went up, Julian had come to a conclusion.

He excused himself to go get drinks for everyone—it was the least he could do with his unlimited supply of money—and as he watched Rami delight in the company of these people, he realized he was fucked.

He also realized…

I should tell them.

The thought rang with the clarity of a bell, and he could've sworn his heart skipped a beat with it.

As he waited for their fourth round of drinks, Julian watched them from across the bar.

Rami giggled, tipping their head back and laughing at something Jesse said after elbowing their side.

He should tell Rami why he's here. He should tell them that he's decided… to hell with the assignment.

The deadline loomed, and Julian was no closer to tempting the angel into selfishness, and he didn't *want* to be.

At least not at Rami's expense.

Julian cursed.

What if Rami was angry? Or disappointed in him? That somehow felt worse than anger.

Their upset would be justified. Julian had been lying all this time.

He frowned, and stared down at the drink in his hand while he waited.

Julian knew exactly what the angel would think. They'd look at this entire week in a new light, colored by their disappointment in Julian. They'd think *everything* was a lie.

His heart dropped, and he froze, hand tightening around the glass.

They'd think everything was a lie.

The bath and, and—

Maybe Julian could explain. He could. He'd reassure them

it wasn't a lie. That maybe he'd come here with certain intentions, but those intentions had mattered less and less the more time they spent with Rami.

A week? A single week?

That would never be enough.

Julian lifted his gaze, staring across the room, at Rami cheering with the small crowd.

As if they could feel him, they glanced up, eyes locking. Their brow furrowed, and Julian wondered if his conflicting emotions were showing on his face.

He cooled his expression into one a little more casual and smiled, lifting his drink.

The angel returned the gesture, and when Jesse elbowed them again, they excused themself from the group.

Julian swallowed as they approached.

"Dance with me?" Rami asked, and before Julian could even respond, they reached out and grabbed Julian's wrist to tug him along.

Julian found himself crushed up against Rami in the crowd. Their cheeks were flushed, or at least what he could see of them between the multicolored lights.

They looked so light and happy, and their arm was around Julian's waist, and—

"I have to tell you something," Julian said softly.

Rami leaned closer to shout in his ear. "What?"

Julian turned them the other way. "I need to tell you something," Julian yelled.

"Do you want to go outside?" Rami asked. "It's loud!"

Julian agreed, but then the music changed, and Rami turned the biggest, saddest eyes on Julian. "Dance with me for this one song?" they asked in his ear.

Julian was helpless against that gaze, and turned his head back, nodding.

Rami beamed, brighter than the lights flashing around

them. And then they grabbed him around the waist and pulled him close.

Julian melted into them. He loved nothing more than feeling Rami against him like this. The curve of their belly pressing into Julian's stomach, their soft thigh slotting between his own as they swayed together.

Julian laid his right arm on Rami's shoulder, threading his left beneath Rami's to grab their waist, just like Rami was doing to him.

Their fingers were sure and confident in their grip on his waist as they danced, and warmth filled Julian.

The beat of the song was slow but heavy, thumping through the building, vibrating the bottom of Julian's feet, rattling his chest.

The crowd shuffled, and they pressed even closer. Chest to chest, Julian was surrounded by everything Rami.

Their soft, sweet scent. Their touch.

He couldn't take it anymore.

Julian slid his hand in their hair and pulled them close, hesitating just as their lips brushed, in case Rami didn't want public affection.

But they clearly didn't care, closing the distance and tilting their head and putting all their practice from the last twenty-four hours to use.

Julian was putty in their hands as they carded said hands through his hair, gripping just tight enough to send shivers over his skin.

I have to tell them. Before it's too late.

Julian leaned into them, bodies still swaying with the beat, Rami's thigh pressing with a little more intent between his legs.

Julian moaned into the kiss, though it was lost to the music, and he ground into them. Warmth trailed down his spine, settling between his legs, and he pulled back.

Rami's lips were kiss-bitten red and twitched in a smile as they stared at him. They brushed a bit of his hair off his cheek, and Julian wanted to scream with the affection that filled him so suddenly.

He was already hard, cock trapped beneath his pants, and he hoped it wasn't visible to the hooting and hollering crowd they'd left at the tables.

"Better get those drinks," Rami said.

Julian nodded, not making a move to do so, at least not until Rami took his hand and pulled him in that direction.

They collected their drinks and Julian followed behind Rami like a lost puppy, grateful for the cover as he tried to think of grandmas and hurt kittens to make his erection go away.

It sort of worked, until Rami stopped right before him to bend over *very* suggestively, placing the drinks on the table as their new friends cheered.

They made room for Julian to do the same, and then he sank into his seat with red cheeks, narrowing his gaze at Rami.

Devious little angel.

Rami *winked* and Julian was dying to know where all this confidence was coming from. Was it the bar? Was it the people? Was it the fact that they'd seen practically every part of each other at this point?

Whatever it was, Julian was loving it.

And that was the problem.

Julian threw an arm over the back of Rami's chair and leaned close to speak into their ear. "If you keep this up, we're going to have to leave."

"What made you think that wasn't my plan all along?" Rami returned with a wicked grin.

Julian smirked and removed his arm before leaning into the table. "Well, kids, I guess we're going to get out of here," he announced, and pushed his chair back to stand.

Rami rolled their eyes, but stood with him, tucking an arm around his waist and—

It went right to Julian's head, that Rami would claim him — a demon— in such a way in front of all these people.

The group shared a set of knowing looks, and Julian found he didn't give a shit if they all knew they were going home early to fuck.

They bid them goodbye and promised to be at the next event before the group let them leave.

Rami kept that arm around his waist practically the entire way home, and Julian wanted to wrap his whole body around them and never let go.

As soon as Julian locked the door behind them, Rami was on him.

Their arms circled his neck and pushed him into the nearest wall, lips crushing to his in a desperation Julian felt all the way to the tips of his toes.

"Thank you for that. I had so much fun," Rami murmured into the kisses.

"I should be thanking you. You're the one showing me around Earth, remember?" Julian drawled.

Rami pulled back, combing their hands through Julian's hair. "Yeah, exactly. I would've never ended up there if not for you landing on my doorstep. So, thank you."

Julian swallowed and nodded because he couldn't find something to say just then.

The next kiss Rami planted on him was slow and so sweet it made his teeth ache.

Then they pulled back with a gasp, and Julian wanted to follow.

"Oh, right, you wanted to tell me something?" Rami said.

Julian's breath left him, and he realized he didn't want to

ruin the moment. He wondered if he could talk himself out of this one.

"I did. But it's not important now," he said.

Rami tilted their head, smiling. "It seemed important at the time. Come on, you can tell me anything."

And Julian believed them.

I can do this.

"Alright, Feathers. I want you to promise me you'll let me finish before you respond."

Rami's smile slipped just the smallest bit. "It is serious, then. I can do that."

Julian sucked in a deep breath. "I—

Just then, there was a knock at the back door. But not a normal, polite knock. It was quick and frantic, panicked.

Both of their heads snapped around, eying the door as if the lock would start turning all by itself.

Rami shared a startled glance with him, and then rushed to the door, slipping from Julian's arms before he could say anything at all.

23
LAST CHANCE

Julian swallowed his words and finally turned toward the door just as Rami pulled it open.

"Melissa? Oh, god," Rami said, and then they were gently directing a woman into their home, shutting the door softly.

Julian's stomach soured as he saw the bruise on her cheek.

"I'm fine, I'm fine; please don't fret," she said, waving a hand. "I just—sorry, this is so inappropriate."

"Nonsense," Rami said. "Here, would you like to go into the office?"

"Oh, no, you have company, too!" she said, catching Julian's eye. "I should leave," she rambled, and attempted to turn toward the door.

"No," Julian called out. "Please stay. I'll get you some water."

And ice, he thought.

For that bruise.

Rami led the woman into their office, and sat her down on that yellow couch.

Julian filled a glass of water, wrapped a gel ice pack in a towel, and grabbed a blanket on his way into the office. He didn't cross the threshold, and Rami's expression melted into one of...

Well, the only way Julian could describe it would be something akin to adoration.

It made his chest tight, and his breath squeezed out of him slowly as Rami collected the items.

"Let me know if she needs anything," Julian said softly. "I'll leave you to it."

"Actually, will you call the police?" they whispered. "Tell them we have a domestic violence victim here and she'd like to make an official report."

His ribs clutched his heart. Julian swallowed and nodded.

Rami stopped Julian from turning with a squeeze of his shoulder. Then they leaned in and placed a kiss on his cheek. "Thank you."

Rami turned away and made their way back to Melissa, who was seated on the couch, staring out the windows. It was too dark to see out.

Julian gave them privacy, shutting one of the doors, and cupped his cheek as he walked away.

His chest was full, like there was something in there too big to contain.

Now wasn't the time to get all lost in his stupid emotions. Fuck.

Julian made the call, and the operator assured him that a unit would be there soon.

Rami stayed with Melissa the whole time, and Julian paced in the kitchen while he waited.

Julian didn't know what had happened, but he didn't need details to know it was foul.

This must be what Rami meant when they'd said that humans went through so much. Melissa, one of Rami's clients, was being abused by the person who was supposed to love her. Her spouse.

It wasn't right.

Julian worked himself up into a mood about the whole thing, anger simmering beneath the surface.

About a half hour passed before headlights washed through the window, and Rami trailed out of the office. Julian wasn't the only one affected by all this. Rami looked downright distraught, but despite it all, Julian was relieved to see them, and some of the spiky anger faded at the sight of them.

Julian was at the door, holding it open by the time the officers made it to the step.

"Good evening," one of them greeted. "We heard there's a report that needs to be made."

"Yes. Melissa is this way," Rami said, and motioned them inside.

"And who are you in relation to the victim?" the officer asked. His little notebook was already out.

"I'm Rami Light, Melissa's therapist. This is…" Rami trailed off, gaze falling to Julian.

Julian saw a chance to make Rami feel a little better, just for a moment. He could tease them in front of the police, ruffle their feathers. Claim to be their partner, watch their cheeks glow in soft embarrassment and softer fondness as they went back and forth. Then, once the police were gone, he'd poke fun at them for that obvious last name.

But now didn't feel like the time for such levity. So instead, "I'm just a friend," Julian said quietly, and stepped back to welcome the officers in.

"Right this way, sir," Rami told him, and led the officers through the living room.

Rami knocked gently, then poked their head in and spoke softly to Melissa before allowing the officers entry. Rami nodded before leaving one of the doors open and making their way to the kitchen.

The officer's and Melissa's voices carried, but not loud enough to make out any of the words.

Rami looked… sad.

Julian hated it.

"She'll be okay," he offered, because it was all he really could offer.

"It'll take some time, but I know," Rami said, leaning against the kitchen counter.

"You did a good thing, helping her," Julian said. He glanced down at his crossed fingers on the counter, practically twiddling his thumbs in the face of these uncomfortable, serious emotions.

"But am I really even doing anything?" Rami sighed. "I just want her to be safe," they said, lips pursed in an unhappy twist.

"She will be. We'll make sure of it, yeah?" Julian told them. He bumped his shoulder into Rami's and the angel returned the movement, a small smile curling their lips.

"You're right. We will."

Julian rubbed a hand over Rami's back and waited with them. They tidied the kitchen, though there wasn't much tidying to do in the first place. They paced and chatted, but not about anything of substance.

It wasn't even that long before the police were exiting the office.

Rami directed them to the back door and after bidding them good evening, returned to the office.

Julian stayed back, trying not to overhear but hearing anyway.

"How did it go?"

Melissa cleared her throat. "I don't want to press charges, so there's not much they can do besides keep the report on file for the courts. I'm going to file for a restraining order, though."

Julian stilled. These human terms didn't mean much to him, but he knew it wasn't anything good.

"Melissa..."

"I know, I know what you're going to say," she said with a huff. "But he's my husband."

It was quiet for a long moment, and Julian wondered if they were having one of those conversations with their eyes.

"What will you do in the meantime?" Rami finally asked.

Julian had the same question. Surely she didn't mean to go home?

"I can go back to the domestic violence shelter. I'll be able to stay there while I get the restraining order filed." She sighed. "There's forms, and I'll have to go to the courthouse, and there will even be a hearing, and—it feels like a lot, right now."

"Go *back?*" Rami asked, and the following silence was telling.

Clearly Melissa had not been forthcoming about everything during their sessions.

Rami's voice lowered, and when Julian could hear them again they said, "You are more than welcome to stay here for as long as you need it."

"No, no. I couldn't. I don't want to put you out."

"Melissa," Rami said, almost scolding. "You'd never. You could take my bed, or I even have a pull-out couch, if that makes you more comfortable."

Julian arched a brow, knowing that absolutely was not true. It was good to know Rami would use magic for someone else's benefit, at least.

"Rami, please. I'd like to take care of this myself, if possible. I don't want to..." She took a shaky breath. "I'm a big girl."

It was quiet again, and Julian knew one of Rami's looks could say a thousand words.

She chuckled softly. "I wouldn't mind a ride to the shelter, though, if it's not too much trouble."

"Of *course*," Rami said gently. "Anything. Anything at all."

"Your *friend* can come," she said, and Julian smirked at the teasing note in her voice.

"Melissa," Rami warned.

"What? I've never heard you even hint at a romantic interest, and here you are with a *man* in your house! You've been sitting on a secret."

Julian could practically *hear* Rami purse their lips. "Well, my dear, it seems I'm not the only one."

"You've got me there," she said. "I really thought it would be different this time." Then she paused. "Never mind all that. We can discuss it in our next session."

Rami cleared their throat. "I look forward to hearing the whole story."

She hummed quietly. "I think I'll miss your little birds. I'm ready when you are."

Rami was silent for a moment, and Julian strained his ears.

"Well, look at that," they uttered quietly. Another moment passed before they asked, "Do you have anything you can take with you?"

A pause. Melissa must've shaken her head because she said, "I left without even thinking. I didn't bring anything. Not even my wallet, because I paid for the taxi on the app."

Julian frowned at that, and waved his hand. A duffle bag full of clothes and necessities appeared beside the back door.

A long moment passed before Rami and Melissa finally came out of the office, and she smiled kindly at him. It made his throat ache.

"Nice to meet you," she said, and stuck her hand out. "I wish it was under better circumstances."

"Likewise," he said. "Would you like me to drive? I can be

the official chauffeur of the evening. At your service," he said, with a bow that made him wince. How stupid of him—

But she giggled, so it was alright.

"That would be lovely, thank you."

Rami's eyes were a little shiny, and they cleared their throat before opening the back door. "After you, m'lady," they said, voice tight.

Melissa went out the door first, and Julian followed behind after picking up the duffle. Had he ever driven a car before? No. But it couldn't be that hard, could it? Besides, he had magic on his side that he wasn't afraid to use.

It wasn't until he slid the duffle into the trunk that she paused and asked, "What's that?"

Julian's cheeks flushed. "I hope you don't mind. My… sister comes to stay with us sometimes, and this is just a few of her belongings she's left here over the years. I figured you might be around the same size."

It was a lie. Quite a complicated one, because Julian didn't have sisters, unless you counted every single demon that'd been created alongside him. And he didn't, for the record.

Rami's eyes were shiny again, and even Melissa cleared her throat.

"That is so very kind of you," she said. "The shelter usually has items, though—"

"Consider these all yours," Julian said, and shut the trunk. "I do."

"Well," she said, voice scratchy from the tears he saw welling in her eyes. "Thank you."

"Of course," he said, and opened the back door for her.

She slid into the seat, and when he closed the door, Rami was there.

"Thank you," they said, and—

Hugged him.

Julian sucked in a breath filled with the clean cotton and

floral scent of Rami, and squeezed his arms around the angel. "Of course," he repeated.

Melissa directed him from the backseat. She knew her way there, and that saddened him, too.

Rami was unusually quiet as Julian navigated the city, directing magic to assist him when he needed it. Eventually, they pulled up outside a nondescript building with an iron gate out back.

Julian popped the trunk with the lever by his left foot, and then… waited.

"Would you like me to come with?" Rami asked.

"Actually, you're not allowed to," she said softly. "But thank you." She hesitated with a hand against the door. "I'll let you know when I'd like to resume my regular appointments."

"Melissa," Rami said. "I'm here, anytime. Even for just a simple phone call. No charge, of course."

She sniffled and nodded. "Thank you."

"Be safe," they said, and with a final nod she pushed open the door and collected her bag from the back.

They waited as she approached the gate.

Julian watched her hit the buzzer, and a few seconds later a kindly older woman and a large, tough-looking man hurried her through the gate.

Rami released an audible sigh as the gate was locked and secured, their hands tightening around the arm rest.

"She'll be okay," Julian promised.

"It's just not fair. It never is," Rami muttered, and Julian put the car in drive before pulling out of the lot. A bit of magic assisted him, but he'd never admit it.

Julian knew what they meant, remembering what they'd said about Atticus. How they hadn't been able to help their friend. And now Melissa.

Julian understood now better than ever just what Rami had meant.

"I'm sorry," Julian said.

There was a moment of silence, nothing but the sound of the tires against the asphalt of the road. "For what?" Rami asked finally.

"I don't know," Julian confessed. "Sorry it has to be this way, I guess."

"It's not your fault."

"I know. Doesn't make me any less sorry, though."

"Well, like you said, she'll be okay. She'll be safe at the shelter, and once she files for the restraining order…"

Rami paused, and Julian didn't want to push.

"Yeah," they agreed, but it didn't feel like enough.

The ride was quiet, headlights from other cars shining through the windshield.

"You know how to drive now?" Rami asked.

Julian chuckled, though he struggled to find levity in the situation. "Not entirely."

Rami pursed their lips, but let it go until they reached the townhome. "Funny how people keep showing up on my doorstep hurt," Rami said as they unlocked the door. Their voice didn't sound like they found it very funny at all.

Julian grimaced, but smoothed out his expression before Rami faced them again.

"Guess you're just a safe person," Julian offered, wanting the ground to swallow him whole.

How was he supposed to do what Hell expected of him when Julian felt like *this*? *This*, meaning… soft, remorseful. Julian was putty for this angel. He hated what he was sent here to do—how could he go through with it?

Rami scoffed and poured themself a glass of water, clearly too keyed up to consider bed yet, no matter how late the hour.

"I just… I don't understand how the police can do *nothing*. They aren't even willing to protect her!" they said.

"That was her call," Julian reminded him. "The restraining order will—"

"It's just a piece of paper. And you heard her, she'll have to go through a court process first. There's just so much red tape, so much concern about following the right processes instead of protecting a real person." Rami sneered, shaking their head.

And Julian, unfortunately, saw his last chance.

The temptation was right within reach.

He could press this, like a bruise, poke at the hurt until Rami did something so selfish…

If it worked… Julian would be able to stay on Earth with Rami. He wouldn't have to leave, and Rami would never be the wiser. Rami could show them more about Earth and Julian could *stay*.

Melissa's husband deserved much worse than whatever the human's justice system would do, anyway.

It would solve all his problems, this temptation.

Nevertheless, he felt sick as he said, "They might not be willing to do anything, but… *we* could."

Rami's pacing halted, and he slowly turned to face Julian, bracing themself on the kitchen island.

"I'm not sure I understand what you're implying," Rami said tightly.

Julian swallowed and tried to put on a brave face. "I'm not implying anything. I'm *suggesting*… we take care of the problem ourselves."

Rami shook their head. "Absolutely not. We are forbidden to meddle in human affairs."

"You're literally a therapist," Julian drawled.

"I'm a *researcher!*" Rami argued.

"Cutting it a little close there, wouldn't you say?" Julian

retorted sharply, unsure why when he didn't even want to do this in the first place. "I know it bothers you. That he can just walk away from this, while Melissa is the one who's afraid and alone."

"She's not alone. She has me, and the DV shelter will take care of her." Rami sounded as if they were trying to convince themself.

"Yeah, but she can't stay there forever. Like you said, the restraining order is just a piece of paper. If he violates it, they'll slap him with a fine and he'll pay it and his life will go on. And you…" Julian sucked in a breath. "You won't be able to protect her forever. Not so long as that asshole's out there," he argued, waving a hand toward the windows.

Rami's gaze snapped in that direction as if he expected the very subject of their conversation to be on the other sides of the panes.

Their voice was stiff as they said, "It is unfortunate that humans have let their world turn into this. However, it is not my prerogative—"

"Oh, *fuck* your prerogative," Julian hissed, annoyed with Rami's moral superiority. "You're an *angel*—aren't you supposed to protect humans? How is doing nothing protecting that one?" He motioned to the back door, where they'd walked Melissa to the car. "You can save her."

"What do you suggest I do?" Rami snapped, back ramrod-straight as they wheeled on the demon. "What is it?"

"We take care of him," Julian said.

"Be. Specific," Rami bit out, teeth gritted.

"Do what the cops won't. Make it so he can't hurt her again."

"And how, exactly, do you suggest *we* do such a thing?" they already knew the answer.

Julian's heart was thundering in his chest. "I think you already know," Julian whispered.

Rami's brows furrowed as their gaze searched Julian's. Their eyes were gray, stormy, with the fury of emotions in their depths.

Then they… nodded. "I see. I think you're quite right."

Then Rami shrugged, and Julian's jaw dropped as their wings unfurled.

They were flawless. Shiny, pure-white perfection, with veins of silver visible beneath the thinner layers of feather, of which there were few. No, this angel's wings were thick as clouds and probably just as soft, aside from the eyes that blinked eerily at him from between the feathers.

Their halo was blinding, silver and beautiful and hard to look at.

Their skin matched, shining beneath the low lighting of the living room.

And despite the way his stomach sank, he couldn't help but think, *we'd look beautiful together.* Silver and gold.

Then the angel snapped their wings, and they were gone.

Julian's stomach dropped.

He stared at the space the angel had just occupied, now glaringly empty.

Oh fuck.

Julian carded one hand through his hair, then both, tugging on the strands.

Oh *fuck.*

Julian had done it: the final temptation.

All Rami had to do was commit a truly selfish act and Julian would be dragged back to Hell. His boss would congratulate him on a job well done, solidify his position on Earth, and then Julian could return here.

To Rami.

All he had to do was wait.

So why did he already regret it?

24
RELIGIOUS EXPERIENCES

Rami reappeared in the backyard of their client's home, Julian's words ringing through their ears.

They hesitated. Rami knew this wasn't a good idea. Knew there would possibly be repercussions. Knew the last thing they should do was listen to a demon...

But it wasn't just a demon. It was *Julian*.

Julian, who had so much kindness in him, who'd been dancing and laughing in Rami's arms not even hours ago. Julian, who'd made up a sibling just so Melissa would have something of her own at the shelter while she went through this awful situation.

They gritted their teeth. If only she'd been honest with them from the start of their sessions. How could she keep something so terrible from them? So many things made sense now... an abusive, narcissistic husband was the last damning puzzle piece.

Make it so he can't hurt her again.

It was wrong. Rami had never done this before, no matter the victim, for a reason.

But Julian was right.

The human justice system was fucked. They wouldn't protect her.

But Rami could.

This time, Rami would save her. Do what they hadn't done for Atticus, all those years ago.

Rami waved a hand over the lock, hearing it click as it opened beneath their vein of magic.

They stepped through the door, adjusting their wings to fit before closing it rather soundly.

Just as expected, the human male came barreling down the stairs, a bat held in one fist.

The knuckles of that fist were red, irritated.

He only hesitated when he skidded into the kitchen to see a literal angel.

The eyes on Rami's wings blinked, seeing and feeling more than Rami usually could. They felt the human's emotions: confusion and anger and disbelief, and amongst it all, not an ounce of regret concerning the bruise he'd left on his wife's cheek, despite the ache in his knuckles.

"This is a dream," Rami said, and snapped their fingers.

Their vein of magic pulsed again, a flutter through the air, barely felt.

The human dropped like a sack of potatoes, and Rami softened the blow with a bit of magic before reappearing the human on the couch.

They pulled open the side drawer next to the refrigerator. Inside, an envelope appeared. Then with a snap of fingers, Rami was at the human's side.

"Oh, look," Rami drawled to the human, making sure their words reached him even in the deep sleep. "You've gotten a promotion. I know how much you love the cold weather—" Melissa had actually stated what a *baby* her husband was during the winter months. "—so you'll accept this research assistant position in the Arctic. After you've settled things with Melissa, adhering to the restraining order and the divorce, you will give her the house and move on. Of course, your travel will include a very inconvenient trip. I see a lot of airport delays and lost luggage in your future. Once you get there, your choices are yours, but you'll leave Melissa alone, and then you won't bother her ever again."

Rami waved their hand, solidifying their intent—protecting Melissa.

The man would be fine. And Rami still didn't feel it was fair that this man would move on with his life while Melissa would be dealing with the trauma from his actions for the rest of hers.

But at least he'd never hurt her again, and she could heal. She'd get the closure she needed from this man and begin anew, without him.

Was it wrong of them to manipulate this human? Possibly.

What was their other option? Stay out of it and let the human authorities mishandle the entire situation? Let Melissa get hurt again?

That, to Rami, was unacceptable. They weren't letting another person get hurt when they had the power to stop it. This would *not* end like Atticus's story.

Rami gazed down at the human man once more, the eyes on their wings attuned to the newfound energy within him: peace—even if he didn't deserve it—and yes, that *was* guilt as well, for how he'd treated Melissa.

Rami nodded to themself. Good. This story would have a better ending—they'd make sure of it.

Satisfied, Rami magicked themself back home. To Julian.

Julian, who was pacing in the middle of the kitchen. At Rami's presence, he froze, glancing around as if he couldn't believe Rami had returned.

"You're here," Julian announced slowly. His hair was a

mess between his horns, as if he'd been scraping his hands through it.

Rami felt it all, his worry and concern, flooded with a healthy dose of guilt.

"I'm here," he said, again, confusion filling his expression. "We're both here."

Rami sniffed and lifted his head high, wings twitching with indignation. "It appears so. Why does this puzzle you?"

"Did you do it?" Julian asked. He rushed over, placing both hands on Rami's shoulders, fingers squeezing tight as if he feared Rami would disappear right from under him.

"I took care of it."

Julian's expression crumbled, head dropping, and he sucked in a breath. He sighed, all the tension leaking out of his shoulders until he slumped down to press his forehead against Rami's chest. "You didn't kill him."

"Of course not," Rami scoffed. "He'll adhere to the restraining order and accept the divorce without argument, and he won't bother Melissa any longer."

A noise was caught in Julian's throat, relief and maybe shock. "Thank god," he whispered, and something in his voice made Rami's heart skip. He picked his head up to meet Rami's eyes. "Do you think she'll be happy with this outcome?" Julian asked.

Was the demon considering someone else's happiness? Rami's lips threatened to curl.

"I think she'll be safe." Now, all those sessions where Melissa seemed distant, skirting around something that Rami couldn't figure out, made sense. "She'll be relieved he's gone, I think," they admitted.

"Good. That's good, Feathers." Julian heaved a sigh.

His reaction touched something in Rami. "You thought I was going to kill him?" they asked.

Julian swallowed, expression distraught. "The thought crossed my mind, yeah."

"Is that what you wanted to do?" Rami tilted their head to the side, studying him.

"What if I did?" Julian asked, stepping away, crossing his arms. "What if I did want him to die for hurting her?"

Rami's halo was casting a soft, white glow across those furrowed features.

Julian was beautiful.

Rami stepped closer, and closer, unsure of this too-big feeling in their chest but giving into it all the same. Julian stepped back, and back, until he bumped into the kitchen island.

They paused scant inches away. Julian's breath had gone quiet, and he gripped the edge of the counter behind him.

"So you care about her? Why?"

Julian sneered, rolling his eyes before his expression dipped into a frown.

Rami didn't know why it mattered to them, but it did. Did Julian care about Melissa just because Rami did? Or was his moral compass stronger than he wanted Rami to believe?

"I wouldn't say that," Julian murmured, letting out an emphasized scoff. "But no one deserves that."

"What?" Rami questioned further.

"To be…" Julian's hands lifted from the counter to fill the space between them, motioning as if he couldn't grasp the words he needed. "Hurt. By someone you love," he finally said. "That's terrible. No one deserves that."

Rami hummed. So he did care. At the very least, he wanted to avenge her, which was a form of caring, they supposed.

"It felt good to protect her," Rami admitted. "I wish I had done it twenty lifetimes ago."

Julian's expression softened. "For Atticus?"

Rami nodded, throat sticking with a swell of emotion. "Yeah," they croaked. "I wish I had saved him."

Julian leaned forward, wrapping his arms around Rami, and they sank into it, breathing deep of the delicious, cocoa smell of this demon. Their arms circled his waist, and they held him close.

A few moments passed as Rami collected themself, mourning a friend and hoping that friend had forgiven them by now.

Finally, when their voice wouldn't betray them, Rami said, "I think you care more than you want me to believe."

"And why's that?" Julian asked, voice muffled in Rami's shoulder.

"You tell me."

To protect himself? From what?

Rami wasn't going to hurt him—

Ah. But maybe Rami had the power to. Because Julian did care. About Rami.

And that scared Julian.

They softened, leaning back, lifting a hand to cup the very cheek they'd kissed earlier. Their silver skin was starkly colored against Julian's human one, and they found themself wondering what it would look like against Julian's demon skin. Gold and silver.

"That was a very sweet thing you did, borrowing clothes from your sister," they said.

Julian's lips quirked, but his eyes were wide as he stared at Rami. "Yeah. Well, she won't be needing them anytime soon."

"I guess she'd need to exist for that, hm?" Rami asked.

"Probably," Julian muttered, gaze dipping to Rami's lips, leaning into their palm.

Maybe a few days ago, the suggestion would've scandalized Rami. Maybe a few days ago, Rami wouldn't have been the one doing the suggesting.

But Julian was *good*. And after a night like tonight, Rami thought they might like the idea of seeking comfort in another person.

Especially if Julian was that person.

They leaned in and kissed him. Julian made the cutest surprised noise in response before melting against them.

His hands lifted from the counter to frame Rami's face, sliding over his shoulders before brushing—

"Your wings," Julian murmured into the kiss and pulled back.

Rami had forgotten. "Sorry, I'll—"

"No!" Julian gasped, and laid a hand against their chest. "I've never seen an angel's wings before. I didn't know they were so…"

"So…?"

"Fluffy," he settled on.

Rami's lips twitched, chest aching. "Fluffy?"

"They look soft," Julian said, shrugging.

"Do you want to touch them?"

Julian's eyes widened, and he nodded.

"Go ahead, then," Rami offered.

They studied Julian's expression as they shifted a wing in his direction, curling around both of their bodies.

His gaze was greedy, taking Rami in, mouth slightly parted and red from their kisses.

Rami shivered as he touched their wing, the sensation like that of someone trailing fingers down their spine.

"They're so silky," Julian mumbled. "They're beautiful. Holy—" He trailed off, and Rami snickered as he corrected with "—cow."

Something in their chest fluttered, too big to fit, too large to put a name to, and they sighed beneath Julian's touch.

"Do the eyes actually… see?"

Rami nodded. "Mostly feelings and emotions, but they're

not, ah, cognizant. So feel the feathers all you want. For now," Rami said quietly. "Because I'm having the urge to have my way with you," they admitted.

Julian's dark gaze flicked up to them. "Is that so?"

"Yes," they said, with no hesitation. "I want to take you to bed."

Julian swayed toward them and it was more intoxicating than any of the drinks they'd had together earlier that night.

"Well, Feathers, what are you waiting for?" Julian purred.

Rami's nostrils flared, and then they were gripping Julian's hand and leading him upstairs.

There was no room for awkwardness or uncertainty in that moment.

They felt empowered after stepping up, protecting someone they cared about. They could be in control of their life, instead of just letting things happen to them.

Rami wanted Julian.

And they were going to have him.

Emboldened, Rami pulled him close, kissing him and wrapping both their arms and their wings around him.

"Like a cloud," Julian muttered into the kiss before their tongues twined.

Rami hummed and felt the growing length of Julian through his pants, just like they'd felt him earlier, too, on the dance floor.

He'd been so open with them, accepting their affections with not even a shrug. In fact, his eyes had lit up, softening every time Rami touched him in front of their new friends.

Their heart did that thing again and they felt like crying from the force of their affection, but instead they pulled away and pushed Julian down on the bed.

"Had your fill yet?"

Julian arched a brow. "No, but I have a feeling whatever you have in store for me will be just as fun."

Rami grinned down at him. "Tell me if it's silly," they began.

"It won't be," he promised, and Rami believed them.

So with a flick of their finger, their halo floated from above their head to hover between them. Julian's eyes widened, mouth gaping. "That's so cool!" he cried.

Rami chuckled and brought their other hand up, spreading their hands apart, and as they did so, the halo widened, too.

"Hands," Rami asked, and Julian gaped.

"Really now, Feathers?" he drawled, but he held them up, completely trusting, pushing his wrists together.

With a swipe of their finger through the air, the halo lowered, circling Julian's hands before settling around his wrists.

A snap made the halo tighten comfortably, and Julian gasped as it touched him.

"I think I expected it to burn," he admitted.

Rami chuckled. "Silly demon," they said, softer than intended. "Ready?"

"For what?"

Rami grinned as they drew their finger in a line, and the halo followed their command, lifting Julian's arms above his head and trapping his hands and wrists to the bed.

His breath caught, eyes darkening. "Feathers, you've got surprises up your sleeve," he teased, but the breathless tone belied his confidence.

"I just might," they agreed, and straddled his waist.

The bulge of him pressed between their legs, and Rami swallowed, arousal sliding through them, hot and divine.

"This has been a fantasy of mine," Rami confessed, and pressed their palms into the bed on either side of Julian's biceps.

Rami rocked their hips, grinding down on Julian, the

zipper of their pants caught just right against them, cunt wet already just from the idea of acting on one of their fantasies.

"Having a demon at your mercy?" he retorted.

"Using my halo like this," Rami said. "It feels… forbidden, doesn't it?"

Julian's gaze was locked on Rami's lips. "It does," he agreed in a way that Rami suspected meant he would agree to anything right then. But then his eyes snapped up. "What else do you want to do to me?"

Rami used a bit of magic to vanish Julian's shirt. He grinned up at them and arched his back in a delightful curve, rolling his hips into Rami and making them gasp.

They directed the halo to tighten in warning, and Julian paused, hips falling back to the bed.

"Well, that's nifty, isn't it," Julian said, breathless.

"I quite think so," Rami answered, and leaned down, pressing a kiss to Julian's lips. It was supposed to be just a tease, a taste, but they went back for more, mouths slipping together easily, fitting like they were meant to.

Julian groaned into the kiss, vibrating against their lips, and Rami shivered, breaking it with a soft smack. "I want to ride you."

Julian's eyes fluttered shut, and he nodded urgently. "Best idea you've ever had, Feathers."

Rami breathed softly. "And you'll tell me if you start to feel otherwise?"

Julian's chuckle was dark and decadent. "I've got an angel in my lap; I don't think we're going to have an issue."

But Rami waited, staring down at him until his brow furrowed. "I'll tell you if I want you to stop."

"Good," Rami said, and kissed him again. They put all their trust and affection into it, savoring the taste of Julian as if he'd be taken away, which was a silly notion.

He's mine.

The thought struck through them, electric and hot, warmth slipping down their spine to settle between their legs, and they rolled into the pressure before sliding down Julian's body.

Their wings twitched as their feet met the floor, expanding only a bit to balance them as they bent over, mouthing at Julian's flat stomach, his hips.

Taking their time, they kissed and nipped at his skin, baring him inch by inch. They bypassed his cock completely, though when they freed it, it was already beading at the tip, tantalizing and teasing.

It took herculean effort not to lower their mouth to him, to move past it and strip his pants off.

They could've magicked those off as well, but it was especially arousing to bare Julian themself, to reveal every bit of his skin, knowing that their own halo was keeping him from interfering.

A dark delight shivered up their spine at the thought, and they wasted no time in stripping themselves, watching Julian, who was arching his neck, keeping his eyes on them as they removed their clothes.

The shirt had to be magicked off, due to their wings, but—

"Are they going to watch me the whole time?" Julian asked, and Rami realized his attention had trailed to their left wing. "The eyes," he clarified.

Rami snickered. "They're not a separate entity; they're all me. Do they weird you out?"

"Not if they're you," Julian said, relaxing down on the bed, gaze flicking back to their bared skin. "Especially not if they're you," he repeated, softer.

Rami melted at the emotion in his tone, and crawled back atop him. They adjusted so Julian was notched between their folds, and his groan was music to their ears.

"Fuck, I can't believe you look like this. You're magnificent," he said.

Rami glanced down, noting their shiny silvery skin against Julian's pale human skin. It was quite a contrast, and they skated their fingers across the plane of his chest, raising goose bumps in their wake.

Even as an angel, with heavenly forces at their back, they had never felt more empowered than when they were with Julian.

He made them feel… special, in a way. And after a lifetime —a hundred lifetimes—of existing in the humans' shadow, it was downright intoxicating.

Rami wanted to show Julian just how much they appreciated being in the spotlight for once.

So they rolled their hips, and Julian tilted his head back with a hum of pleasure. Rami followed the long, lean line of his body with their gaze, appreciating the flex of his arms as he tested the bond of the halo.

"You're going to ruin me," Julian murmured.

"That's the idea," Rami promised, and rocked their hips again, and again.

His cock slid alongside their clit, and Rami released a shaky breath, their arousal slick between their lips, making the glide against Julian slippery and smooth.

"T-touch yourself," Julian asked. "Let me watch you get yourself ready. *Please*," he tacked on, begging for Rami.

A demon, begging an angel.

Rami had no choice but to indulge him, and they rolled to the side, slipping a hand between their legs. They knew their face was red, embarrassment threatening to ruin the moment, but they also knew they had nothing to be ashamed of. Julian wanted this as much as Rami did, was *begging* for them.

And they very much liked it.

They liked knowing Julian was desperate for them, so for that reason they drew their left leg up, blocking his line of sight, and kept the halo pinned to the mattress. Their breath went sharp and weak as they brushed a finger through their arousal, dragging the slick up to coat their clit. They stroked the pad of their finger over themself, similar to the way Julian's tongue had, and their breath caught as they shifted their hips into the movement, giving into every urge they had just so Julian would feel like he was missing something.

"Angel, come on," Julian whined. *Whined.*

And angel. *Used like a human endearment.*

"Just—just a moment, dear," Rami breathed, and slid their hand lower, pressing a finger at their entrance before slipping in.

It was never at the perfect angle like Julian could accomplish, but it was an experience nonetheless, feeling themself tighten around their own finger. They moaned, adding a second digit when the first became too easy, and curled their hips up, wishing they could manage something *better.*

Julian cursed, and Rami knew that something better was right beside them, waiting eagerly, and Rami hummed.

"Be good, or I'll—I'll finish this myself," Rami said.

And even though they stuttered through the command, it had the desired effect. Julian swallowed, and in the silence of the room, so close to each other, Rami heard it loud and clear. He stopped writhing against the sheets, and the only sounds from then on were Rami's own. Their fingers in their cunt; the slick, wet glide of them; their own breaths, growing sharper and needier with each thrust.

By the time they added a third, even they were growing impatient, so finally—bless it—*finally,* Rami withdrew their fingers.

"Oh, that's different," Rami said, watching the way the

gloss shimmered on their hand. It had a silver sheen to it, just like the rest of them.

They went to wipe them on the bedspread, but Julian bucked, huffing out, "Don't!", and Rami paused.

Their gaze trailed up and Julian's dark eyes were wide and intent. "Give them to me," he said, wetting his lips.

Warmth inflamed Rami from the inside out as they straddled Julian once again, settling over him, grinding their cunt along the length of his cock, a promise.

Then they lifted their hand to Julian's lips, and he parted them, opening for Rami without hesitation. He even arched his neck, lifting his head to take them faster, and his eyes fluttered shut as he sucked at their fingers, at Rami's silver slick coating them.

Arousal struck them like a bolt at the sight, at Julian's tangible *want*.

He laved at them just like he had Rami's cock, and—

If Rami didn't have him inside them, they were going to perish.

Utterly and irrevocably.

So they lifted up on their knees and dragged their fingers from Julian's mouth, and though he tried to follow, he realized what they were intending faster, and whined.

"Please, please, come on," Julian groaned, and then lifted his head to stare at them. "M'your first," he said, dazed gaze flicking to their own and then back down to where their bodies would join.

"Virginity is a human-made concept," Rami informed him.

He shuddered beneath them, and they smirked, pausing with their hand wrapped around Julian, brushing the head of him against their core. "Unless you like the idea, of course."

Julian's lips parted, sucking in a deeper breath, and Rami's lips twitched with confidence.

"You *do* like the idea," they declared, and let gravity do the work.

The head of him popped inside Rami and they stilled, soaking in the experience for the first time.

Julian cursed, arms flexing as he tried to touch them, but couldn't, and bit down on his lip.

Rami's hands pressed into Julian's chest as they slowly lowered themself, taking him deeper. They retained their composure, even though their eyes wanted to roll back in their head. Julian felt so perfect, filling them exactly how they wanted, reaching places Rami could never manage with their own fingers.

Once the back of their thighs were flush with Julian's, their cunt squeezed, adjusting to the sensation. "What is it, exactly, that you like about the idea?" Rami managed to ask, grinding their hips down for emphasis. "Being the first? Ruining me for anyone else?"

Because he was well on his way. Rami couldn't imagine this with another person. A pleased noise escaped them as they rocked against Julian's pelvis.

Julian shook his head. "Never ruined," he blurted, head falling back to the mattress, hips jostling them above him, stirring his cock deep inside them.

They tightened the halo in warning, their nails digging into his chest, until Julian relaxed again, cock twitching so forcefully inside them that they felt it.

"I like being the first to show you this. To… to know that I taught you these things."

"Oh," Rami said, mind blanking as they pressed into their knees, lifting up only to sink back down, pleasure striking them just right.

"I like that you've never felt this way before, that I'm the one making you—feel it," Julian panted, words stuttering as Rami moved again.

"I haven't," Rami agreed. "I haven't felt this before."

Rami wondered if Julian heard the double meaning in their words, the sentiment going unsaid.

"Good," Julian rumbled, and the possessive inflection echoed something in Rami.

A tiny, blooming part of Rami wondered if they'd secretly been waiting for this, for Julian. Because they were glad it was Julian showing them this, letting them explore and learn and *feel*.

Feel the drag of him inside them, his breaths inflating the chest beneath their hands, the hush of their wings as they used them to balance. Their thighs burned, but the pleasure burned better, and so Rami chased it atop Julian.

The rhythm wasn't *easy* to regulate at first, because each sensation was brand new. And it was good, so fucking good that Rami wasn't certain if they wanted to roll into the pressure against their clit or lift up just so Julian could fill them again.

Julian attempted to lift his hands and groaned. Knowing he had no choice but to lie there and let them *play* gave Rami a certain freedom.

But when they let their weight sink onto Julian again, they leaned forward and sought his lips, a hand pressing into the bed beside Julian's arm. Their mouths slid together, locked, tongues brushing as they shared a breath, two, three.

"I wanna touch you," Julian panted when they broke apart. "Please," he added again, and Rami *loved* hearing that word uttered so politely from such filthy lips.

And suddenly Rami wanted nothing more than Julian's hands on them, so with a swipe of their finger they loosened the halo, and it floated to situate itself above their head again. It settled into place like a lock of hair, and then it was forgotten.

Julian lowered his arms and the first place he touched

Rami was their thighs, framing them on the outside before dragging his palms over them.

His hands were warm against their skin, fingers digging in and squeezing before shifting an inch in another direction and groping again.

"You're so fucking shiny," he murmured, and Rami chuckled softly, gasping at the way their muscles tightened around Julian with their laugh and dropping their head to watch Julian touch them, the silver light reflecting against their skin.

He slid his hands up just as Rami began moving again, grasping their hips.

Julian began to rock his hips with them, and tilted them in a way that made their breath catch. The angle made them stiffen, a moan breaking over the clench of their teeth.

Rami wanted to feel that *again,* so they followed Julian's lead, chasing their pleasure with him until his hands fell away.

"You feel so *fucking* good," Rami groaned.

They couldn't believe they had waited so long.

But that was just the pleasure talking. They'd been waiting for Julian—they knew it.

Knew it as certain as they felt the swell of an orgasm, a wave, building in height, each rock of their hips filling it a bit more, close to bursting. They sensed it looming overhead, but knew if they stared too hard it would take forever to crash.

"I'm so close," Rami said, nails digging into Julian's chest. His hands were on their thighs again, possibly leaving bruises in the shape of his fingers, until one of them lifted, drifting between their thighs to stroke their clit.

Rami let their head fall back, hips jerking out of the rhythm as they sought the crash in Julian's lap, his cock filling them again and again.

"I want my novel experience, Julian," Rami told him, voice uneven from the exertion. Their thighs were shaking, but they melted into it like warm water. "I want you to come with me."

"I'm with you, angel," Julian promised, and worked them in his hands like putty. "I will, I will."

Everything was so sensitive; everything felt so good. Their clit between Julian's fingers and the way his length brushed over that sweet spot inside of Rami.

"Oh, fuck," Julian muttered, head tilting back.

Rami went taut as the wave crested, their rhythm stuttered, and it crashed.

They cried out, quivering around Julian, their voice cracking as Julian thrust up beneath them, chasing the squeeze of them in two, three more strokes before—

He came, following right after them into the balmy depths of the swirling sensations, spilling inside them.

They stayed tense together at that peak, nails digging and hands tightening and mouths agape, before they sank together, riding out the waves in lazy, messy movements.

Rami managed to lean down and slot their mouths into one with weak accuracy. They chuckled into it, groaning as that sent them both on another spiral.

Finally, they melted together, and Rami dropped their head to Julian's chest.

His hand rested on their back and Rami threaded their fingers through Julian's hair, the strands like silk.

Rami listened to the steady, slowing beat of Julian's heart through his chest.

They floated in the afterglow like this, and Rami wondered, for all intents and purposes, *was* this *the cuddling Julian really wanted that first night?*

Rami liked it *very* much.

"Rami," Julian murmured a while later, chest still shifting with each breath.

"Hm?" they asked, so sated they could barely open their eyes.

"I think I just had a religious experience."

Rami huffed out a laugh, and Julian gasped, still inside them.

"Guess I'm not the only one having *firsts* tonight, then," they retorted, heart too big for their chest.

25
DELIVERANCE

Julian was still asleep when Rami woke, for once.

Rami was curled into him, an arm over his waist while Julian sprawled across the bed. Their wings and halo had long dissolved into Rami's human form.

Their lips twitched at the sight of him, disheveled with sleep and twice as adorable.

Something wiggled loose in their chest.

Rami studied him in the low light, the sun barely giving the room a soft glow. It must still be so early, but Rami knew they wouldn't be able to fall back asleep.

Not with this new feeling in their chest they were too afraid to name.

They tried to slip from the bed without disturbing Julian, and at first they thought it worked.

But just as they slid their feet to the floor, arms curled around their waist and Julian hummed.

"S'too early."

"Go back to sleep. I think I'll get some work done. Reply to some emails. I'll bring you coffee in a bit, how's that sound?"

"Okay," Julian murmured, and gave them one last squeeze before letting them free.

Julian was already nuzzling himself back to sleep in Rami's pillow, taking up far more of the bed than was required.

Rami smiled as they practically floated down the stairs, making quick work of their own coffee.

The morning sun was cheerful as it shone prisms through the windows, and Rami sat at their desk with a smile.

It'd only take a moment to reply to a few emails and send the automated texts to confirm the upcoming appointments.

Melissa's emergency had only reminded Rami that the world kept moving even when they didn't get to see their clients. They were still going about their days, and Rami needed to get back to work helping them get through it.

It was time for their little vacation to end. Even if Julian was still around, he could busy himself with something while Rami was with a client.

They spared a moment of heartache that Melissa wouldn't be attending the sessions for a while, and made a note to themself to check in soon.

Even though they knew that damned husband wouldn't be laying his hands on her again, Rami still worried.

Their brow was furrowed as they remembered the bruise on her cheek.

Rami still had good to do; they couldn't lay around with Julian forever.

Rami rescheduled and confirmed appointments with a new vigor, which didn't take long at all.

They would resume in three days, just in time for the new work week to begin.

Rami would just have to find somewhere to put Julian. Maybe they could send him to the grocery store.

Their lips quirked at the idea. They'd give it two days before Julian ended up on the news for assaulting some human.

Rami was staring into space, laughing to themself, when they heard a coo and a tap on the window panes.

A bird was sitting on the other side. A dove, to be specific, and it was holding a letter in its beak.

Their heart dropped.

"Oh dear," Rami said. They'd forgotten all about the correspondence they'd sent to Heaven, asking after Julian.

Took them long enough, they thought, even as they also wrestled the guilt of essentially checking up on Julian.

They rolled out their chair before crossing the office and pushing the left pane of the window open.

"Hello there," Rami said softly to the little bird.

They gently accepted the envelope and stroked the back of a finger along the dove's head before it flew away in a flutter of white.

"Now, let's see what we've got here," Rami murmured.

They were more interested to see what Heaven said than they were concerned about the demon's purpose now.

Warmth flashed through them at the memory of Julian whining beneath them.

How absolutely inappropriate to be thinking of such a thing while holding Heaven's property, and yet Rami found themself not caring.

They plucked open the envelope and pulled out the letter with silver scrawl on it. They read it aloud as they walked back to their desk.

"Thank you for reaching out—blah, blah— the demon in question is in fact Julian from the Sixth Region of Hell, previously from the Seventh, blah, blah…"

A word caught their gaze as their eyes skipped ahead, and they paused, one hand on the desk.

Temptations.

Rami blinked, then started from the beginning to absorb all the context.

The letter read, "Current job description: Temptations. Current location: Earthbound. Status: Active."

Rami didn't breathe for a long moment, reading the letter again. And a third time. Then a fourth.

Julian was a temptation demon. Not a messenger.

The assignment began on the date Julian first arrived. And apparently it ended…

Tonight.

Their hand tightened on the desk, and they sank into their seat, legs going weak.

Demons usually tempted humans. So what was Julian doing here, with Rami?

He'd hardly left their side the whole week.

Was that Julian's game? This whole time? Showing up hurt on their doorstep? Latching onto them, refusing to let go?

They buried their head in their hands.

It all made so much sense now!

The frivolous magic, the gambling, the—

Their head snapped up.

Was it *all* an act?

Rami's chest caved in, deflating as all the air rushed out of them as if they'd been kicked in the solar plexus.

Had Julian seduced them for a *temptation?*

Their throat closed up, tears threatening to well at the realization.

Of course that was it.

Rami let out a bitter, airy chuckle.

Of course.

Of course the first person Rami let themself care about in *centuries…* was only there for an assignment.

Rami was Julian's assignment.

They dropped their head, staring down at the letter as if

the words would rearrange themselves into something that would make more sense. Anything else.

How could Julian do this? How could he just—just—

Was none of it real?

They wanted to laugh and couldn't find the energy.

Rami *knew* better, was the thing. They knew better than to let anyone in. Angels on Earth didn't get to have *friends* or *lovers* because they all *died.* Rami outlived them all, forced to mourn them for the rest of their existence.

They didn't know why they'd thought befriending a demon would be any better.

They shook their head.

Fuck! No wonder Julian hadn't wanted to leave once he felt better. Not because he feared he'd be hurt again, or because he had nowhere to go, but because if he left, he wouldn't be able to tempt Rami. And with only a handful of days to do so…

They choked back tears and shut their laptop more harshly than it deserved, patting it once to apologize. Then they shoved the letter out of sight, into the drawer, and slammed it.

They didn't apologize to the desk.

They sipped their coffee to wash away the lump in their throat, then leaned back in the chair and looked at the ceiling.

Rami didn't even know what to do from here.

None of Julian's temptations had worked, and part of them felt some form of pride at that fact.

But now what?

Just then, Rami heard the house settle from Julian's waking steps.

Rami sat up straighter, rubbed their shaky hands against their thighs, and stood.

Then they sat back down.

They weren't even sure what to do. How to act. All they knew was the crater of hurt in their chest.

The stairs creaked as Julian came down to the first floor and Rami's breath ran short, heart thumping beneath their ribs, thunder in their ears.

"Rami?" Julian asked, and stopped at the entrance to the office.

Rami's gaze snapped to him and—how fucking dare he look so comfy and soft and, and lovable, in nothing but a pair of pajama pants and one of Rami's pullovers.

It hung to his mid-thigh.

It made him look adorable.

"Are you okay?" Julian asked. "Can I come in?"

That didn't make sense. Why would Julian care about Rami's boundaries if he was here only to tempt them? Was he that good an actor?

"I—" they began, and then stopped. "Why are you here?"

Julian's expression went guarded, hand tightening against the door jamb.

"What?"

"Why are you here? On Earth? Really?" Rami asked.

They knew the answer. And Julian knew.

And as Julian's gaze shuttered, lips turning down into a worried frown, Rami knew that Julian knew they knew.

Did that even make sense?

Rami didn't care.

"I wanted to tell you," he said. "I almost did. Yesterday. But then we were having such a good time and I didn't want to ruin it. And then Melissa. And then…"

Oh my god, Rami thought.

They sat back down. When had they even stood up?

"Of course," Rami whispered. "Trying to talk me into hurting Melissa's husband. That was all part of the temptation."

Julian's lips tightened, and he crossed into the room. Rami didn't tell him to get out. "I hated it, but yes. I saw the opportunity, and I took it. Because if I complete the mission, I'll be able to stay! With you! Here!" Julian moved closer, standing across the desk from them.

Rami shook their head. "What makes you think—"

"I wanted to tell you! I wanted to come clean. But if I don't complete the assignment, I get sent back to Hell. I get put on a waiting list for *centuries* until another Earthside opportunity comes around. So when I saw how distraught you were about Melissa, I... I ran with it. I figured, that guy deserved it, whatever you would do to him. And then I'd get to stay. And we could..."

Rami stared up at him.

"We could what? Live happily ever after? Even knowing this was all a lie?" they asked.

Julian leaned onto the desk, expression pleading. "But it wasn't! That's what I'm saying. It wasn't a lie."

"You showed up on my doorstep *bloody*, asking for help. You're telling me that wasn't part of the plan?"

His lips thinned, a hand lifting to drift over his healed horn. His fingers didn't make contact. "They wanted to make sure you kept me around for a bit. It wasn't my idea," Julian said. "But the rest of it... getting to know you, that—"

Rami turned their head away, biting the inside of their cheek.

"I took the assignment because I wanted to experience Earth. I didn't think I'd meet *you*."

"What does that mean?" Rami bit out.

"Someone so infuriatingly good. Untemptable," Julian said, lips quirking. "I wanted to tell you yesterday because the deadline ends tonight. If I don't complete the assignment, they're going to take me back. So I wanted to tell you I was leaving. I didn't *intend* to finish the assignment. To hell with it."

Rami couldn't even appreciate the humor in the moment.

"But you tried anyway. The final temptation," Rami muttered.

"Yes," Julian whined, running his hands through his hair. His voice cracked on the word and Rami's heart thumped. "I did. Because I'm *selfish*. One last try, because I want to stay here. With you."

"Even if it meant I killed someone?" Rami snapped.

Julian's expression softened. "You weren't going to kill him, Feathers."

"But you didn't know that."

"Yes, I did."

"How?!" Rami shouted, and stood.

"Because you're *you!* You wouldn't hurt a fucking fly," Julian told him.

"Well, it's a good thing you just know me so fucking well!" Rami said, shaking their head. "Then why did you imply it? All your nonsense about making sure he never hurts her again?"

"I…" Julian gnashed his teeth. "I did imply it, fuck. I know I did. I guess because, even if by some miracle the selfishness won and you *did* hurt him, at least…"

"Your assignment would've been complete. You would've got what you wanted."

No matter the cost.

Rami sat back down, the fight going out of them.

"What did you think would happen?" Rami asked.

Julian shook his head. "I don't know. I hadn't figured that out yet. I told myself… maybe you never had to know."

"You hoped you could just stay and play house with me forever?"

Julian chewed on a lip. "Yeah, I guess I did."

"You wanted to build a fake life on a lie?" Rami asked.

"When you put it like that, it—" He shook his head.

"Like what?" Rami bit out. "Like the truth? You showed up here under false pretenses and then tried at every turn to—"

"It was my *job*. What else was I supposed to do?"

"Be a good *person!*" Rami snapped. "Like I thought you were."

"I still *am* that person. Yes, when I arrived, it was with the intent to tempt you, but you're just… not temptable!"

"What about the sex? Was that another temptation?" Rami finally asked, dreading the answer.

Julian rounded the desk and sank to his knees, finding Rami's gaze and refusing to release it.

"When I took you to the sex shop, I was trying to get a rise out of you, yes. Trying to, I don't know, frustrate you, or piss you off. But using sex to tempt you was never and will never be part of the plan."

Rami wanted to believe him.

But how could they?

So much had already been a lie, and Rami hadn't been able to detect it then. It meant nothing that he didn't detect it now. This—Julian, on his knees, apologizing— it could all be just another part of the ruse.

"I *can't* believe you," Rami told him. "I don't trust you."

Julian's expression tightened, his hands lifting to lay on Rami's thighs before pausing, hovering, hesitating. "You don't mean that."

"How am I supposed to trust anything you say ever again when you've lied so thoroughly?"

Their chest ached so viscerally they wanted to reach between their ribs and grip their heart to keep it from seizing.

They stood and paced away from Julian. Couldn't look at him.

"Rami, please," Julian asked, and the vise around their torso tightened.

"Stop," Rami whispered, and ran both hands through their hair, wanting to grasp it from the roots and pull.

When they spun around, Julian was right *there*.

"I love you," he said.

Rami froze, and yet it felt like the world around them kept spinning.

Tears welled and they slammed their eyes shut, hands sliding down to cover their ears so they couldn't hear anymore.

But oh, how they'd wanted to hear those words from someone, anyone at all in the past... forever.

Rami had been so lonely.

And Julian was using it against them.

The realization seemed to shock them back into the moment. They blinked.

The worst part was... They loved him, too.

Julian, this demon sent here to tempt them, to corrupt them, to *lie* to them.

"You know what? You win," Rami said softly, unseeing. "I —I must be corrupt. Otherwise how could I love someone like *you?*"

The quiet after Rami's statement was tangible, the hurt furrow in Julian's brow severe.

They both felt it, the shift, a silent ringing through the air.

Rami had just hurt someone on purpose, the intent behind them exactly what Julian was looking for.

Julian's eyes went wide.

"Rami, wait, I—"

A flash of golden light filled the room where Julian stood.

When it faded, he was gone.

Rami blinked at the spot Julian had just occupied, and sank onto the yellow couch.

26
PROMOTION

Julian's words were torn from his lips as he materialized in Hell.

No, no, no, no!

He blinked at the familiar cream-colored walls of a plain office, and lowered his gaze to a demon sitting in an office chair, wings out, horns on display.

His boss.

"Well, Julian. It seems you managed to complete your assignment."

"Carl, send me back," Julian said, planting his palms on the edge of the desk. "Please."

Carl arched a brow at him, ignored his plea entirely to glance down at a tablet, lips twisting.

"You tempted the untemptable. How ever did you manage it?"

Julian's nostrils flared. That's right. He technically had succeeded, even if he hadn't wanted to.

He'd tempted the angel.

That meant Julian had completed the assignment. He could go back to Earth!

He'd win Rami over eventually. He'd done it once, and he could do it again, this time with no ulterior motives. He could just find Rami again and they could work this out. Together.

So for now, he just had to play along until his position was permanent and he could return.

He took his hands off the edge of the desk and shoved them into his pockets, standing straight like he was right where he was supposed to be.

"Right. Well, I learned it helps if you… befriend the target first. If they trust you…" Julian's chest ached, but he fisted his hands to keep from rubbing at the sore spot. "If they trust you, they're more likely to listen to the temptations."

Carl hummed. "Quite a success for your first assignment. Color me impressed. I think this means I can make your promotion permanent."

Julian nodded, smothering his urgency. "Thank you, sir."

"In fact," Carl said, looking satisfied as he slapped the cover on his tablet shut, "I'll do you one better."

Julian's stomach lurched with nerves. "How so?"

"I'm promoting you to a trainer," he said, leaning back in his chair. "It's simple. You'll train the newly appointed demons on how to tempt. Here. In Hell."

Julian blinked. "But when I took this job, you said—"

"Oh, I know what I said." Carl waved a hand, ring winking in the too-bright light of his office. "This is a much better deal, honestly. More respect; a new, fancier house. Working internet," he drawled.

Julian's eye twitched. "With all due respect, I'd like to remain in my current position."

"With all due respect," Carl sneered, "I don't give a shit. You'll be staying here in Hell, just like the rest of us."

Julian suppressed his anger. "You know I took this position for one reason."

"I do," Carl said, not an ounce of remorse. "I didn't think you'd manage to corrupt an angel, of all people."

"Let me get this right," Julian bit out. "You set me up, hoping I'd fail, hoping to deny me the promotion. But now that I've *earned* said promotion, you're not giving it to me."

"Right on, dickhead," Carl said, smug with power the asshole should've never had.

"You're a miserable old cunt," Julian growled, and planted his hands on the desk, leaning over. "Just because you couldn't trick some poor, unsuspecting human into marrying you, you think everyone deserves to be as miserable as you are."

Carl shrugged, not even showing a hint of give. "Maybe so. Do you feel better now?"

Julian grunted and pushed away from the desk, heading toward the door. There was nothing he could say to change Carl's mind.

He was stuck here.

"You'll be just like me one day, Julian, just wait!" Carl called.

What a selfish, smarmy *bastard*.

Julian slammed the door, the sound echoing down the long, never-ending hallway in one of the many office settings of Hell.

Julian lifted his hands to tangle in his hair, bumping into his horns in the process.

He felt the shorter length, remembered the way it felt for Rami to touch them, and his heart sank at the same time anger flared.

He turned and kicked the door to his boss's office. "Fuck you, Carl!" he shouted.

It did little to curb his frustration, and he—

"Julian?" a familiar voice asked.

Startled, he turned, finding none other than Galen, the Devil of the Seventh Region of Hell. Julian's former boss, before he'd shifted to the Sixth to take the temptation position.

Now he had an asshole for a boss *and* he was stuck here.

"What are you doing here?" Julian asked. It wasn't often that the lead devils visited another region.

"I was here for a meeting," he said, tilting his head at the door behind Julian.

Oh. Julian stepped to the side. "Enjoy," he muttered.

"How's the Sixth Region treating you?" Galen asked, then frowned. "What happened to your horn?"

Julian shot him a look filled with a thousand words, and he winced.

"Ah." Galen stiffened, his gaze trailing to the door before sliding back to Julian. "It looks like something's come up. I can't make my meeting," he said. "Want to walk with me?"

Julian had nothing better to do, and nodded. He shoved his hands into his pockets and walked, wings tucked tight to his back so he and Galen could walk alongside each other.

"How's Maeve?" Julian asked.

Galen got that dopey smile on his face as he glanced over. "Oh, she's great. Wanna say hi?"

"Sure—"

Before Julian could even finish his response, Galen winked them into his office, where Maeve was sitting in his chair behind his big, ornate desk.

"Julian!" she said, and hopped out of the chair, rounding the desk to hug him.

His eyes burned and he swallowed. No one in Hell was as nice as Maeve and Galen. They deserved each other.

"Glad to see you fully clothed this time," he teased, voice tight.

"Well, it's your fault for not knocking," she scolded.

"Actually, I think the fault falls on the people who were using the desk in such a manner at the peak of the work day," he drawled, staring at Galen with an arched brow. The humor felt hollow.

"Call us selfish," Maeve said with a wink. She slapped him playfully on the shoulder. "I'll find someone else to terrorize while you two talk."

"Thanks, babe," Galen said, and leaned down for a kiss.

They were so tender with one another it hurt to watch. They might as well just break his other horn off.

I must be corrupt, otherwise how could I love someone like you?

God, what had Julian *done?* He was so stupid! He should've come clean as soon as he started to feel something for the angel. But he hadn't.

And now he was stuck here.

In Hell. He'd never see them again.

"Catch you later," Maeve said to him, and then she was gone with a wiggle of her fingers as she slipped out the door.

"Alright!" Galen said with a single clap. He perched his ass on the edge of his desk. "Tell me what's going on."

"What's the point? You're not my boss anymore; you can't help."

"Tell me anyway. I take it the assignment didn't go well?"

Julian deflated, sank into the couch along the opposite wall of the desk, and tried not to think about the bodily fluids—knowing those two—he was probably sitting on.

"They assigned me an angel," Julian began.

Galen cocked his head to the side and sat in one of the chairs in front of his desk, spinning it to face Julian.

"They do that now?" Galen asked.

This must be what Rami's clients feel like, he thought with a pang.

"Apparently," Julian muttered.

"Sounds like something Carl would do," Galen groused. "Tough mark?"

"They were, at first," Julian admitted.

And then the whole tale spilled out of him.

The beating, which tightened the lines around Galen's eyes. Meeting Rami. He got a laugh out of the therapist nonsense, just like Julian had.

He told Galen how the angel had tentatively nursed him back to health, and how the angel had slowly grown on Julian, infuriating as they were.

The simple, Earthly pleasures. The *other* pleasures.

Because if Julian had to listen to Galen and Maeve's sexcapades for the past two years, there were no secrets between them.

"And before I knew it, I was in too deep and I realized I didn't even want to finish the stupid assignment. But I fucked up," Julian groaned, and buried his face in his hands. "I tempted them anyway and it almost worked, and I felt sick about it." Julian pressed the heels of his palms to his eyes. "Then they figured it out—why I was there. And I confessed everything and now they hate me and Carl won't even give me the promotion and now I'm *stuck here!*"

Julian finally lifted his head, spreading his palms wide as if to say, *well, there you have it.*

"I fucked up." Julian finished, and stared at Galen. "And now I have this stupid short horn as a permanent reminder of my failure. That's how the Sixth is going," he spat.

Galen's expression was crestfallen, and suddenly Julian felt a little guilty for venting. "I'm sorry, man, I didn't mean to dump this all on you—"

"I asked," Galen reminded him, and Julian snapped his mouth shut. "I knew Carl was an asshole and I let you go anyway. Sorry," he said, one corner of his lip quirking in sympathy.

"S'not your fault," Julian said. He crossed his arms and leaned back. "I should've known better. There's no way outta here. I just gotta accept it."

He'd never see Rami again, and by the time Julian ever got back to Earth, the angel would've moved on and Julian would never find him.

His throat hurt.

"You know, it's really unfortunate that you fell in love with an *angel,* of all people," Galen sneered.

Julian lifted his head, a rebuttal on his tongue, ready to defend Rami, but then he caught the almost playful expression on Galen's face.

"Most demons would say angels are our natural enemies, all selfless like that. Kinda shitty of you to value one over your job, which is a high honor, by the way," Galen told him.

Julian swallowed.

"I mean, after all that Hell has given you…" He shook his head. "I think you deserve a punishment," Galen said. "You even spoiled the temptation. Rather selfless, wouldn't you say?" He wrinkled his nose. "In fact, I think there's only one punishment befitting a demon the likes of you."

"Galen—"

"For the betrayal of loving an *angel,* I, the Devil of the Seventh Region of Hell…" Galen declared with a wink, "…cast you to Earth."

Julian's heart began pounding, a steady thump in his ears.

"Humans are running the Earth into the ground anyway, so I say you should stay long enough to learn Earth isn't all it's made out to be. You'll live a *long* life, so you have plenty of time to regret your selfless decisions."

"Galen…" Julian choked out. "What about the Sixth Region? Carl?"

"Fuck Carl," Galen scoffed. "I'll handle him."

Julian surged up out of the chair and hugged Galen. "What the fuck, man," he said, throat tightening with emotion.

Galen chuckled, hugging him aggressively.

"I want to meet them, one day. We can go on a double date," he said once they separated.

"Assuming they'll even talk to me," Julian murmured.

"They will," Galen insisted. "Now go get your angel."

"I can just… go?" Julian asked.

"Well, not on your own," Galen said.

He snapped his fingers, and before Julian could even respond, gold filled his vision.

When he blinked, he was standing outside Rami's house, on their front door step.

It was eerily similar to that very first night, except the sun was shining brightly and Julian didn't have the shit beaten out of him.

Reeling, Julian spun and knocked on the door.

There was no answer, so he knocked again, and waited.

And waited.

Julian tried the knob and it opened right away.

"Feathers," Julian called out warily. "You need to lock your doors—I've told you this."

There was no indication the angel heard him, and Julian stepped inside. It looked like it had when Julian had come downstairs just that morning. Sun shone through the windows, though it had moved past Rami's chair as the day trailed on.

With careful steps, he made his way through the small living room to the office. The door was still half-open, but there was no angel inside.

Heart dropping, Julian retraced his steps back through the living room and headed for the stairs.

He took them two at a time, knowing Rami would hate the fact that he was wearing shoes on their stairs, but—

There was no Rami to scold him. Not upstairs.

Not in the bathroom, not in the bedroom. Not hidden in the closet.

He raced back downstairs, and rechecked the office just for fun before he let his worry run rampant.

The car.

Julian sprinted to the door and threw it open before running along the little path hidden by hedges to the short driveway.

The car was there, sitting still. No angel inside.

So where the fuck were they?

Julian ran a hand through his hair, his breath sharp.

They wouldn't leave just like that, would they? They hadn't collected all those books overnight. They wouldn't leave *everything* behind. All the books and their little bath necessities, and their stupid comfy chair.

Maybe... maybe the angel went for an emergency pastry run.

Yes, that seemed like something they'd do.

Gulping in air like he'd run a marathon, Julian followed the path back to the door and pulled it shut before sitting down on the front step.

The least he could do was not break and enter.

He'd just... wait.

Right here.

Rami would be back soon.

There was no other option.

27
MORAL COMPASS

One moment, Rami was on their yellow couch, contemplating the life they'd led to end up in that very spot, anger and unfairness still raging through them in Julian's absence.

The next, they blinked and found themself in a place they hadn't returned to in a very long time.

"Heaven," Rami breathed.

As with all angels in Heaven, Rami's wings were out and instinctively adjusted to balance them as they caught their bearings. They splayed their hand out before them, feeling nostalgic at the silver shine to their skin under the light of Heaven.

"Welcome back," a voice said, and Rami spun.

"Hello," Rami said, a little wary of the other angel, Raguel. Their halo shone quite a bit brighter than most, like with all angels of the council, and Rami gulped before their gaze trailed to their surroundings.

Heaven was still as they remembered, green and untouched by human pollution, beautiful and natural, as it should be. Peaceful, quiet.

"Wow," they said, taking it in.

Rami felt their anger fade just at the peace of it all. They'd forgotten how pure and wonderful it was here.

That's what happened when one spent most of their existence on Earth with humans, they supposed.

"It has been a while, hasn't it, Rami?" the other angel asked.

"Indeed, Raguel," they agreed, and finally turned their attention to them. They were dressed in loose-fitting clothes of many colors, none of them matching. It made Rami smile.

"Actually, these days, it's Ginger," they said.

"I think that rather suits you," Rami told them with a smile.

They were silvery perfection, with long hair flowing down their back and wings as white and fluffy as Rami's own. The eyes on their wings were squinting at them, knowing.

Perhaps theirs were a little better groomed than Rami's.

My own fault, they thought.

"Why am I here?" Rami asked.

Ginger's expression was gentle, pearly eyes bright and perceptive, and they began to walk, pulling Rami with a barely-felt touch on their sweater. "Well, we noticed a bit of a pattern with you lately, something a little peculiar, and wanted to check in, is all."

We referred to the council, once known as God's very own confidants.

"What happened?" Rami asked, worry tightening their chest as they took the footpath along Ginger's side.

"Well... why don't you tell me?"

Rami's lips thinned, all their raging emotions bubbling up again. "Well, I don't know if you're aware, but I've been dealing with a *demon* that Hell sent to *tempt me to evil!*"

Ginger's brow furrowed, lips quirking. "Evil?"

"Yes!" Rami cried emphatically. "He tricked me!"

Ginger brushed their hand over a tree as they passed. "Tell me more," they said.

Rami huffed, unsure where to even begin.

"Start at the beginning, if you wouldn't mind."

Rami drew in a deep breath. Right. The beginning. "A demon showed up on my doorstep. You must know; I sent a correspondence about him."

"Yes. Julian, I believe. A temptation demon."

Rami waved their hands. "Yes! Tempting me to do bad!"

"Bad like what?" Ginger questioned.

"Like—"

Rami's frowned, and they paused as they considered their words.

"Like *gambling*," Rami said. *Even though I quite enjoyed it.*

Ginger hummed and glanced over at him. There was a smile on their lips, and Rami's cheeks heated. "What else?"

Rami racked their brain. "Using magic frivolously."

Rami didn't very well want to confess to the drinking and the eating. Not to mention the—

Their cheeks flamed.

"Why did you gamble?" Ginger asked.

"Because… I wanted to win. We were betting chocolates."

"Mhm. And why were you using magic frivolously, as you say?"

Rami crossed their arms. "Because my coffee was cold. And sometimes getting dressed is just so tiring."

"And the sex?"

Rami snapped their head around to stare at Ginger.

"I'm not obtuse. What else would have someone in such a tizzy?" They paused. "It *was* consensual, wasn't it?"

"Of course!" Rami blurted, offended at such a suggestion, even on the behalf of a demon.

"Okay, then. Why'd you do it?"

"Well. It… felt good, I suppose," Rami admitted,

wondering if an angel could pass out from the amount of blood settling in their face.

"So, by committing all these grave *sins*," they said with a laugh, "it sounds like you were just being selfish."

"I— yes, I suppose I was."

"You know human nature—their motivations for most things are either *selfless* or *selfish*."

"I know that," Rami said warily, something niggling in the back of their mind.

"Rami," Ginger said, pausing and waiting for Rami to face them. "Manipulating that human man to protect your client is one thing, but lashing out at someone, hurting them just because you are hurt, is a very selfish thing to do."

"I—I know," Rami said, throat tightening.

"Even though both actions were equally selfish, only one of them actively caused harm, even if emotionally, to someone. And someone who cares about you, no less."

Ginger shook their head. "And hurting someone is much worse than any chocolate gambling or all the consensual sex in the world." Rami swallowed as they continued. "There's nothing inherently *wrong* with being selfish, Rami. Not unless you're hurting someone."

Their gut twisted as they reexamined the past week.

"I suppose I haven't been very selfless as of late."

I hurt Julian. On purpose. Just because I could, and because he hurt me first.

Not very angel-like of me.

"Well, it sounds like Julian was successful in tempting me to evil," Rami admitted.

Ginger chuckled, and then paused. "Again with this *evil* nonsense. What are you going on about?"

Rami frowned at them.

"Hold on," Ginger said, waving a hand. "Do you think demons are evil?"

Rami's brows furrowed. "Of course. They're demons."

Ginger's lips twitched, humor filling their eyes until they couldn't contain it, and it spilled out in loud laughter, echoing in the naturistic scenery around them.

"You know what I think?" Ginger finally asked, once Rami's cheeks were redder than ever.

"What?" they asked, feeling small.

"I think you've been on Earth a bit too long. These things —gambling and using magic and having sex—they're not bad things, Rami. Neither is enjoying food or drink. And neither are demons, for that matter. But you believe them to be. Why?"

"Because..." *Because they are,* Rami wanted to say.

But if Ginger, an angel of the council, was telling them they weren't... then...

Rami's eyes went wide. "Oh my god."

Ginger giggled, the sound like chimes. "That's a very human phrase. Which is fitting, because it seems you've embraced a bit of their moral superiority, too, I think."

Rami ran a hand through their hair.

"You've tried so hard to be selfless, staying on Earth, observing humans, that you've internalized some of their own beliefs, whether you realized it or not."

"But demons..."

"Just like us, can be selfish or selfless. Though they tend to lean one way, just like we do."

Rami was at a loss. Now they were questioning everything. How much of their own beliefs were adopted from their time on Earth?

"You know, Rami," Ginger began hesitantly. "It has been quite a while since you've shown up for your therapy appointments."

Rami's mouth dropped open. "But I *am* a therapist."

"So?" Ginger glanced over them from head to toe. "If this

conversation has proven anything, it's that we all need someone to talk to. Even you." A beat passed. "And also maybe we should put together an Angel 101 for those posted on Earth."

Rami laughed before realizing that Ginger wasn't. "Wait, you're serious?"

"Quite," Ginger said, and continued walking.

Rami walked alongside them in silence, losing themself in their thoughts.

If demons weren't evil, and Rami had been *wrong* this entire time…

"I fucked up," Rami whispered. The last several days flashed through their mind. Putting Julian down even without realizing, just because he was a demon. Thinking he was there to do some great evil when really… it was all for the selfish amusement of some higher-up in Hell.

It wasn't about good or evil, or who was better than the other—it was about selfishness and self*less*ness.

The last time Rami saw Julian flashed through their mind.

Ginger was right—Rami had been *very* selfish to hurt Julian like that.

"I can't leave it like this," Rami said suddenly, and stopped walking. It was only then that Rami realized Ginger had led them to a building. Through the window they could see a group of angels sitting in a circle of chairs.

"Then fix it," Ginger said, a kind, knowing smile on their lips.

Rami swallowed, throat tight, eyes threatening to burn. "Is it that easy?"

"Up to you," they said, shrugging. "Listen, I know you think you are all alone down there, but that is very much not the case."

Rami met their gaze bravely. "I'll admit I have felt quite… separated from Heaven, recently."

Ginger's expression softened. "I promise, you're not alone down there. The doves have enjoyed watching you help your clients, after all."

Rami blinked at them as another piece of the puzzle fell into place.

I think I'll miss your little birds, Melissa had said just the night before. Rami had finally seen them, doves perched on the branches and nestled into place like they'd always been there.

Rami was realizing just now that maybe, just maybe, they really had been.

"Thank you, Ginger," Rami whispered.

They dipped their head graciously. "We're here for whatever support you may need." Then tilted their head toward the building, at the angels inside. "Sharing hour."

Rami nodded, a bit of guilt nestling beneath their feathers.

"And I promise we're not going to yank you back if you use a bit too much magic on your morning tea," Ginger drawled.

"I actually drink coffee," Rami said, chuckling. "I suppose I've been down there so long I just assumed… Well, I don't know what I assumed." Ginger was right. Rami had begun to fear consequences that didn't exist, just because the humans had.

"And in case you need to hear it…" Ginger waited until Rami's gaze flicked up, meeting theirs. "You're allowed to exist however you see fit. You don't have to fear we're going to take it away from you, unless you deserve it. And having a spat isn't quite what we mean."

They supposed that was a very human fear, too. Rami sucked in a shaky breath and nodded. "Thank you."

"Like I said, we're here for whatever you may need, even if that's a chat."

They clapped him on the shoulder and stepped back. "Well, anyway. I can't wait to tell the others you've had your first lover's quarrel. Oh, they'll be thrilled. In the meantime, if you'd like to stay awhile and hide from the ex, we are happy to have you."

Rami didn't know how they felt about being the source of entertainment for the council. But what were they to do about it?

"You should stay for a bit, have a think," Ginger suggested. "And whe—*if* you're ready to go," they said with a soft laugh, "just wish yourself back home. Use a bit of that magic you've been so afraid of."

Rami's cheeks heated. Maybe it *was* that easy? "Thank you."

"And come back sooner. For therapy," they said. "That's an order."

"I will. As soon as I sort this out," Rami said, and meant it. "Thank you."

"Anytime. Now, it's taco night, so I'll be seeing you soon for your next appointment. I'll send a dove," they said with a lifted eyebrow.

Rami's lips curled in a smile. "I look forward to seeing them."

Ginger hummed as they walked away, and it took Rami a moment more to process their words.

"Wait a second—" They raised their voice. "Taco night? Angels don't need to eat!" they called out.

Ginger turned, walking backwards as they shouted, "Guess we're selfish, Rami! We can eat tacos if we want!"

Rami laughed, a little breathlessly, as Ginger walked out of sight.

Selfish.

That's what it was all about. No wonder Julian had kept using that word.

It was true that Rami had volunteered to go down to Earth, to study things, to keep an eye on the happenings of humans. That was selfish, even way back then, because they'd simply wanted to be around humans.

So when, exactly, had Rami started to internalize their beliefs, their moral compass? In fact, when had they started to fear Heaven?

Maybe not Heaven itself. Maybe they feared they weren't good enough.

The longer they had stayed away, the scarier Heaven had seemed. The less they felt like they deserved it.

Was now their chance to rectify that? To stay here?

The silence of the nature around them was loud, a roaring backdrop to the jolt of their thoughts.

But the idea of never seeing Julian again—something lurched in them, violent and urgent.

In fact, the idea of leaving things just as they were…

Rami's breath grew tight, chest and throat squeezing, and a sudden revelation crashed into them, just like the waterfall crashing somewhere in the distance.

Rami shouldn't have said what they did. They'd lashed out because they were hurt. But that was no excuse.

They'd *hurt* Julian.

Now they just had to fix it.

Rami tucked their wings in and with a slight tug of the magic that always existed just out of sight, they left Heaven to return… home.

They could start there, at the very least. And then they'd —well, they'd find Julian, some way. Somehow. And they'd use however much magic it took.

Rami blinked, and the sound of rushing water disappeared, replaced with the silence of their home on Earth.

Usually Rami reveled in the quiet, the peace, but this time it just felt… wrong.

Their gaze trailed to the couch, to the open doors of the office across the way.

All empty.

"Okay, how do I fix this?" Rami asked the couch quietly, beginning to pace.

Their pale human-colored hands were sweating and they rubbed them on their pants before huffing a breath. If Julian wasn't on Earth, how was Rami supposed to find him?

"Can we go to Hell?" they asked, as if something would answer. "I suppose I've never tried. But magic—it can do anything, right?" Rami rambled nervously.

With every passing minute they felt as if there was no solution, as if they'd fucked up monumentally. What if there *was* no fixing this?

They shut their eyes and drew in a deep breath.

"Calm down," they told themself. *Focus.*

I can go to Hell. Find Julian that way. And then...

Thump.

Rami's eyes snapped open, the pulse in their ears fading as they zeroed in on the sound.

In quick succession, *thump, thump, thump.*

Slowly, Rami turned toward the door.

The sound didn't return, but Rami's feet carried them the few steps, and their hand was turning the knob before they even realized.

They pulled the door open.

"Oof," the person said as they spilled across the threshold.

Julian gazed up at them from the ground, upside down.

"Oh," he breathed. "You're back."

28
STUBBORN DETERMINATION

Rami reached down, taking Julian's hand and pulling him to his feet before tugging him closer.

They collided, chest to chest, and Rami wrapped their arms around him, relief filling them until they couldn't even take a breath. Their throat was tight and their eyes were definitely more than a little damp.

When they could finally take a breath, they pushed Julian away just far enough so they could look at him, blurry as he was from their tears.

"I don't think you're bad," Rami said in a rush. "I was just hurt—"

"—and you had every right to be—" Julian said at the same time.

"—and I lashed out. I didn't mean it—"

"I should've told you sooner," Julian blurted. "But I knew you'd be disappointed in me, and—"

"—but really, that's very quite human of me, if you think about it—"

"—and I was afraid you'd never talk to me again, and I was almost trapped in Hell—"

"So Ginger was right about one thing after all—wait

what?" Rami said, absorbing Julian's words. "You were almost trapped in Hell?"

"Who's Ginger?" Julian asked simultaneously.

They both paused, Rami's hands twisted in Julian's shirt and Julian's hands gripping Rami's shoulders.

A beat passed, and they studied one another, and then they were chuckling, and hugging, and Rami was so relieved Julian was *there*.

"I'm sorry," Rami said, sobering, squeezing him just a bit tighter.

"I'm sorry, too," Julian murmured into their neck.

"What happened?" Rami asked.

"It's a long story," Julian said, pulling back.

Rami swallowed. "Well, I have until my next therapy appointment for you to tell me."

Julian's brows furrowed at that. "What?"

"They're mandatory, I'm afraid. I also have to go through…" They grit their teeth. "Angel 101."

"You get to come back, though, right?" Julian asked, hands tightening around Rami.

"Yes, yes. I just have to make sure to attend," Rami said.

"Okay, good," Julian said, blowing out a breath. "Because I'm officially banished from Hell."

"What?" Rami asked, eyes widening. "I didn't even know that was possible."

"Me neither," Julian admitted. "It's all thanks to Galen. Said I committed a selfless act by spoiling the temptation to the subject in question."

"So you get to stay?" Rami asked, almost afraid to hope.

"Yep. No getting rid of me now," Julian said.

Rami hugged him again. "Oh, thank god. Because I really didn't want to have to storm Hell to find you."

Julian snickered, the sound warm and soft in Rami's ear. "Had a plan, did you?"

"More like blind determination."

Their chuckles faded, and Rami still hadn't released Julian. Part of them still couldn't believe it was real.

"I'm sorry," Rami said again. Words didn't seem like enough. "I don't know how to make it up to you."

Julian pressed a kiss to Rami's pulse, still racing from the fear of losing him. Then his hands trailed down Rami's back, to their soft waist. They squeezed. "It's me who needs to make it up to you. And I can think of a few ways."

"Julian!" Rami cried, and then… paused.

Sex wasn't *bad*. Being selfish wasn't… sinful.

In fact, Rami needed to train themself to stop thinking of things in such a manner. Such *human* manners.

They weren't human, after all. They were an angel. And Julian was a demon.

They pulled back, trying for innocence and missing the mark. "Is your tail… prehensile?"

Julian winked. "Want to find out?"

Later, when Rami was giving Julian every detail of their Heavenly dressing-down, he stopped Rami with a hand against their lips.

"Are you telling me. That this whole time. You thought I was tempting you to be *evil?*"

Rami whined and covered their face. "I'm so embarrassed!"

"I was tempting you to be selfish!" Julian cried.

"I know that *now!* I—I just… forgot."

"You forgot your own *history?*" Julian asked, teasing.

"Well! You try spending thousands of years on Earth and see what happens!"

Julian chuckled, pulling Rami back down to lay beside him. He pressed a kiss to Rami's cheek, and they reveled in the warm fuzzies in their stomach from the sweet action.

"Gladly, as long you're here," Julian returned.

And Rami didn't have very much to say to that.

Well, except—

"I love you," Rami said, hand pressed to Julian's chest as they stared down at him. "And I'm sorry for what I said. I'll never stop being sorry."

His golden eyes softened. "I love you, too. And I've already forgiven you. Besides, you did plenty of apologizing when you put your tongue—"

Rami surged up and kissed him before he could finish that thought.

Their lips locked together, and Rami melted into Julian, until they were pressed chest to chest and Rami was straddling him.

They trailed their mouth to his pulse, his collarbones, his chest, memorizing him by touch and taste alone.

"Should I keep apologizing?" Rami drawled.

Julian swallowed. "Could do, if you wanted."

"Might as well," Rami said. "Just to be safe."

EPILOGUE

6 *months later*
"What if they don't like me?" Rami asked. Julian would've scoffed, except he recognized the actual worry in their voice.

Julian reached over and shut the car off, laying his hand on Rami's thigh. "Angel, they're gonna love you."

"There's absolutely no way you can know that," Rami pointed out.

"Can, too," he argued, just to see Rami roll their eyes. "I love you, so they will, too. I promise."

Rami sighed. "At this point I have to take your word for it."

They dropped their hand atop Julian's and squeezed, and Julian felt the full force of his overwhelming fondness for this angel.

"Come on. He's the whole reason I'm here, after all," Julian reminded them.

They squeezed his hand again and released a breath. "You're right. I like him already."

"And Maeve is a hoot," Julian added. "I told you, she works—"

"For a sex toy company, yes," Rami answered, chuckling. "I'm sure she has some excellent stories."

"Oh, don't get her started," Julian drawled. Confident Rami wouldn't flee back to the comfort of their home, Julian leaned away to open the car door. "Come on, then."

"Alright, alright," Rami whined a bit dramatically, but pushed open their own door and met Julian around the back of the square car.

"If you can handle Jesse and the crew from the gay bar, you can handle Galen and Maeve," Julian told them, wrapping an arm around Rami's shoulders.

"I know, you're right. I'm just nervous," Rami admitted, fingers tapping against Julian's waist. "What is this place, anyway?"

"It's an others-only restaurant. So..." Julian let his horns free once they were through the threshold and Rami gazed up at him appreciatively.

It took no time at all to locate the couple in the back of the restaurant. Maeve was all cuddled up to Galen's side in an adorable display of affection.

"Keep your pants on," Julian told them as they neared.

Maeve's head snapped up, Galen grinned, and Julian felt Rami tense under the scrutiny of his previous boss's gaze.

"Galen, Maeve, this is Rami," Julian introduced them. "Rami, this is Maeve and Galen."

Maeve stood and wrapped Rami in a hug with no preamble. They *oofed* and hugged her back gingerly. "It's lovely to meet you," Rami said. "I've heard so much."

"And I'm sure none of it was good," Galen teased, offering his hand once they separated.

Rami shook it politely and Julian had a surreal out-of-body experience.

Here he was, six months free of Hell and enjoying every single minute with Rami, introducing them to his *friends*.

Something that never would have been possible without Galen.

So as they both took their seats, Julian said, "I'm so glad to see you guys again."

"It's really nice to see you too, Julian," Maeve said. "Galen's excited, too; he's been talking about it nonstop for the last few days."

Galen's cheeks colored as they all snickered.

"Despite how nervous I am, I've been very curious about you two. So thank you for the invite, I suppose," Rami said.

"Of course, of course. I told Julian I wanted to meet the angel that stole his heart," Galen said with a wink.

Julian groaned and covered his face. "Galen, please don't embarrass me."

"Please," Galen retorted. "I'm going to embarrass the hell out of you. Do you know how long I've been waiting for you to meet someone?"

Beside him, Rami chuckled, and Julian pinched their thigh in a tease. Their smile softened as they glanced over. "Well, I, for one, want to thank you for what you did," Rami said, turning to Galen. "I mean, without you sending Julian back, I don't know what I would've done."

"Nothing to thank me for. Carl was an asshole, and I shouldn't have let Julian go in the first place," Galen said, lips curling unhappily.

"Kinda glad you did, though," Julian interjected. "I mean, if I never went to work for Carl, I never would've met Rami."

Rami bumped their shoulder into Julian as Galen said, "Well, fine, I guess. But I come bearing good news!"

"What's that?" Julian asked.

"Carl's been sacked," Galen announced, looking very proud of himself.

Julian laid his hand on Rami's thigh to share the excitement. "What happened?"

"Replaced him with someone else who doesn't beat up their employees for assignments," he grumbled, gaze flashing to Julian's horn.

He tried not to feel self-conscious about it, what with Galen's horns all perfectly curled and blending into his hair.

Then Rami's hand covered his own atop their thigh and squeezed softly. The horn, at first, had been a reminder of what had happened, how he'd fucked up. But after months of affection lavished on him by Rami, Julian couldn't help but feel *thankful* every time he saw the damned thing in the mirror.

Thankful for Rami, thankful for meeting them, and *yes,* even thankful for the temptation.

Because if Julian hadn't accepted that position, if his horn hadn't been broken, if he hadn't been sent to Rami, they never would've crossed paths.

Now, his horn was forevermore a reminder of how they met, and how'd they be spending the rest of their lives *together.* Julian would never feel the sting of loneliness again, and neither would Rami.

Rami, his angel, beamed. "You're right, that is excellent news," they said. "Fuck Carl."

Maeve snickered and elbowed Galen. "I didn't know angels cursed."

"We do all kinds of things," Rami said, relaxing further into their seat.

Julian hoped their nerves were finally dissipating. "Damn right, they do," Julian said, waggling his eyebrows.

Rami groaned, shaking their head despite the amused grin on their face, and Galen chuckled.

The waitress returned with their wine, and Julian watched Rami's fingers curl around the stem.

"You look happy," Galen announced suddenly, shrugging. "So I guess I don't have to offer you a job to escape."

Julian glanced over at Rami and squeezed their thigh before they could get any ideas.

"Nah. I like it here," he said.

"Well, let's toast to that, then," Maeve said, lifting her glass.

"To what?" Galen asked.

"To love, of course," she said, as if it was obvious.

And it was. Galen and Maeve had something pure, and now Julian didn't have to spend his days wondering what it was like.

Because he knew.

"To love," Rami agreed, and lifted their glass.

Julian joined in with a smile.

"Okay, well, it's not my fault the story turned so scandalous," Rami hissed through their laughter as they debriefed over dessert in the kitchen.

"I don't know what you expected, bringing up the sex shop like that. I told you Maeve had stories!"

Their giggles died down as they sobered, and Julian nudged his hip into Rami, who nudged back.

"I had fun," Rami admitted. "They were just as lovely as you said."

"Glad you think so. Would you do dinner with them again?"

"In a heartbeat," Rami agreed, and sat their fork down to thumb at Julian's lip. "I do not, however, appreciate Galen having a back-up plan to whisk you off to Hell again."

Julian chuckled, heat stirring as Rami sucked the chocolate mousse from Julian's lip into their mouth. "He was not going to whisk me away—he's just looking out."

"Good," Rami retorted, and stepped closer, closing Julian into the island. His lower back pressed into the edge, but Rami was all softness as they collided. "Because you're not going anywhere."

"Didn't want to," Julian whispered, gaze dropping to their lips.

Their mouth quirked. "Good."

And then they kissed him, burying a hand into his hair. Julian's hands landed on their waist, yanking them closer.

Already he felt the hard line of them pressed into Julian's hip, and he shivered.

"How tired are you?" Rami asked into the kiss.

"Wide awake," Julian returned.

"Excellent," Rami purred, and grabbed Julian's hand. "Let's go upstairs, then."

"You sound like you're plotting," Julian mused, and followed eagerly.

"Maybe I am," Rami said. The steps took no time, and then Julian was being pushed down on the bed, the nice slacks and button up magicked off him with a snap of his own fingers.

Rami pouted. "You know that's my favorite part," they chastised.

"I want to hear more about this plot of yours," Julian answered.

"So impatient," they noted, and began unbuttoning their own shirt, shrugging off their sweater.

Julian arched a brow, waiting, dropping a hand between his legs to stroke himself.

"Bringing up the sex shop made me remember something," Rami said, and curiosity struck Julian sharp.

"Yeah? Like what?"

"Like the toy you kept fondling," Rami said, shirt finally sliding off their shoulders, baring their chest and round stomach.

"Which one?" Julian asked.

"The tentacle," they answered, and Julian squeezed his cock.

His gaze trailed down their body, staring at the bulge beneath the zipper they slowly worked open. "No way," Julian scoffed. "You can do that?"

"Of course I can," Rami answered. "Unless it's weird?"

"Not weird. Hot," Julian corrected, and held out a grabby hand. "Come on, show me."

Heat flashed through him, rising just beneath his skin as he watched Rami strip, the confidence they'd built over the last several months obvious as they stared down at him.

"It didn't occur to me until dinner, actually. I figured if I could magic one appendage, why not another?"

"I love your brain," Julian moaned.

Rami finally pushed their pants down their hips and Julian's breath caught at the sight. "Fuck."

"Yes, that's quite the idea," Rami retorted, and pressed a knee to the bed before crawling toward him. He spread his legs, and Rami settled between them, a real-life actual tentacle brushing against Julian's hard cock as they slotted together.

Julian swallowed. "You gonna fuck me with that?" It was a similar size to the toy, nothing outrageous, and colored like their angel skin, with suckers and everything.

"If you're amenable," Rami teased, sliding their hands down Julian's chest.

Shivers broke out from their touch, and Julian arched into it, curling his legs around Rami's waist. "Very much so."

Rami leaned down, and as they did so, their tentacle pressed into Julian's cock, both squished between their stomachs as they kissed.

Julian groaned at the sensation of the slick tentacle against him, the suckers latching onto him.

He jolted against Rami, who smirked into the kiss—devious bastard—and pulled away to glance down at him. "Think you can be patient enough for me to open you up?"

Julian nodded, rocking against them, breath catching.

Rami dropped another kiss to his lips before moving, shifting down his body and dragging their lips along Julian's skin, nipping teasingly at his throat and shoulder before continuing down to his chest.

They curved their lips around his nipple, and were only satisfied once they chased shivers over his skin and it was beaded on their tongue. Julian's hands were tight in their hair, but were forced to release them once they sat up.

Julian dropped his legs from their waist and made room for them, tilting his hips up, eager and impatient, just like they'd said.

Rami stroked themself, the tentacle curling around their hand, leaving a shiny residue behind.

Julian couldn't contain the needy noise that escaped, cock pulsing against his belly, a bead welling at the tip.

"I know, dear," Rami said softly, and then readjusted. The pet name hit him like a brick and Julian melted beneath them, even as disappointment filled him from the distance between them.

But then Rami was leaning down and their breath was hot on Julian's cock and—

He moaned as their lips wrapped around him, and at the same time a finger, smooth and sure and experienced at this point, pressed against his ass.

Julian focused on his breath, and gripped the sheets tight as pleasure ravaged him.

"Rami," Julian whined, but he kept his hips pressed to the bed like he was supposed to.

Don't rush, he reminded himself.

Rami's answer was to swallow him deeper, tongue pressing to the underside as their slick finger moved inside him.

Julian threaded his hands back through Rami's silver hair, tangling the strands and gripping tight, because he'd learned these past few months that Rami didn't mind a tug, either.

They hummed around Julian, and he cursed, biting down on his lip and scratching lovingly at Rami's scalp.

It was so good it was a blur, Rami adding a second and a third finger, and pulling off Julian just when he shouted a warning that he was close, so close—

He slumped back to the bed, breathless as Rami finally settled between his legs.

"I need to see this," Julian said, voice wobbly as he pressed up into his forearms, tilting his head down to watch the tentacle— "Oh fuck," he panted as he felt the slick tip of it brush against him.

"My sentiment exactly," Rami said, voice rough from taking Julian so deep. Just the reminder of it sent another spiral of warmth through him.

He tilted his hips eagerly, the tentacle catching and slipping past his hole. It was tapered, thinner at the tip and thickening to the base. Rami's hands circled his hips and held him still. "Patience," they reminded him.

"I know, I know," Julian said, hand gripping the bedclothes tightly.

Rami arched a brow, and Julian forced himself to settle down. "I am—I'm patient," he lied.

But Rami must have been just as eager, because they let it slide, and the tentacle was pressing, pressing—

Julian shuddered as the thin tip entered him, no thicker than a single finger when he'd had just three inside him, but the texture was new and different and *so fucking good.*

He let himself collapse to the bed, and laid a palm against the side of Rami's thigh, fingers sinking in, holding on.

"That's… new," Julian mumbled, mouth falling open as Rami slid deeper.

The suckers weren't just for texture; he could *feel* them grasping inside him, curious and exploratory, and he arched his hips for more against Rami's hold.

"It's so good," he rambled, and Rami nodded, gazing between them until he was too close, too deep to see clearly.

"It is," Rami agreed. "You always feel so good," they breathed.

Julian pressed the heel of his foot into Rami's low back and urged them in until their hips smacked together gently. The fullness was the same and yet entirely different.

"I can feel it move," Julian panted, and jolted against Rami as the tentacle did just that, the tip searching, pressing right into that perfect point inside him.

Julian dropped a hand between his legs, circling the base and squeezing tight. He didn't want this to end so quickly. "Too fast," he warned.

Rami backed off, the tip relaxing instead of pressing, and in Julian's peripherals there was a soft, silver glow. It neared, and he blinked, seeing Rami's halo floating between them, growing smaller, and smaller.

"This can help," Rami murmured.

"Oh, no way," Julian breathed as it circled his cock, sliding down to the base and cinching, snug but not uncomfortable. "Now *that's* forbidden," Julian teased. He would never tire of teasing Rami for forgetting their own lore.

"Oh, I'm sure," drawled Rami, who'd actually taken quite well to Angel 101, and then they pulled their hips back.

Julian swore he could feel every sucker as it passed his rim, and he moaned, grateful Rami at least had no neighbors to worry when they were positively taking him apart like this.

"Yes, yes, I know," Rami groaned, and moved their hips. They were slow at first, and Julian felt their intense gaze, knew they were cataloging each expression Julian made, paying attention to every sound they forced out of him.

But eventually it all melted into nothing but pleasure, and their hips were slapping against Julian's. The halo-turned-cock-ring kept him near the edge without sending him over. The tentacle's thickness felt so good on every plunge, and it even pulsed like a cock did, too. The slickness from it made every stroke sound filthy, and it wasn't long before it coated the pair of them, their thighs and Julian's ass and certainly the bed beneath them.

Noises spilling from both Julian and Rami, and the edge was nearing and this time Julian didn't want to back away from it. He grasped at Rami's thigh, lifting his hips, and Rami nodded.

"You're close, I can tell," they said, and kept the rhythm steady. Their breath was sharp and tight, too, hands gripping Julian's hips hard.

Julian's moan devolved into a soundless gasp as the tentacle pressed deep, the tip sliding over his prostate with each thrust. Rami dropped a hand between them, wrapping around his cock.

"Oh fuck, Rami, please," he whined, tilting his head, back bowing into each plunge, each stroke.

The halo loosened, and pleasured barreled toward him, like watching a storm roll close. Julian opened himself to it, felt the lightning sizzling in his spine, his stomach tensing with it.

"Come for me—with me, come on," Rami pleaded, and snapped their hips in again.

Julian came, arching his back as if struck, and spilled over Rami's fist. It flayed through him, hot and electric, and he felt as if his hair should be standing on end. He clenched around Rami's tentacle cock, heard their shout as they joined.

They rode the aftershocks together, and Rami tilted forward, bending Julian practically in half so they could kiss. It was sloppy and as messy as the fluids between them and he loved it so fucking much.

"I fucking can't believe how much I love you," Julian muttered lazily, lips brushing Rami's with each word.

"I can," Rami replied. "Because I love you, too."

It was such a sweet moment, considering Rami's magic tentacle was still inside him. They were pliant and relaxed, and if Julian was going to ask, now would be the time.

"So is this the *only* item we saw at the shop that you might be open to trying out?" Julian asked as casually as possible.

Rami arched a brow at him. "Is the item in mind the item I think it is?"

Julian shrugged, envisioning the faux feathers and the low neckline and the— "You don't have to wear the halo," Julian told them.

"Oh, well, thank heavens for that," Rami drawled, and tilted their head in thought, gaze narrowed down at Julian.

"I might have been wondering about trying the... equipment to fill something like that out," Rami mused.

Julian gulped at the thought. "Yeah?" His voice came out higher pitched than normal.

Rami chuckled and leaned down to kiss him. "I would wear fake feathers for you."

"That's the most romantic thing you've ever said," Julian murmured, lips bumping.

Rami rolled their eyes, affection in the curl of their lips.

They separated with a slick noise and Julian, a mature individual, snickered at the state of the two of them.

"Sorry I got cum on your halo," Julian whispered, biting down on his lip.

"It wouldn't be the first time," Rami retorted, teasing.

Julian grinned. It also wouldn't be the last.

AFTERWORD

Meowdy!!
I wanted to share some fun lore bits that didn't make it into
the story:
Angels and demons were created at the same time and
balance one another out. That's why they're silver and gold,
two sides to the same coin. Which means yes, when Julian is
in demon form, his cum is gold. More on this topic (with art)
on Patreon.
It was so fun to piece Rami and Julian's story to together, and
I'd love to know if you felt the same. Please consider leaving
a review, and I'd love to know what you thought—tag me in
your posts or reach out via dms or email.
Much love,
Lana

ACKNOWLEDGMENTS

I cannot thank Owen, my sensitivity reader, enough for being so open to questions as this story was shaped and broken down and reshaped into its current form.

Thank you Meg, Zoe, and Chloe for reading, brainstorming, and cheering me on.

Thank you Sonny for always being just as thrilled as I am for my characters, and making amazing art of them along the way.

And lastly but certainly not least, thank you to all my Patrons for your support! I promise to spoil you.

ALSO BY

Visit my website to learn more about my books and how to get your paws on signed paperbacks.

www.lanakoleauthor.com

Cautionary Tails Series

How Not to Date a Demon

How Not to Date a Dragon

How Not to Date a Griffin

How Not to Date an Angel

Short & Sweets

Seasonal Spice & Everything Nice 1

Seasonal Spice & Everything Nice 2

Seasonal Spice & Everything Nice 3

Monster Vacation Series

The Abdominal Snowman

Tentacle Difficulties

In the Sweetverse w/ Kathryn Moon

Baby + the Late Night Howlers

Lola & the Millionaires Part One

Lola & the Millionaires Part Two

Lyric & the Heartbeats

Fighting Instincts

Bad Alpha

All Packed Up

Faith + the Dead End Devils

Knot That Serious

Ashley & the A-Listers

Crystal Clear Series

Illusion of Escape

Illusion of Death

Illusion of Darkness

The Unlocked Series

Chaos Unlocked

Betrayal Exposed

Misery Undone

Truth Revealed

Hope Lost

Death Defied

Standalones

Feline Good

LANA KOLE WRITING AS LOGAN GREY

Heartbelt Records Series

The Deeper You Go

The Longer You'll Stay

Love in Progress

ABOUT the AUTHOR

With a southern twang that's all charm, Lana Kole hails from Tennessee with their four feline roommates. Lana's most likely busy writing stories, but not without a cat purring in their lap. Their work brings life to characters who don't fit the mold, romance as sweet as it is sexy, and worlds better than this one.
Author of paranormal, sweet omegaverse, monster romance, and queer love stories with a happily ever after.